White Vampyre

Europa City 1

LEON STEELGRAVE

ICE PICK

BOOKS

Published by Ice Pick Books

ISBN-13: 9798682193332

LEON STEELGRAVE

Books by Leon Steelgrave

Europa City 1: White Vampyre
Europa City 2: Though Your Sins Be Scarlet
Europa City 3: The Violet Hour
Europa City 4: A Life Owed

Europa City One-shot: Cocoa Psycho Killer

Darkness Visible: The Complete Short Stories

For Tom,
    Who willingly accepts the blame for all this!

With thanks,
    John and James, for proof reading and comments
    Steve, for poetry and madness
    Helen, for faith, encouragement and healing

Fast Vampire

There's a Vampire wrapped in pretty paper,
There's a Vampire pure and white,
She will steal your mind and drain your body,
But you'll treat her like a cure.

You will race headlong through nights of madness,
As the Vampire sucks your veins,
But she'll come on like a friend and lover,
And she'll ease your aches and pains.

You will learn the joys of frenzied passion,
Feel the blood run hot and fast,
You will hurtle into red-washed future,
Leaving vapour in your past.

But there's a price to pay for God-like power,
And for fury swift and fresh,
And she'll take it when you least expect it,
She must have her pound of flesh.

Then as power fades and sleep enfolds you,
After many sleepless days,
You will waken after briefest hours,
Weak and feeble in the haze.

And you will crawl around like helpless infant,
Hollow, empty, in despair,
Seeking out your new-found Mistress,
With your powdery blood-shot stare.

Steve Thomson

CHAPTER 1

The hinges groaned in protest as the door opened, casting a triangle of light into the otherwise dark alley. Brecht cursed silently and listened for sounds of response to his unauthorised entry. He waited two minutes before slipping inside the storage facility. A stack of cardboard cartons occupied most of the available floor space, the dim glow of the overhead light just sufficient to pick out the stencilled legend "Gehennah Games" on the side of each box. Brecht selected one at random and split it open with his thumbnail. He folded the flap back to reveal neat rows of Virtual Reality game discs. The titles kindled a hot knot of disgust in his stomach and confirmed his source was telling the truth; this was the headquarters of a major Virtual Reality child pornography ring.

Such people, in his opinion, were the lowest order of scum. They existed only to pander to the whims of the city's degenerate and idle rich; thrill seekers after the taboo high of violating children, or that of becoming the children themselves, without the risk of physical contact. The VR black market provided clean, clinical perversion at the flick of a switch. Few users gave so much as a moment's consideration as to how the producers formatted the discs; that they recorded the psychological and nervous stimuli from live test subjects, reducing countless brutalities and emotional traumas to a series of digital bits, which the end user could then conveniently play back. Unless someone stops them. Brecht had his own brand of justice – no jury, no appeal and no chance of re-offending. Not in this life.

Conflicting emotions of rage and duty fought for reconciliation as Brecht made his way toward the exit on the opposite side of the room. He had too many black marks on his record and Sajer had made it clear during his last briefing that he could no longer cover for him. The officers of the Internal Affairs Department were suspicious about the high fatality rate of his arrests and wanted to suspend him for use of excessive force.

Brecht pushed the thought from his mind and drew the Walther PP10 from his shoulder holster. There were only two kinds of undercover officers - professionals and corpses. Checking left and right, he thumbed off the safety and turned the door handle. He heard the faint click of a contact switch closing and then the door erupted in a shower of molten plastic and burning foam. The shockwave threw him across the room and into the cartons. Stunned by the blast, he struggled to rise against the darkness that leapt up to claim him.

Brecht regained consciousness to find himself staring down the barrels of a pair of heavy calibre automatic weapons. The only things uglier than the guns were the men holding them, who could have been twins with their shaven heads, wraparound shades and black t-shirts.

'Don't even blink fuck-head. Unless you want to add being dead next to stupid on your list of problems,' growled the man on his right. He punctuated the statement by cocking his gun.

Brecht played for time. 'I know what this looks like but everything's cool, all right? I got caught short on my way home and your door was open - I just stopped off to use the facilities.'

'You know something? You're a real comedian. In fact, I think you're dead,' the man paused for effect, 'funny.'

Brecht, forewarned by the tensing of the thug's muscles, made his move. A flick of his wrist fired a spring-loaded knife into the throat of the man doing all the talking, severing his carotid artery in a spray of blood. Brecht snatched the gun from unresisting fingers as the hired muscle folded to the ground. He thumbed it to semi-automatic, fired two bursts and rolled clear of the other thug's retaliating fire. The first volley hit the man in the chest, the high velocity shells lifting him from his feet in time for the second burst to strike him in the head.

Brecht ended his roll by coming up into a crouch and swung the gun round to sight on each of the fallen men in turn. Satisfied that both were dead, he stood up and walked over to retrieve his "snake-killer". He wiped the blade clean on the man's t-shirt before replacing it in the sheath strapped to his forearm. 'I guess you just added dead stupid next to ugly on your list of problems.'

The door the gunmen had entered through led to a medical facility. Three stainless steel operating tables dominated its centre, each connected to banks of sensory and life support equipment, currently active as it monitored the children strapped to them: two fair-haired boys and a redheaded girl. Brecht estimated them as being aged between eight and twelve years old with the girl as the eldest. Siblings, judging by the family resemblance. They looked malnourished and a liberal assortment of bruises and welts coloured their skin varying shades of blue, green and purple.

The girl stirred as Brecht examined her restraints. 'Please don't hurt me anymore,' she whimpered.

'It's okay,' he reassured her, 'I'm with the police. We're going to take you somewhere safe. Nobody's going to hurt any of you anymore.'

He unzipped a jacket pocket and pulled out his com-unit. 'This is Brecht, do you copy, Control? I have three children in need of Med and Psych. Present locale 1412 Ostenstrasse. I also have a pair of corpses for the meat-wagon. Run an ID on them and get me a list of known associates.'

A burst of static echoed over the com-unit, 'We have you positive on all points. ETA of Med assist five minutes. Do you require backup?'

'That's a negative at this time, Control. Will keep you apprised of developments. Resuming radio silence.'

The table rocked on its gimbals as he unbuckled the girl's restraints.

'Can I have something to drink… Please?'

'Sure.' Brecht slid out of his jacket and wrapped it about the girl's shoulders before fetching her water from the sink. He left her sitting on the edge of the table while he turned his attention to the boys, who were strapped face down. Fresh disgust surged through him as he checked their vitals. Pulse slow, breathing shallow, pupils fixed and dilated by narcotics. Sensing the girl needed the comfort of another human voice, he spoke over his shoulder as he worked on releasing the children from their bonds. 'Don't worry, the boys are going to be fine. Hey, you never told me your name.'

'Rachel, and that's Tim and John. They're my brothers. Did you kill the bad men?'

'Yes, Rachel, I killed the bad men. They won't hurt anyone else ever again. But…'

'Good,' she interrupted him, 'I'm glad. They hurt me. Killed Mummy and Daddy. I wish you could keep on hurting them like they hurt us.'

Brecht suppressed a shudder. Rarely had he heard such a clinically cold and emotionless voice, let alone from a child, but he had to continue; he needed more information. 'There are other bad men out there that will hurt other families unless you help me catch them. Can you do that, Rachel, can you help me?'

'I'll try,' she said, hesitantly. 'But I don't know how.'

'There must be someone else besides those two men. Perhaps they operated some of the machines. Was there someone like that?'

'Yes.' Her voice was barely more than a whisper as she continued, 'He comes every night. I don't like him. He touches me and calls me his little girl. He was the one who told the bad men to hurt us. And after, he'd sit in that chair.' She pointed to a padded chair beside a control console on the opposite side of the room. Keypads were set into each armrest along with several jack sockets and disc ports. A helmet with an opaque faceplate mounted on a sliding ratchet, completing the Virtual Reality gaming chair.

Slip into your neuro-link suit, jack into the chair, select your disc and you were away. It made sense of course. The fucking pervert would want to check his merchandise before selling it.

He spoke to Rachel again; 'Do you think he's going to come back tonight?'

'Yes,' Rachel drew her knees up to her chest and hugged them. 'He said he was looking forward to playing me. He had a special new game.'

'What you've told me is good, Rachel. You've been really helpful. I'm sure your mother and father would've been proud of you.' The words sounded hollow and pathetic to him, a series of empty platitudes that carried no more weight than the breath that uttered them.

Rachel rocked back and forth sobbing; quiet at first and then in great agonised gulps. Brecht approached her cautiously, tentatively reaching out to hold her, but frightened of doing more harm than good. Her arms wrapped around his neck and hot tears coursed down his back. He lifted her chin gently and looked directly into her eyes. 'I'm going to make you a promise, Rachel, and that promise is the man who hurt you will never hurt you, your brothers, or anyone else ever again. Someone will be here to collect you soon and take you to the hospital, but I'm going to stay and wait for that other man to return. Then I'm going to punish him, hurt him worse than he ever hurt you.'

'Am I going to be safe afterwards, when you've hurt him?'

'Yes, you'll be safe. The people at the hospital will take care of you. It's their job to look after children like you and your brothers.'

Harsh fluorescent light flooded the room in response to Hagen's spoken command. He noticed the absence of the children immediately and cursed aloud to himself.

Brecht swung the VR chair round and confronted him. 'Evening, Doctor,' he gestured nonchalantly with his gun, 'I trust you're not about to do anything stupid? I'd hate to have to kill you right away.'

'Who are you and how did you get in here?'

'Believe me, that's the least of your problems right now. Let's just say the Department has its resources.'

'Ah, you're the police.' Hagen relaxed slightly.

'No, I'm not one of your business rivals come to take over your operation.' Brecht laughed humourlessly. 'On the other hand, I'm not here to take you to a nice five star prison either. A couple of hours from now you're going to wish I was some gangster heavy.'

'W...w... what do you mean?' Hagen stammered. Beads of perspiration broke out on his forehead and his left leg started to tremble uncontrollably as his fear increased. 'You've got to arrest me. It's my constitutional right.'

'You don't have any rights,' Brecht spat. 'You surrendered them all the second you violated those children. I'm giving you justice.' He kept the gun trained on Hagen as he reached for the neatly folded garment draped across the armrests of the VR couch. He threw it at Hagen who caught it clumsily. 'Put it on.'

'What are you going to do to me? I want to know what you are going to do to me. You can't just kill me!'

'Wrong.' Brecht pulled the trigger, the explosion of sound deafening in the confined space. Shards of concrete flew across the room as the bullet tunnelled into the ground beside Hagen's feet. 'I definitely could. In fact, I was planning to, but that would be far too easy. Then a little girl called Rachel gave me a better idea. She was sorry I'd killed those other two scumbags you'd hired. Y'see, they could only die once.' He produced a couple of VR discs from his pocket. They were black, five centimetres in diameter, with no visible markings. 'With the aid of these I'm going to be able to kill you again and again. Out of the mouths of babes and innocents, eh? Now put on the suit before I have to hurt you.'

Hagen was shaking to the point of palsy by the time he finished stripping, prior to pulling on the skin-tight neuro-link suit. He shuddered violently as he zipped the suit up and felt its tiny needles penetrate his skin and establish contact with various nerve centres.

'Please don't do this to me.'

Brecht remained silent as he grabbed Hagen by the hair and threw him back into the couch. He closed the wrist restraints and jacked the suit's lead into the port on the armrest, completing the neuro-link. His finger paused over the play button as he slid home the disc and stared into Hagen's eyes.

'In these civilised times the justice system rarely sentences a man to death for his crimes, and when it does it's usually by means of lethal injection – a relatively painless method. Not like previous centuries - they used all sorts of nasty methods. Like the electric chair.'

Brecht's finger stabbed down and a wry smile twitched at the corners of his mouth as he watched Hagen's frenzied jerking.

Hagen couldn't believe the pain. Streams of spittle flew from between his teeth as his body writhed from the effects of the simulated electric current. Waves of agony lashed up and down his spine, through his innards. Electricity paralysed his lungs. The smell of burning flesh mingled with the stench of excrement as his sphincter relaxed and his bladder emptied. Then, as abruptly as it had begun, the pain ceased.

Hagen blinked sweat from his eyes as Brecht leaned close to whisper confidentially, 'Of course sometimes that first shock didn't kill the prisoner.' His finger pressed down again sending a new wave of agony through his victim. Hagen started to blackout but the neuro-link dragged him back to consciousness. Brecht grinned at him, 'No escape that way, Hagen. The software designer who engineered this baby made sure of that.'

The pain ceased again. 'You'll never get away with this!' Hagen screamed. 'It's torture. For the love of God, have pity!'

'Did you show those children any pity?'

Hagen hung his head, unable to face Brecht but desperate to find a way out of his predicament. Words spilled from his mouth in a rush, 'If you let me go I'll give you the name of my backer. You can get the headman, wipe out the ring and be the big hero. They'll probably give you a promotion.'

Brecht laughed, 'Oh, don't worry about that. Long before this is over you're going to tell me everything you know.' There was an ominous click as he switched discs. 'Tell me, have you ever heard of the Spanish Inquisition? They were religious fanatics who turned torture into an art form during the sixteenth century.'

Hagen barely had time to consider the statement before the room faded away and he found himself transported to a fresh hell.

His first awareness was that of the circle of silent inquisitors that surrounded him. Although hoods shadowed their faces, he could sense their eyes upon him, their voyeuristic hunger an emotion with which he was well acquainted. His next sensation was of his nakedness, bound to a rough wooden table with coarse hemp ropes that chafed his body. He had a cage secured to his stomach and could feel a number of warm fury bodies against his skin. The creatures began to move, scurrying about the cage on clawed feet. As it became apparent that they were trapped the scampering became increasingly frenzied. At that same moment Hagen had a terrifying realisation of his own, the creatures in the cage were rats; large black rats intent on digging their way to freedom. Then the pain began as they burrowed into his flesh with teeth and claws, gnawing first through skin and then muscle to reach the soft tissue of his intestines, the tortured screams that accompanied their feasting only served to urge them to greater effort.

Sajer was reading a report at his desk when Brecht entered the darkened office, his face deliberately shadowed by the harsh under lighting of a desktop lamp, a cheap psychological trick Brecht found more amusing than effective.

Sajer threw the report across the desk. 'Well?' He arched an inquisitive eyebrow.

'Sir?'

'Don't play dumb with me, Brecht. It doesn't become a man of your intelligence. This, as if you didn't know, is the medical report on Doctor Hagen. Perhaps you'd care to explain how he came to be in his present state of traumatised catatonia?'

Brecht coughed to cover his growing impatience with his superior's loaded questions and an awkward silence developed between them as Sajer awaited his reply. Brecht finally ventured, 'I guess the strain of being caught was too much for him. It can happen. You know how high strung some of these academic types can be. After all, he was a respected man in the community. The thought of the scandal alone probably sent him over the edge.'

Sajer rose from behind his desk and stood with his hands clasped behind his back, his face clearly revealed for the first time. Brecht gazed at his superior, seeking some indication as to how Sajer had received his explanation. The calm grey eyes mounted above sculpted cheekbones, an aquiline nose and bloodless lips gave nothing away. It had always been so for as long as Brecht could remember, since that fateful day when he had witnessed his mother's murder. Sajer had seen to it that he was cared for afterwards, paying for his education and ultimately guiding him to his present position in life. Brecht felt a surge of guilt over his irritation. He owed everything to Sajer and knew he would not ask such questions without good reason.

Sajer's voice cut through his reverie, 'And that is your official statement? You don't wish to change it in any way?'

'No, sir. I believe that's what must have happened.'

'Very well. I should inform you that the medical report on Doctor Hagen indicates that he had recently used a neuro-link. Not that I'm suggesting that you would be party to something as illegal as mentally torturing a suspect. But, as you know, my superiors in the Department are men of an altogether more suspicious and cynical turn of mind.'

Suddenly it fell into place. The interview must be an act for the benefit of IAD. 'My statement stands, sir. I'm sure you've read the girl's testimony. Hagen was in the habit of testing the newly programmed discs. That would account for the findings of the Medical Examiner.'

'I'm sure you're right, just as I'm sure you understand that these facts must be noted for the record. As an officer of the law one must always consider due process.' Sajer leaned forward and toggled off a switch on his desktop console. He continued in a more informal tone of voice. 'Ah, Kurt, what am I to do with you? I sympathise with your point of view but there is only so much I can do. Weill is pressing for your suspension and I must be candid and tell you that if your shooting of those two enforcers hadn't been vindicated I'd be asking for your badge and gun.'

'I understand, sir.'

'Do you? Let's hope so, for both our sakes. In the meantime, your zealous behaviour has left us without any leads or further suspects in this case. Even if there were, we could not hope to get Hagen to testify.'

A look of indecision crossed Brecht's face. 'Actually, that's not quite true. Hagen supplied me with several names and addresses before he suffered his… breakdown.'

'I never heard that, Kurt. But should you acquire any fresh leads from your sources feel free to pursue them. Now,' he handed Brecht a buff coloured disc, 'here is the file on your next assignment, an illegal prostitution operation inside the French Quarter. Although why anyone would be willing to risk such services when we have neuro-link parlours and state sanctioned brothels, I do not know.'

'Human nature - thrills and profit. The clients get off on doing something illicit and the owners make a higher profit by not paying tax and using prostitutes desperate enough to accept any kind of fee, usually drugs. But you know all that, just like you know why this particular case would be of special interest to me.'

Sajer looked uncomfortable. 'Perhaps that is so, but you know my position. All I'm asking is that you show a little restraint. It will make things easier for all concerned.

'Now, do you have any questions?'

'How's the girl - Rachel?'

'That was not what I meant but since you ask, physically she and the boys will heal soon enough. The mental trauma is another matter. I think we could be looking at the possibility of neuro-surgery coupled with selective memory implants. Erase the horror completely, let them believe their parents were killed in an accident and have them adopted.'

'I thought as much. If that's all, sir, I best be getting along. I'll review the case files and be in touch.' He hesitated, needing to say more but unable to, and then the moment was gone.

A look of melancholy flitted across Sajer's face as he watched Brecht leave. He shook his head, reached into the top drawer of his desk and removed a framed photograph. He was still brooding over the photograph when the message light on his vidphone flashed red. Snapping alert, he replaced the picture in the drawer before keying the receive switch. The features of a swarthy-skinned man with dark hair flickered on to the screen.

The man spoke in a low, guttural voice, 'I think that interview pretty much summed up my argument, Sajer. So you needn't bother making any more feeble excuses for that rabid dog of yours. Brecht is quite clearly beyond salvaging.' He smiled triumphantly, malice in his eyes. 'You've no choice except to sanction Damocles.'

'Congratulations on your promotion, Weill. I had no idea that you were now in a position to give me orders.'

Weill's smile froze. 'I meant no disrespect, Guyon. I was merely giving my recommendation. Perhaps I was a little over-enthusiastic but I thought you and I were friends? We both, after all, have a stake in Damocles and all that that entails.'

'Indeed,' Sajer replied in a cold voice. 'I understand you perfectly. You, however, do not appear to understand me. Please indulge me while I clarify matters, Captain Weill. Internal Affairs has no jurisdiction over my operatives. I and I alone shall handle Kurt Brecht as I see fit. Should it become necessary to take action against him you may rest assured that I will not hesitate to do so. Finally, in future you shall both remember and respect my rank, addressing me as Commander Sajer. Have I made myself clear, Captain Weill?'

'Perfectly clear, sir.'

'Then this interview is terminated.'

CHAPTER 2

S ajer drew up alongside the patrol car and lowered his window. The uniformed officer nodded a greeting and quickly broke eye contact. His knuckles showed white as he gripped the wheel, his attention fixed upon the dashboard.

'You called in the ten-double zero?'

'No, sir. Falconer responded to an anonymous tip off. He and his rookie are in the alley with the crew of the meat wagon.'

Sajer drove on and parked the cruiser on the sidewalk. A cordon had been set up around the entrance to the alleyway, on the other side of which stood the usual rubberneckers and press parasites. Sajer ignored the pointing video cams and ducked under the yellow incident tape. He badged the uniform guarding the cordon and entered the alley. Temporary spotlights silhouetted two paramedics as they secured a body to a backboard. Another pair of uniform officers stood off to the side watching them work. Sajer recognised the older uniform as Sammy Falconer, a fifteen year street veteran. The boy next to him looked barely old enough to be out of school, surely a sign of his own advancing years.

Sajer took in the scene with a disciplined eye, noting the police issue automatic and com-unit lying next to the victim, the surrounding blood splatter black in the sodium glare. The drawn weapon meant he had seen his attacker and either been too slow or otherwise dismissed the threat, the latter unlikely in a dead end alley.

One of the paramedics turned as Sajer's shadow fell across him. The movement gave him his first clear view of the victim's face. He recognised Brecht even through the oxygen mask.

'What are his chances?'

'About eighty-twenty against. There's an infected GSW to the right shoulder, plus your man took three shots to the gut – hollow points,

11

judging by the tissue damage. If he lives, he'll probably spend the rest of his life shitting into a bag.'

The paramedic motioned Sajer aside and gestured to his colleague. They lifted Brecht on to a gurney and wheeled him in the direction of the waiting ambulance.

Sajer squatted beside the pool of semi-congealed blood and lifted the com-unit. He wiped the blood from its case with a handkerchief before slipping it into his overcoat pocket. His knees cracked as he stood. The wail of a siren marked the ambulance's departure. A one in five chance. Not odds he would personally care to play.

Sajer addressed Falconer. 'I want the scene processed and scrubbed. No press access. No comment. Keep this off grid. Understood?'

'What about the com-unit, sir?' the rookie interrupted. 'Isn't it evidence? I mean you shouldn't handle it like that.'

Sajer's gaunt features turned pale. 'There are a couple of things you should learn if you intend to have a career in the Department, son. First, never quote procedure to me. Second,' he looked at Falconer, 'did you see a com-unit?'

'No, sir. Duvall must be working too hard - imagining things. Y'know what these double shifts are like.'

'Ah,' Sajer sighed. 'Perhaps it's time he had a rest? Have him transferred to Records.'

'Very good, sir.'

Falconer ran a finger around the edge of his grime-stained collar as he watched Sajer exit the alley. 'Bad move, Duvall. You just couldn't let go, could you? Have you listened to a single word I've said over the past month? Apart from Internal Affairs, Vice is the one other squad whose men you never question. Sajer's unit is an autonomous state all of its own. When one of his people goes down everyone else with an ounce of smarts starts looking for a rock to hide under.'

Sajer polarised the cruiser windows, shutting out the glances of the curious. He ran his fingers through his iron-grey hair before pulling the com-unit from his pocket. Department issue, same as the pistol that he'd left in the alley. Sajer keyed in his master code, a backdoor password held by each squad commander, and browsed through the file timestamps. The most recent entry was less than two hours old.

21/12/85, 21:40: Lady Methedrine has made it clear that she'll never relinquish her claim on me. I've been running on luck for far too long now, but Slinky finally delivered the goods and I might just have a chance to get out from under before she plays her end-game.

Sajer slammed the door to his office, strode angrily to his desk and threw his coat across the back of his chair. His emotions seethed as he tried to rationalise his actions. Brecht was as good as dead and he might as well have pulled the trigger. It didn't matter how much he tried to dress up the truth or justify his actions, one fact remained the same; his was the hand that had authorised the sanction.

He slumped into his chair and stared at his hands, seeing, like Lady Macbeth, imaginary bloodstains that would never wash clean. 'So it was wrong!' he shouted. 'But if I have a credo it is "never regret, never apologise", and by God I am going to live by that.' Voicing a defence against his self-doubt lent him strength and composure. He retrieved Brecht's com-unit from his coat and flipped open the case. His finger hovered uncertainly over the touchscreen, but he had already come too far to shy away from the truth. He navigated to the first of the journal entries and started to read.

11/10/85: I've seen a lot of strange shit in this city, met a lot of weird people, but I reckon last night at the Paradiso deserves an award. I'd gone there on the off chance that Slinky might've dug up some dirt on Doctor Hagen's associates, but my informer proved to be a no show. Guess that's what you get for relying on a junkie.

Seeing it had just gone midnight - early by the club's standards - I decided to hang around and see who or what turned up. It had been a long day so I ordered a double, propped up the bar and scanned the crowd to see if I could score a little something to pick me up.

I'd about given up hope when a familiar voice shouted, 'Garth, don't tell me you've started hanging out in this dive, honey?'

Garth, the pseudonym I used in the French Quarter, a junkie fuck-up with an eye for the main chance. Assuming character, I hunched my shoulders and turned to face the five feet of peroxide blonde and animal cunning that went by the name of Marian. 'Beggars can't be choosers,' I replied, flashing a quick smile.

'Broke again, Garth? You never change.' She pouted, nonchalantly fluffing up her blonde curls with a languorous hand. Film Noir; eat your heart out.

'So, is my baby hurting?' she asked with vulture-like intensity.

'Not really,' I said far too quickly as I relaxed into my role. A hint of desperation to colour my voice. 'But something fast wouldn't go amiss.' My fingers drummed nervously on the bar top.

Marian sidled up to me. 'How much you got?'

'Fifty.'

Her voice was husky, 'Not enough, honey.'

'Yeah, but…'

'Shush.' She silenced me with a finger against my lips, which she drew slowly down until she was holding my chin between her thumb and forefinger. 'I trust you, Garth. So I'm going to let you have some anyway.' Her fingertips walked across my belly and then her hand dropped to rub my crotch. 'I'm sure you'll find some way to make up the rest of what you owe me.'

'Oh yeah, you can bet on it.' I grinned and slid my hands around her back, cupping her buttocks to draw her closer. I'd slept with her before, ostensibly in payment for drugs when I was really after information. It wasn't a chore. I heard the zip on my jeans slide down and nimble fingers tucked something inside my underwear, paused, and then withdrew. I bent to kiss her and she gently shoved me aside with a giggle.

'Sorry, honey, got to go. I'll see you at the close.' Her statement was an order, not a suggestion.

She paused, looked over her shoulder, and called out loudly, 'Garth, honey, your fly's undone.'

I laughed, pulled up my zip and went to the toilet to powder my nose.

Ten minutes later I was back at the bar nursing a splitting headache. They were beginning to be of concern. Their frequency had increased of late and dizzy spells and blackouts often accompanied them. I decided to take a seat until the attack passed and was making my way to the booths on the opposite side of the dance-floor when my knees buckled. Strong hands caught me under the elbows and steered me to a corner booth. I mumbled my thanks to my rescuer and stared. Then I stared some more for good measure. She was the most beautiful woman I'd ever set eyes on. Her hair, long and black, contrasted with a pale complexion and complemented her sapphire blue eyes. Well-toned muscle rippled with the promise of pleasure beneath the white leather of a figure hugging catsuit.

We sat in silence for over a minute before she spoke. 'Hello, Kurt. You're late. I've been waiting for you.'

Her voice a sibilant whisper, it stirred primal emotions. Yet something nagged at my subconscious. Then it hit me. She'd used my real name. 'I'm pretty certain we've never met before and yet you're using a name that could get both of us in a lot of trouble. Who are you?'

'Who's anyone at the end of the day but the product of other people's perceptions? We're something more and less than we appear when we try to be all things to all people.'

'Save the philosophy for someone who gives a shit and answer the question.'

'Who am I? Who do you want me to be, Kurt?'

Cruelty shone in her eyes and I stared dumbly at my reflection in the tabletop. After a time she started to speak, a whisper at first which grew in volume with each phrase.

'I am the psychic fall-out of the ravaged and bastardised minds of the twentieth century's children. I am a concept made flesh, personified. I am the true ruling power behind the governments of the world, the maker and breaker of kings and queens. I am the loan shark extraordinaire, who grants your wildest desires, but always at a rate of interest greater than you're able to repay. I am fear and loathing, ecstasy and joy. I am the White Vampyre, the androgynous amphetamine,' she paused, 'but you, Kurt, may call me Lady Methedrine.'

I chewed over this wild and obviously rehearsed speech and extracted the one thing that made any sense to me. 'So you're trying to tell me you're a fast woman?'

She threw back her head, her hair cascading over the back of her chair, and laughed. 'That's what I love about you, Kurt, your refusal to believe the evidence of your own senses.'

She was clearly mad, either that or she was on something. Not wanting to scare such a fascinating woman away, I pushed her gently. 'I'm flattered, but you still haven't told me how you know my name.'

She treated me to a mysterious smile. 'You're not the only one with contacts, Kurt. All you need to know for now is that I'm on your side. And from what I've seen you could use a little help.'

Her words stung, enough for me to forget the demands of my libido and abandon the softly, softly approach.

'That tells me precisely shit, and I'm a man who gets annoyed when people don't tell me what I want to know. You're playing in the big league now. People get hurt in my world. So do us both a favour and quit with the games. You know my name, which means you probably know my profession, which in turn raises the question of what you want from me. I'm waiting.'

She gave me a coquettish glance and took a sip through the straw of her drink, playing the little girl flirting with one of her Daddy's friends. I could tell I wasn't getting through to her and was considering slapping her about when she fixed me with the cold stare of a killer. She went from fourteen to a hundred years old in a glance. Her voice took on a hard edge, 'That would be a very stupid thing for you to do, Kurt. Just because I need you, don't make the mistake of thinking you're indispensable.' Her eyes clouded and her expression grew vague, as if she had gone back to reading from some internal script. 'I've been growing for centuries now. Coalescing from the psychic screams of the victims of Belsen, Hiroshima, Nagasaki, and the Great Flood of 2049. A distillation of human suffering and misery, each injustice adds another facet to my being.'

A cold shudder rippled down my spine at her words; I might not have believed her nonsense but she clearly believed it herself. I decided to try a different approach. 'All right, we've established who you are, so what brings you here?'

'Curiosity as much as anything else,' Lady Methedrine said. 'I wanted our first meeting to be casual,' she leaned closer, 'to inspect the goods, as it were.'

'Really? So tell me, do you like what you see?'

'Yes. I can use a man like you.'

'You've implied that already. Use me for what?'

She laid an ivory coloured hand on top of my own. 'That, I'm afraid, will have to wait until our next meeting.'

'If you think...' A wave of dizziness cut short my reply. It passed in seconds but I wasn't surprised to find myself alone when I looked up. A quick scan showed no sign of my mystery lady and I headed back to the bar.

The entire episode left rather a bad taste which, coupled with Slinky's non-appearance, had me feeling more than a little pissed off. I was still in a foul mood when Marian turned up and suggested going back to her place several drinks later. I conceded anyway. It turned out she had nothing to say I hadn't heard before but what the hell, it was fun.

Fast food cartons littered the floor of the living room, the half-eaten contents congealing over a mound of empty bottles and cans. Kurt lay sprawled on the sofa in a drunken stupor, the epicentre of the debris. An empty whisky bottle and a dirty glass lay abandoned on the coffee table surrounded by rings of spilt drink. A framed photograph rested face down on his stomach, gently held in place by his hand. Unshaven and dressed in a soiled t-shirt and boxer shorts, Kurt reflected the seediness of the apartment.

The harsh tone of the vidphone cut through his slumber, causing Kurt to groan until the auto-record system switched in and silenced it. Some time later Kurt swung his legs off the sofa, causing the photograph to fall to the floor. With a grunt, he retrieved the photograph and placed it on the table. He cleared his throat and commanded, 'Playback messages.'

The distressed features of a young woman with dark hair appeared on the screen. Her eyes were red and swollen as though she had been crying recently and her voice choked with emotion when she spoke. 'Kurt, pick up, goddamn you.'

Kurt turned away. 'Voice only.'

'Shit! I didn't want it to be this way. Not a message. Not over the phone. It's over, Kurt. We're finished. I'm sorry.' There were sounds of hysterical sobbing followed by an angry outburst, 'Fuck you! Why should I be sorry? It's your own fault, you lousy bastard! You don't call for weeks; then you turn up out of the blue and expect to be welcomed with open arms. Giving me lame excuses about how it's your job or some case you've been working. Bullshit! More like some other woman. You must think I'm pretty stupid if you expect me to believe you got all those scratches and bites in the line of duty. From now on you can go screw one of your whores, or yourself, 'cause you're never gonna fuck my little pussy again!'

The vidphone went dead and Kurt picked up the whisky bottle. 'Happy fucking birthday to me! Thirty-one years old and none the wiser.' He looked dejectedly at the empty bottle before picking up the picture from the table. It was a portrait shot of a girl with blonde hair and garish make-up.

'Perhaps it's just as well you're dead, mother. This way you'll never know what a lousy, worthless piece of shit your son's become. I know I made you a promise but I'm running out of time and options. IAD are set to crucify me and Sajer can't keep deflecting the flak.'

A new message began playing on the vidphone. 'Hey, Kurt, my bitchin' force multiplier of justice. How's it fixing?'

Kurt sat bolt upright at the sound of the new voice. It was Slinky, his AWOL informer. 'Resume visual playback.' The rat-like and emaciated features of a man appeared on the screen.

'Obviously fixing good, Kurt, if you can't answer the phone, or are you still coming down because of my no-show the other night? Well don't be. Slinky was busy meeting with some very sketchy characters on your behalf and has just the info-fix you're hurting for. The Mr Nasty of Pederasty behind Gehennah Games is Joseph van Meyer. I told him you were looking to make a tax-free investment in the entertainment business and fixed a meeting for tomorrow evening. If you want to sour this pervert's trip, you had better be at Maximilians for midnight tomorrow. Payment's in the usual manner. Stay on that up-elevator, baby.'

Kurt punched the air triumphantly, instantly sobered by the prospect of hunting down his quarry.

14/10/85: Marian either sold me some seriously fucked up shit or else I've finally lost it. One way ticket down the rabbit hole. And yet there's enough evidence to suggest that the events of last night actually happened. But I'm getting ahead of myself. I'd better begin at the beginning.

It was shortly after Slinky called to let me know he'd arranged a meet with Joseph van Meyer, the owner of Gehennah Games – the company responsible for fronting the VR child pornography ring I'd been assigned to investigate. I'd been after this sleazy sonofabitch for months, so decided to celebrate my good fortune by doing a couple of lines of the sulph Marian had fronted me. That and the fact that I'd been on an all-day drunk and needed to straighten out fast. I cleared off the table and fetched the wrap from my coat. Finding a generous half-gram, I chopped out some fat lines with my Vice ID laminate, snorted them and sat back to enjoy the rush. Come on like a bastard. That familiar sense of clarity and invulnerability. Tightness in the lungs. The need to move, to find a task. Pure shit. Unstepped on. Elevator going up. Taking me all the way to the top floor.

Ten minutes passed, or maybe a lifetime. Time always came unstuck. I became aware of my reflection in the glass of the table top. As I watched, my features morphed into those of the woman from the Paradiso. I looked round and found only empty space behind me. Laughing at my paranoia, I turned back to discover her standing directly in front of me. She'd fashioned her hair into ringlets and was wearing a ball gown, but it was undoubtedly the woman from the night before, the so-called Lady Methedrine.

'How the fuck did you get in here?'

She threw back her head and laughed. It was harsh and forced; laughter intended to punish. 'Ah, Kurt, polite as ever.' She pointed to the table. 'You invited me in.'

I'd experienced hallucinations before during a meth binge but this had to be the mother of them all. Hyper-real, involving not only sound and vision but also touch, taste and smell. Just what the fuck had Marian cut this shit with? I closed my eyes and opened them again. It was no good - she was still there.

'I don't know and I don't care how you got in here, but one thing I'm certain of is that I didn't ask for your help. I don't need or want it, so if you know what's good for you then you'll get the fuck out of my apartment.'

'Such ingratitude, but I forgive you. I know you love me really. As for asking for my favours, you receive them every time you take those chemicals into your body. Every ounce of energy. Every logical thought. You owe them all to me. And I expect to be paid in full for them.'

Her words were gibberish. I shook my head in denial. 'You're a parasite, an illusion, a product of guilt and fear!'

'My, how you love your pain, little man. You sit there and nurture it like a small child, watching it grow with a perverse pleasure. Does it help her?' She pointed to the overturned picture. 'Does it make your mother's soul rest any easier? I don't think so.'

I jumped to my feet, shaking with rage. 'What would you know? You're not even real. You're just some fucked up dope hallucination. How can you hope to gauge my suffering? My pain!'

'Your words prove my point exactly. Where has all your precious pain got you? Nowhere. But I'm offering you power. You want to make a difference? Then side with me and I'll give you the strength to fight your crusade. I'll help you to punish those who imprisoned and destroyed the woman who gave you life. You can take your revenge on them and others like them, such as those you found exploiting children for the sick pleasures of the rich and idle. Just remember that getting what you want always comes at a price.'

'Very profound,' I sneered. 'Now, if you've finished preaching, how about you do me the favour of getting the fuck out of here?'

'What? Are you honestly trying to tell me that you're not in the least bit curious as to what I'm going to demand in payment for granting your wildest desires?' She glanced round examining the disarray of my front room. 'Perhaps you're right. We should leave your apartment. The atmosphere in here is not conducive to concluding our arrangement.'

Lady Methedrine snapped her fingers and I felt a sudden surge of movement. It felt as if the ground beneath me had turned through ninety degrees while I remained stationary. The physical sensation confirmed what my eyes were trying to tell me. Instead of four walls, tall fir trees now surrounded me. The thick pile of the carpet had transformed into mossy grass, the illumination from my down-lighters replaced by brilliant sunshine slanting through the trees.

'Is that better?' Lady Methedrine inquired. 'This is the forest Sajer took you to play in as a boy.'

I looked around, astonished at first, filled with pleasant memories of a more innocent time. Then I realised I was being manipulated. 'You can quit with the mind-fucks and mental rape right now, bitch! These memories, the past, it's all I have left to me that's clean.'

Lady Methedrine frowned as though she were genuinely surprised by my reaction and then snapped her fingers again. I experienced that peculiar shifting sensation once more and I found myself in the familiar surroundings of the Paradiso. Flashing strobes highlighted the frenetic revellers throwing shapes amidst the clouds of dry ice on the dance-floor, their bodies synchronised to the repetitive drumbeats and throbbing bass lines.

'Do you prefer this, one of the squalid clubs you run to when you feel the need for forgetfulness?' Her fingers snapped once more. 'Or perhaps this?'

It was dark and a certain dampness in the air suggested we were somewhere below ground. My eyes slowly became accustomed to the gloom, allowing me to make out the rough blocks of stone that formed the walls. It bore a strange sense of the familiar, yet I was certain I'd never been here before. 'Where are we?'

Her laughter was sharp. 'The darkest dungeon of your mind.'

My patience was beginning to wear thin with her games, but before I could reply to her latest assault on my psyche we were suddenly back in my apartment. I slumped down on the sofa and attempted to rationalise the events of the past few minutes. It had to be a trip or some form of hypnosis. Neither of these hypotheses could dispute the fact that Lady

Methedrine was standing directly before me.

She became impatient with my silence; 'Do you accept my offer?'

I decided to humour her in the hope that she would go away. 'Okay, you win. What do you want, my soul?'

'Not quite. Merely your life, your love, nothing short of your complete devotion.' Her voice and features softened, recalling our first encounter. Having got what she came for, she relaxed her dominatrix persona, returning to her girlish flirtation. 'But rest assured you won't find me a hard Mistress to serve.'

Lady Methedrine gave me a look that spoke volumes. A sinuous shrug of her shoulders caused her breasts to rise and fall beneath the tight fabric of her dress.

'No one will ill use you but yourself,' she continued, 'and in the end I'll grant what you most desire.'

'And what might that be, apart from the obvious?'

'Oh I think you know the answer to that, Kurt. Enough talk; let's drink a toast to seal our bargain.'

Two glasses of wine materialised in her hands and she offered the left one to me. I accepted the glass and we linked arms and drank. The wine was golden, bitter-sweet and cool.

Lady Methedrine's expression became whimsical as her body faded to a ghostly shadow. 'Until we meet again, which I'm certain won't be long. You can't seem to help yourself.'

I woke up a couple of hours later with a splitting migraine, jagged lines flashing across my vision. The migraines had reached such intensity I'd considered consulting the squad physician, but given my recent lifestyle I gave it up a bad idea. There were plenty of underground quacks could do the job just as well and their discretion was guaranteed. Despite the pain, I felt a huge grin creep across my face when I realised it had all been a dream - unusual with stimulants but not impossible. I looked at the table and my grin froze. Two long-stemmed wine glasses sat there, the rim of one stained with blood red lipstick. The shock, like a kick to the stomach, awoke my other senses. I noticed an unfamiliar scent in the air similar to cherry blossom, further proof that my mystery woman was no illusion. The sense of enervation I felt was enough to make me seriously entertain the idea that Lady Methedrine truly was some form of creature of the night. One that was hell bent on sucking me dry of life.

Sajer poured himself a fresh drink, engrossed and dismayed by Brecht's journal in equal measure. Brecht had clearly been in the grip of a powerful psychosis during the last few weeks. As his commanding officer he should have seen it and reached out to him. Instead, he had let Weill coerce him into a Damocles Sanction.

Sajer looked up at the clock. It read a little after three o'clock in the morning. He keyed in the number for Saint Jude's Infirmary and having run the gauntlet of the admissions desk finally got through to a Doctor Rauch.

'Still in surgery,' Rauch said in the clipped tone of a man who had more pressing concerns than answering Sajer's questions. 'Rest assured your man is in capable hands. Anike Nystrom is one of the best trauma surgeons in the city. If it were me on the table I'd want her to be the one operating.' Rauch looked at something off screen and nodded. 'I have to go. We'll notify your liaison once Brecht is out of surgery.'

The cognac burned pleasingly as Sajer swallowed. It kindled a knot of warmth in his otherwise cold gut. He had no business calling the hospital. Too close for objectivity. Better for all concerned that he remove himself from the investigation. No point giving Weill fresh ammunition.

CHAPTER 3

The same sequence played repeatedly inside Sajer's head; the walls tilting at unnatural angles as he sprinted down the never-ending corridor, the gun a heavy but comforting weight in his hand. He tried not to think about where the blood and brains on the front of his shirt had come from. He heard a woman's screams and a man's harsh laughter. The door drew closer, his heart thumping in rhythm with his pounding feet. Memories of the recent past, unbidden, played in a continual loop, forming a mental late night horror show.

The level of tension in the car was rising steadily. Sally, sensing the younger man's unease, tried to make light of it. 'Relax, Guyon. I know this is your first bust since getting your detective's shield, but believe me, it's gonna be a piece of piss.' He adopted a faux Mexican accent, 'We don't need no steenkin' backup, keed.'

Sajer forced a smile as he combed his fingers through his sweat drenched hair. 'Just you and me, Sergeant. We can handle whatever they throw at us.' He pulled back the slide on his gun, flicked off the safety and looked at his partner. 'Well?'

Sally drew his pistol and opened the car door. 'Okay, kid, let's rock.'

Their target was a run-down hotel with a garish neon sign proclaiming it to be "The Garden of Earthly Delights". They crossed the road and took up position on either side of the hotel's rear fire exit. Sally nodded and Sajer kicked open the door. He dived inside, rolled to the right and came up into a crouch. Sally slipped around the left side of the door and stood with his back against the wall, covering Sajer. Both men relaxed when it became apparent that the small vestibule was empty. Across from them, a set of stairs led up to another door. Sally took the lead and made his way cautiously up the staircase. He paused at the door and listened. Muted sounds of conversation and laughter filtered through, warning him there was somebody on the other side.

'There are at least two of them. Be ready to shoot when I open the door,' he whispered.

Sajer nodded and adopted a two handed grip on his gun as he flattened himself against the wall. Sally threw open the door and crossed the threshold to one side. Two men dressed in dark suits and armed with machine-pistols spun round in surprise. Ignoring Sally's shout of, 'Armed police officers, drop your weapons,' they tried to bring their guns up to fire.

Sajer's pistol thundered twice, accompanied a split second later by Sally's gun. The bullets hit the men high in the chest, the impact propelling them backward to land in a lifeless heap. An eerie silence fell over the corridor as the echo of the shots died away.

Sally grimaced, 'I guess we just lost the element of surprise, kid.'

'Quite,' Sajer replied, 'So we'd better…' A woman's scream from the far end of the corridor interrupted Sajer. He glanced quickly at Sally and a silent communication passed between them as they both sprinted in the direction of the cry. Up ahead a door slid open and the ugly snub nose of a pistol peered out. Everything slowed down as Sajer tried to shout a warning to his partner. Sajer saw the muzzle flash and heard the boom of the shot in quick succession, felt something warm and wet splatter against the front of his shirt and face. He returned fire instinctively as the gunman stepped into the corridor; his first two shots bit chunks out of the door frame before the third found its mark, hitting the gunman between the eyes. With the immediate danger past, Sajer's mind allowed itself to process what it considered the less important details. Blood and brain matter covered his shirt: Sally's blood and brains. Reaction set in and he stood trembling, staring at his partner's headless corpse. Then the woman screamed again and his training took over. The walls tilted at unnatural angles as Sajer sprinted down the never-ending corridor, but no matter how fast he ran he was never in time.

Sajer sat bolt upright, fighting with his sweat drenched sheets. As he fought for calm, his breathing gradually changed from ragged gasps to a slow, even rate. The weight of the last twenty-six years crushed relentlessly down on him, forcing him to recall the next part of the story.

He had crashed through the door with his gun at the ready. A burly half-naked man stood over a naked blonde woman. She was sobbing bitterly, her face puffy and starting to swell from several recent blows. Sajer shouted a challenge as the man struck her with a powerful backhand blow that sent her flying across the room. She slammed into him, knocking the gun from his hand. His opponent seized the opportunity, reaching for the gun tucked inside the waistband of his trousers. 'I don't know who the fuck you are, but you're dead anyway.'

The woman screamed, 'No, Lars! For God's sake!' and leapt at him.

Lars snarled and she jerked as he shot her twice at point blank range. She collapsed against him, her arms wrapping around him in a twisted parody of a sensual embrace. Sajer used the distraction to recover his gun. He rose to one knee and fired as Lars disentangled himself from the dying woman. The bullet penetrated his left hip and angled upwards to exit below his right armpit. Lars' mouth formed an "o" of astonishment as he sank to his knees, the gun falling from nerveless fingers.

Sajer walked over to Lars. 'This one is for Sara, you filthy bastard,' he said and shot him between the legs. He watched Lars writhe in agony for a few moments before shooting him twice more, this time through the heart.

Sajer knelt down and examined the woman in the hope that she might still be alive. A cursory inspection killed that hope, both bullets having struck close to the heart. Further examination revealed a series of needle tracks up and down both arms, confirmation that the brothel was a "locked box", the owners keeping the girls prisoner by hooking them on hard drugs and forcing them to work for their fixes.

Sajer was just about to leave when he caught a movement out of the corner of his eye. A bundle of sheets beside the bed was shaking rhythmically. He approached cautiously, gun in hand, and reached out and pulled back the sheets to reveal a small boy. He looked past Sajer and cried out, 'Mamma! What's wrong with you?'

Sajer grabbed him as he tried to scramble by and held him tight in spite of his frantic efforts to escape. He was still holding him twenty minutes later when two uniformed officers burst into the room.

The Department ordered a full inquiry into the incident. Why had they not reported in? Why had they not requested backup? Sajer had remained stoically calm throughout the proceedings. His answers were short and terse; 'There was not enough time. It had not been deemed necessary,' and so on. In the end Sally, as the senior officer, was apportioned most of the blame and Sajer had retained his detective's shield. The state took Kurt into custody and there the matter might have ended had not Sajer taken it upon himself to act as a surrogate father to the boy.

Everything appeared fine at first; the trauma of witnessing his mother's death so deeply suppressed as to appear forgotten. Childhood was a period of learning, exploration and the development of a keen intellect, all under Sajer's careful guidance. For a time Brecht looked set to pursue a career as an architect or an engineer, helping rebuild the shattered world he had been born into. Afterwards, Sajer never knew if such ambitions were real or merely a calculated plan on Brecht's part to deceive his protector. Whatever his true motivation, Brecht announced his decision to join the ECPD shortly before his graduation and no amount of skilful oratory or desperate cajoling on Sajer's part could persuade him otherwise.

Despite Sajer's concerns, Brecht graduated from the Academy with

Honours and enjoyed an exemplary career while in uniform, making detective after four short years and transferring to the Vice squad two years later. Then the cracks began to appear, it quickly becoming apparent that Brecht had been biding his time until he was in a position to exact vengeance from the drug pushers and pimps he viewed as responsible for his mother's death. An expanding pattern of violence and the use of deadly force eclipsed the glory of his early career.

The episode involving Doctor Hagen proved one mistake too many, providing Weill with the justification for a Damocles Sanction. Much as it galled Sajer to admit it, Weill had been correct, Brecht having become a danger to himself and to the public. Hindsight, a wonderful thing. He should have removed Brecht from active duty following the conclusion of the van Meyer case. They might have salvaged something that way instead of cleaning up an unholy mess.

Sajer sighed and swung his legs off the bed. There would be no more sleep that night. He crossed over to the window and looked out at a thousand lights. Europa City, a modern day Sodom and Gomorrah. A cruel mistress, one that often left him ashamed of the lies and deceit used to maintain her. Like all lovers, he knew her intimately. The good and the bad.

Construction of the vast conurbation had commenced early in the sixth decade of the twenty-first century following the Great Flood, its purpose to provide a fresh start for millions of refugees. Situated on the hilly and mountainous lands of the former Umbria region of central Italy, the rocky slopes of the Apennines defined and protected its eastern borders. The city, home to more than forty million inhabitants, formed a melting pot of creeds and colours, composed largely from the original members of the now defunct European Community. Each of the former countries ran their own section of the city, the Quarters subdivided into districts named after famous, long drowned, cities. An elected Council governed the city, its laws enforced by the Europa City Police Department. To them had fallen the onerous and, as Sajer knew only too well, thankless task of maintaining order against a rising tide of crime and violence fuelled by cramped living conditions and ancient racial prejudices.

Beyond its environs, scattered communities farmed the surviving lands of Tuscany to the west, the Marche to the east and Lazio to the south, linked to the city by the steel umbilical cords of a massive monorail system. It stretched over the peninsula like a giant spider's web, providing transit routes for the food, supplies and raw materials used by the city's manufacturing industries, the latter vital in maintaining trade with the surviving communities of America and Asia.

America. Even the word conjured a foul taste in Sajer's mouth. A land of religious zealots intent on trying to keep hold of an empire that had long since slipped from their grasp. The oil conflicts were now into their third decade with no sign of a resolution. A bitter war of attrition between Christian and Muslim driven not by ideology but greed. At least sanity had prevailed with the break up of NATO, leaving the Americans to fight their own wars.

Light drizzle fell as Brecht strolled through the busy night time streets of the Naples district. Ten minutes to midnight and the roads coursed with a steady stream of traffic. In the rain diffused glow of neon signs clubs, brothels and casinos offered him their various pleasures. Girls, boys, gambling and drinking were all his to enjoy in this safe and sanitised environment. These were state-licensed businesses, the legally accepted face of Europa City's vice, which provided the government with tax revenues in excess of three billion every year.

Brecht paused on the opposite side of the road from Maximilians; a high-class pleasure complex that offered a heady mix of services ranging from night club facilities to VR neuro-link sex parlours.

Two heavily muscled men dressed in immaculately tailored suits stood on guard outside its expansive glass doors. On their left, a bored looking girl huddled under a street light. She wore the costume of a hooker from the twentieth century, the management's feeble attempt at conjuring up a risqué ambience for its clients. Dressed in a scarlet basque and a pair of black lace panties, the girl was shivering with cold, goose-pimpled flesh more likely to inspire feelings of pity than lust. Brecht crossed the road and stopped beside her. Close up she looked young and vulnerable, maybe sixteen or seventeen years of age, but hard to tell for sure beneath all the makeup. Hair dyed red, left arm covered in bright tattoos from shoulder to wrist, typical street kid.

Brecht handed her his leather trench coat. 'Here, this will keep the rain off you. You can flash the customers. They'll get a buzz out of that.'

The girl smiled at him but her eyes had a desperate glint as she looked beyond him at the two bouncers in the doorway. 'Thanks. Look, I'm not sure…'

Brecht winked. 'Don't sweat it, kitten. I'm about to become a very good friend of Mr van Meyer.' He turned and stepped in close to the two men as they approached, leaving them no room to manoeuvre. 'John Dumas. Mr van Meyer is expecting me, gentlemen.'

The slightly taller of the two pressed a cautionary finger against Brecht's chest. The ugly puckered scar that ran from the corner of his left eye into his hairline enhanced his menacing appearance. 'That's as maybe, matey. But it don't give you no license to get cute with the staff.'

Sensing the possibility of a fight, Brecht sized the two men up. Both were over six feet tall with powerful physiques. Their fluid movements suggested efficiency in at least one form of martial art. Dangerous adversaries. Discretion was definitley the wisest course of action. 'My mistake,' he said, showing his open palms. 'Just thought she looked a little cold. No harm done, eh? C'mon, let's go and meet Mr van Meyer. I'm sure he doesn't like to be kept waiting.'

Scarface subjected him to a withering scowl and grunted, 'All right, Dumas. Just so long as you know the score in future.'

'No problem, man,' Brecht replied, adding to himself, 'Yeah, next time I'll make sure I bring a gun.'

He followed the bouncers through Maximilians' foyer, up two flights of stairs and into a casino. The air was thick with wreaths of smoke from the cigars and cigarettes of the wealthy patrons. It coiled lazily upwards to be chopped and dispersed by the blades of the ceiling fans. The well-dressed guests were either engaged at the gaming tables or sitting at the bar drowning their sorrows. Scarface motioned Brecht forward and led him past the roulette wheels to a horseshoe shaped baccarat table. He nodded to a thin man wearing gold rimmed spectacles, who sat to the left of the dealer. 'Mr van Meyer, Mr Dumas.'

Van Meyer stood up and removed his spectacles, an unusual affectation in a day and age when most opted for corrective surgery or fusible contact lenses. He held out his hand to Brecht, 'Pleased to meet you, Mr Dumas. Shall we adjourn to my office to discuss details?' Brecht nodded his agreement and van Meyer turned to the other players. 'I trust you'll forgive my leaving? Terribly bad form in the middle of a game, especially when one is winning.' He handed a stack of chips to the croupier, 'George, please divide my winnings between my guests by way of an apology.' He flashed the other players a twenty-four carat smile, 'Now, I really must leave you.'

'I never had you figured for an altruist, Mr van Meyer,' Brecht whispered as they moved away from the table.

'I'm not. George will ensure that the House recovers its losses before the night is out.'

Van Meyer ushered Brecht into his office and indicated that he should make use of the chair in front of his desk. He waited for Brecht to sit before seating himself. Scarface and his silent partner moved to flank their employer, standing three paces behind him on either side.

'I'm led to believe by that piece of gutter-filth you sent that you're interested in taking out a franchise in my adult entertainment industry. I don't trade with just anybody, and you may rest assured that I've had your credentials thoroughly checked before letting you in here. Luckily, for you anyway, I liked what I was told. You're a man with his finger on the pulse - drug trafficking, prostitution, even arms dealing. And now you want a piece of the lucrative market in illegal neuro-link games. My market, Mr Dumas, the one I've fought tooth and nail to build. I'm telling you this so you will understand that even getting a foot in the door is going to cost you dear.'

'I'm well aware of that, Mr van Meyer. If your sources are as good as you say then I'm sure you're aware that I'm a man of no little means myself. So let's cut the crap, shall we? We both know I'm not here to waste your time.'

On Brecht's right Scarface's silent partner tensed. Van Meyer caught sight of the movement and waved an airy hand. 'Relax, Simone. I appreciate a man who speaks frankly. None of this fawning "respect" nonsense. All of that went out in my grandfather's day. I like this man. We can do business together. So tell me what you're offering.'

'An initial investment in gaming discs and machines of forty million euro-dollars, to be used in supplying the three parlours I've already started to equip in Amsterdam. You will of course retain the rights to a percentage of the gross profits. Looking at the long term, if profits are good, I would be looking to invest a further fifty to sixty million, starting in Hamburg with a multiplex in the Reeperbahn.'

'That's serious capital, Dumas, but the returns will be good in the long term. Thirty-percent.'

Brecht grimaced. 'Not that good. Twenty-three.'

Van Meyer chuckled. 'God, you've got balls, Dumas. But you've nothing else without me. True, you could get the equipment and the discs elsewhere but then I'm certain your establishments would develop a nasty habit of burning down or being raided by the police. Regardless, I like your attitude. Twenty-six.'

'Done. Now I've another proposition for you.' Van Meyer raised his eyebrows questioningly as Brecht passed across two black discs. 'Neuro-link torture simulations. We could cut a new market in the sado-masochism field, or export them as an interrogation aid. Guaranteed not to leave signs of trauma on the victim.'

'Tried it, have you?'

A cruel smile twisted Brecht's lips as he remembered Doctor Hagen. 'Oh yes. If we knew who was manufacturing them we could get a wholesale supply.'

'I take it your own enquiries have been unsuccessful?'

'Correct. But I'm betting a man with your connections would have no problem finding out. Particularly since I'm led to believe they're originating in the Italian Quarter. I'm willing to split this one fifty-fifty.' Brecht held out his hand. 'Do we have a deal on that?'

Van Meyer gripped his hand firmly and shook it to seal both deals. 'I'll have my people draw up the necessary documentation and as soon as the money changes hands you'll be in business. My people will be in touch as to when and where you can take delivery of the merchandise.'

'Through Slinky?'

'Yes, that would be best. As for the other matter - I'll have my sources look into it.' He stood up. 'Simone, Anton, please escort Mr Dumas to the door.'

They led Brecht back across the casino to a set of stairs. Anton and Simone remained silent as they opened the concealed door at the foot of the stairwell, which exited on to a side street at right angles to the main strip. Anton bowed mockingly. 'I hope you have a pleasant evening,' he said, closing the door.

Brecht felt the tension drain from his body. For a brief instant he thought his cover had failed and that van Meyer had ordered the guards to dispose of him. The rain had turned from a drizzle to a downpour. Brecht pulled up his shirt collar and started towards the nearest underground station. He would take the Fast-Bahn home and contact Sajer.

The rain continued unabated, leaving Brecht soaked through by the time he reached his apartment. He pulled off his shirt, grabbed a towel from the bathroom and briskly dried himself. Ten minutes later, he stood in a fresh set of clothes drinking a steaming mug of coffee laced with brandy. He picked up the vidphone handset and dialled Sajer's secure number. The screen flickered to life.

Sajer yawned, his eyes still blurred with sleep. 'Who is this? It's a quarter past two in the morning.' His eyes focussed, 'Oh, it's you, Brecht. Good, I was hoping you'd be in contact.'

'And bearing good tidings, sir. I've just finished my meet with Joseph van Meyer and he's agreed to my expansion into the neuro-link child pornography market.'

Sajer came wide awake, a calculating look in his eyes. 'Excellent. How soon do you envisage closing the case?'

'Once the credit transfer's complete I should be able to take delivery of the equipment within a week. We can take him and his men down there and then. Bad news is that I'm going to need you to authorise a payment to my John Dumas identity of forty million euro-dollars from Department funds.'

'Do not concern yourself about that, Kurt. We've been after van Meyer and Gehennah Games for a considerable period of time. The Commissioner will authorise the funds. Now, is there anything else? What are you planning to do for the next week?'

Brecht took a swig of coffee. 'You know those neuro-link torture discs?'

Sajer's face hardened, 'Yes,' his voice was tight.

'I've conned van Meyer into tracing the source for me. He thinks I'm looking to invest in them so with luck we'll get two for the price of one.'

'Devious. But then you were always one of my best men. Is that it?'

'More or less. I'll probably check out a few clubs, see what I can pick up. I'm still looking for leads on that locked box prostitution case. Trouble is they keep moving locale every few days. But don't worry,' his voice took on a hard edge, 'I'll get the bastards in the end. I always do.'

Sajer looked uncomfortable. 'Yes, well, you might like to keep in mind what I said about taking things easy. Weill is not a man you want to cross. He has influence far beyond his rank. You'd be wise not to underestimate him.'

'Don't sweat it, I understand. I'll keep the paper work clean.'

'See that you do. I will ensure that the payment is authorised in the meantime. Get in touch the instant van Meyer is ready. I don't want any mistakes when we arrest him. It's an election year and the Council would like a big show trial for the voters.'

Brecht snorted, 'They would. Never mind the trade in human misery behind it all. Parasites are what they are. But you can tell them not to worry. I'll make them look good to the voters.' He ended the transmission and relaxed back into the sofa, sipping his coffee. Tomorrow would be a busy night but for now he had time to unwind.

Sajer stared at the blank screen in consternation. He should have informed Brecht that he intended to assign the prostitution case to another detective. The man had been working deep cover for too long, with all the stresses and strains that went with it. Fast approaching burn out, Brecht needed a rest. Even if he couldn't see it for himself. Problem was that it might put him irrevocably over the edge if handled wrong. In the interim Sajer had no choice but to play out the events as they fell. He keyed the vidphone again and dialled out. 'Put me through to accounts.'

CHAPTER 4

The receiving light blinked out and the Damocles Assassin removed the bundle of transmitted information. He leafed through the various pages of text until he came to an image of a corpulent looking man in his late forties. The accompanying documentation listed the target's name, address, next of kin, known associates and habits. The full details of his professional and personal life. Information on the time he started and finished work and the route he used to travel there; the clubs, theatres and galleries he liked to frequent during his leisure time, everything the assassin required to plan the hit. As he read the dossier his preconditioned mind carried out a logistical analysis of the target's habits. Hard-wired implants selected the greatest window of opportunity in which to complete the termination. He would carry out the sanction tomorrow evening as the target returned from the Empire Theatre. The target always walked home, taking a short cut through the Kohl Memorial Gardens. It was there that Sword would wait for him.

Few remarked on the dark figure as it drew up along side the main entrance of the gardens. The rider of the sleek motorcycle dismounted; a tall, sinewy figure in oiled black leather that gleamed in the harsh sodium glare of the street lights. The assassin projected a sinister ambience that inclined those that saw him to forget what they had seen. He had honed the skill over many years, composed in equal part of physical and mental presence.

Sword paused to adjust the mirrored visor of his helmet and the night turned bright through its thermal imaging lenses. A courting teenage couple were necking on a bench ahead of him. He stepped from the path and moved silently through the shrubbery with fluid ease. Reflex instinct noted that both were male as he evaluated their potential threat. Two hundred metres on, he took up position at the side of the path to await his prey.

Right on schedule, at eighteen minutes past eleven, the assassin's victim entered the gardens by the west gate. Sword unzipped his jacket and drew a silenced pistol. The action, aided by hard-wired reflexes took two hundred milliseconds; a series of micro-amplifiers speeding the electric impulses of nerve signals across his synaptic gaps. Engaging the targeting system built into his helmet, he aimed, fired two short bursts, and was already turning away as the bullets hit their target. Death was instantaneous, the first burst striking the man in the heart, followed by the now redundant second salvo to his head. All six shots passed through the target's body, the impact of the high velocity rounds causing massive tissue-quake and propelling him backwards. The whole sequence, from the time Sword reached for his gun until his mark hit the ground, lasted less than two seconds. By then Sword was threading his way back through the undergrowth towards the garden's east entrance. During this time neither of the two teenage boys had looked up from their petting session and so remained ignorant of the body when they left by the east exit half an hour later.

At approximately the same time Weill received a coded transmission on his personal channel direct to his office. It read, "Sanction completed" and was signed Sword. He pressed the intercom button. 'Get me a secure line to Commissioner Haynes.'

News of the assassination broke the following morning in a media frenzy fuelled by the bottom-feeders of the press. Brecht caught the details on the early morning news broadcast. The newscaster's face was impassive as he read, 'The body of Paul Costello, Socialist Liberal candidate in the forthcoming elections, was discovered in the Kohl Memorial Gardens in the early hours of this morning. Fears for his safety were raised when Mr Costello failed to return home from the Empire Theatre the previous evening. A police spokesperson issued the following statement: "We have yet to establish a motive for the killing, although we are pursuing several leads, which I am not at liberty to discuss. We have no other pertinent information to disclose at this time."

'The statement has caused mass protest from the Socialist Liberal Party, which has accused the police of attempting to stage a cover-up. Mr Costello was a vocal opponent of the "Police Emergency Powers Act", which is due to be read in Council chambers later this year. If successful, the Act would entitle the ECPD to hold suspects on suspicion of guilt for an indefinite period prior to making formal charges. The Act additionally allows the police to monitor all electronic correspondence. Failure to hand over personal encryption codes would result in an automatic custodial sentence. Opponents of the Act have claimed that these kinds of draconian measures would send the Justice System back to the Dark Ages. Had he been elected, Paul Costello had promised to dismiss the Act and curb existing police powers.

'Mr Costello is survived by his wife and two children.'

18/10/85: My mystery lady continues to dog my footsteps. I ran into the disturbing (or should that be disturbed?) Lady Methedrine last night at the infamous Hamburg Docks club. If a premier place exists in which to encounter the city's lowlife scum the Docks is surely it, which made it the perfect place to pick up a lead on the prostitution case. With that in mind, I went in the guise of "Garth", all twitching nervous energy, waiting to explode. A quick snort of ice made getting into character easy - just a little something to keep me going, you understand. It's not like I'm an addict or anything. I hadn't slept the last couple of nights and in this game you can't risk the kind of fatigue that leads to. Failing to stay alert usually has fatal consequences.

I mingled with the crowd, buying a drink here, greeting a familiar face there. Somewhere among the pimps, whores and junkies was the kind of person who could put me in touch with some locked box action. I merely had to put it about that I was looking for a house where the girls might not be too clean or too willing.

I spent a good hour cruising, getting slowly drunk and nowhere fast. All the while developing another world class migraine that I'd started to suspect was the result of a brain tumour or similar terminal illness. It was damn painful, whatever it was, and I resolved to give the whole sorry business another half-hour at most before going in search of my personal physician. Meantime, another drink would anaesthetise the pain. Things started to get a little weird as I approached the bar, a gleaming monstrosity in polished marble, brass and steel. My voice sounded muted, as though heard underwater, as I ordered a double Pernod but the barman seemed to understand me well enough. I watched, fascinated, as he turned and poured the drink. Traces of after image fanned out beneath his arm as he raised it, giving the impression of a great bird's wing slowly flapping. I took a deep breath in an attempt to clear my head and reached for my credit card as he handed me my drink. It helped, but I couldn't quite shake the suspicion that I was being served by a giant bird. The barman swiped my card and slid it back to me.

He bent close, 'Hey, buddy, I hear you're looking for the Shifting House?' I nodded. 'Well, there's a lady in the corner who can put you in touch with the action.' He pointed and I followed his finger to one of the ubiquitous corner booths that were an integral part of these clubs.

I picked up my drink and flinched as the barman snapped his beak at me, cawing: 'Nevermore!' He gave me a strange look as I hurried away from the bar, a beady eye searching for prey.

It's easy to say I should have known whom I was going to find in the booth but at the time, confused as I was, it came as a genuine surprise to find Lady Methedrine sitting there. Dressed once again in her provocative leather catsuit, her right leg drawn up beside her on the seat. She smiled demurely and beckoned me to take a seat opposite. I tossed back my drink and did as she bid, almost collapsing into the seat as a violent stab of pain lashed through my head. Lady Methedrine's eyes narrowed with concern as she reached across and placed her fingertips on my temples. Her touch felt very cool and produced an immediate sense of calm. We sat like that for several minutes until I realised the pain was gone, not merely reduced to a dull ache in the background as it had been for the past few weeks, but completely absent. I stared at her unable to voice my thanks, my gratitude overcome by my need to discover if she had any information for me. 'Well?'

'Well what? Well, a hole in the ground or well, have you got the information I want, or are you merely toying with me? Or do you simply wish to know if I am in good health? Which do you mean, Kurt? You really must learn to express yourself in more explicit terms. Say what you mean and mean what you say.' She gave a little breathy sigh. 'Still, in this case I think it would be safe to assume you want information.'

'That would be nice. I might also want to bend you across this table and teach you some manners. But let's take things one step at a time.'

She laughed in my face, her scorn almost palpable enough to blister my flesh. 'Why steal something when you can have it for free? Just say the word and I'll play with you later, although it will be my decision. But first, you want to know who's running those girls in the French Quarter, don't you?'

I nodded warily. This wasn't a question I'd been putting round the club, but maybe she'd deduced it by herself. Not a particularly great feat considering she already knew I was an undercover vice cop. That of itself raised questions. That and how she always knew where to find me.

'Lay this on the table.' She handed me a piece of black silk about three-quarters of a metre square and I obligingly spread it flat on the table, wondering what game we were playing. Next, she produced a deck of cards and shuffled them before dealing the top card face down on the silk. 'This is your enemy.'

I turned the card over. As I had expected, it was a Tarot card - The King of Swords. 'Guess it shouldn't be too hard to find a man wearing a crown and carrying a big sword.'

'Don't be so tiresome. The card shows the nature of your enemy. He's a man of intellect, possessed of a powerful personality. Someone in a position of authority, a man who has fought many battles in life.'

'Someone with a name and address, I hope?'

'Behave,' she warned. 'I said I was going to help you and I will. That's the nature of our deal, remember? When you leave the barman will give you a contact number. It will allow you to arrange a visit to the Shifting House, where all of your questions will be answered. Satisfied?'

'It'll do to be going on with.'

'Good.' Lady Methedrine's expression suggested she was less than satisfied with my reply. She tapped an elegantly filed nail on the table. 'Next, I'm going to show you one of a number of possible futures, so you may better understand the choices you have to make in this matter.' She handed me the deck. 'Shuffle the cards, being sure to reverse some of them, then cut the deck into three and reassemble it with the bottom pile on top. When you're satisfied return the cards to me.'

I started to carry out her instructions. 'You're really something, you know that? An informer and circus sideshow performer all rolled into one.'

Pain shot through my skull greying out the edges of my vision. Lady Methedrine hissed, 'I can give pain as well as pleasure, Kurt. You'd do well to remember that.'

'I'm sorry, all right!' I apologised. The pain receded.

Pouting sulkily, she began to lay the spread, placing the first card face down in the centre of the cloth, with the next right angles across the first. She followed this with one above, one below, one to the right and one to the left, to form a cross. Four more cards completed the spread, laid one above the other starting at the bottom right of the cloth and finishing in the top right corner. Ten cards in total.

Lady Methedrine turned the first card face up, gently removing the second card from on top. 'The Knight of Pentacles. This card,' she stated, 'represents your current situation and in some ways is also a reflection of your character. This is the card of a man who knows total dedication to a cause, even though that cause may be lost or impossible to fulfil.

'The next card may reveal more - ah, The Emperor - reversed. The undermining of law and order will block the pursuit of your cause. Perhaps by one who would use you to his own end.'

She pointed above the card. 'The Five of Cups. There's a sense of loss and sorrow hanging over you in this matter. It's possible that your emotions run too deep in relation to this problem. You would do well to tread carefully.

'Your fifth card is The Knight of Swords - reversed. This might best be said to represent your psyche. I see brashness and incautious action. The need for extreme behaviour in both your professional and personal life.'

She turned over the right arm of the cross. 'The Three of Swords. The past is filled with a sense of regret, pain and emotional torment.'

I caught her hand as she pointed to the sixth card of the cross. 'I've heard enough, you fucking bitch! I thought you wanted to help me? This occult shit isn't going to put anyone away.'

'You will let go of my hand, Kurt.' Her voice was quiet, without any force, yet I felt compelled to obey her. I sat back, fear knotting my stomach, and let her continue with the reading.

'The Two of Wands. This card represents forthcoming influences in your life. There is a sense of striving, a conscious focusing of your will as you struggle to act in the world.

'The seventh card is The Nine of Swords - a dark card. It foretells of a cruel and painful situation in the near future that you must endure, one that you'll refuse to turn from for good or ill.

'Temperance - reversed - is your next card. Those around you have noted your excesses. They fear that your emotions blind you, that you are in danger of losing all sense of self.

'The ninth card, The Ten of Cups. This is representative of your hopes and fears. I sense that you are striving for inner peace and contentment but fear what achieving such happiness might bring.'

Lady Methedrine paused dramatically. 'The last card shows the final outcome of events if you follow your present course. It is another of the Major Arcana - The Tower. There will be violence, a time of pain and destruction. Through this, at the end, you may finally find your liberation.'

She gathered the cards, wrapped them in their silk and said, 'The reading is concluded. Take from it what you will.'

I decided not to take much at all, mainly because I didn't care for her last prediction. It chilled me to the core, cutting through my outer shell of scepticism and bypassing more rational thought. I reminded myself that this was practically the twenty-second century and that there was no way that a random selection of cards could tell me of my past or future.

Lady Methedrine said, 'Don't be so ready to dismiss the cards.'

Had she read my mind? Such an unsettling idea didn't seem as far fetched as I might once have thought, not where Lady Methedrine was concerned. A shiver ran down my spine and I had an eerie premonition of what she had meant when she claimed the price of her favours was always more than what one was willing to repay.

Drops of moisture spattering across my face broke me from my reverie. I looked up to see Lady Methedrine dipping her fingers into a drink that had mysteriously appeared on the table. She smiled, all sweetness and light again, and flicked another couple of drops at my face. I wiped the liquid off with my forefinger and tasted it, deciding to play along with her latest schizophrenic change of mood. The drink gently stung my tongue - vodka

Martini - if I was any judge.

She leaned across the table and breathed in my ear, 'Teach me some manners,' before sliding round the booth to kneel beside me.

I placed an arm about her neck, pulled her forward and kissed her. She responded instantly, her lips parting for me, her tongue a fiery dart of inquisitive movement. I tried to remember we were in a public place as I felt her hand caress my body through the thin material of my shirt. I managed to win against my growing arousal and gently pushed her away.

She rocked back on her heels. 'Not man enough to play with me, Kurt?' she mocked. Pouting, she raised a languorous arm and began to unzip her catsuit. The leather, already stretched tight by her breasts, slipped apart as she drew a deep breath. She reached out and took my hands, placing them against her flesh. Her skin, though cool, was not as cold as I had expected.

She let her breath out in a long, shuddering sigh. 'Tell me, can you feel the beat of my heart? It is strong, frantic. Stronger than you or any other man alive. It lusts for life.'

It was true; her heart pounded beneath my right hand with a force that said it would never be stilled. I swallowed, my throat felt suddenly dry. I've had my share of women over the years; my classic Aryan looks are a fatal charm. Yet here was a woman who surprised me at every turn. She was confident of her sexuality and appearance but capricious with her charms. Her moods shifted like quicksand, flitting between playful, serious or angry almost at random. Who was the enigma that knew so much about me? She knew my haunts; had broken into my apartment, spiked my drink and treated me to a hallucinogenic mystery tour of the past. And I still didn't know her real name or where she came from. I resolved to put my contacts to work before I slipped any further.

My attention was slipping in other areas as well. Lady Methedrine began to roll her shoulders, gently rubbing her nipples against my inattentive palms. I felt them harden and swell and bent to kiss her breast. I expected to feel the sharp bite of her teeth at any moment, so I shuddered violently when she brushed my jaw with her lips.

Laughing, her voice low and husky, she breathed, 'I don't bite, Kurt. Not like that anyway. Well, maybe in certain situations.'

Her feather-light kisses danced across the skin of my throat as she bent over me once more. Her hands moved to unfasten first my shirt, then my zip; those gentle kisses followed her progress steadily southward and suddenly all thought of our potential audience was gone. I leaned back and closed my eyes in anticipation. There was a faint clinking sound and moments later my breath exploded from me as she poured her vodka Martini, ice and all, into my lap.

'Consider,' she paused to get her laughter under control, 'consider yourself bitten, Kurt.'

'Jesus Christ, you bitch! What's your fucking problem?'

'Anything you like, Kurt.' She zipped herself up and stood. 'Remember to get that number from the barman before you leave.'

'Don't you worry, I'll remember. Everything.'

'Poor thing, all fired up and nowhere to go. Why don't you try to find Marian? Maybe she'll blow you.'

'How…' I didn't even bother to finish the question. Instead, I just stared at the rhythmic swaying of her hips as she walked out of my life once more. Not that I intended to let the matter slide. I was going to find out who she was and then things would really get interesting. If she liked games, she was going to discover that I could play with the best of them.

The barman gave me a pink slip of paper with an eight-digit number and the name Georgio printed on it. He also gave me a lurid wink as he called last orders but I decided to let it go. With a bit of luck I'd get the pleasure of catching him in the act when I busted the Shifting House.

A habitual sense of caution led me to run a check on the number before using it; a decision I started to regret when I had to wait over two hours for Records to call back. The number belonged to an office in the Lyons district of the French Quarter. The Tessler Corporation was currently renting it: a major league arms manufacturer whose main field was the Research and Development of cybernetic weaponry. A rather unlikely organisation to be involved in white slavery, but then you never can tell. With that in mind, I asked Records to start digging for dirt on Tessler's Chief Executive, Isaac Vaughan. Vaughan was a decorated veteran of four Middle East tours and a fast rising political star. He struck me as being just the type to have more than a little shit on his hands. In the meantime, I had a call to make.

The number had been configured to provide voice only at the caller's end while giving the receiver full visual. Unperturbed, I opted for the straightforward approach. 'Is that Georgio?'

The man who answered spoke with a pronounced American accent, something of an anomaly in Europa City. 'Yeah, buddy, whatcha want?'

'Barman at the Docks said you might have a ticket for the Shifting House.'

'Well, there's still one or two left, but it'll cost ya. Credit transfer of a thousand up front. That a little rich for ya?'

'No. That's fine by me. You get what you pay for.'

Georgio snorted. 'Maybe, buddy, but don't hold your breath. If your credit's good and ya vet positive, we'll be in touch seven to ten days from now. 'Nother thou' will buy you a time and a place. Ya sure you still want in?'

'I already said so, damn it!'

'Max and relax, buddy. Just checking. Make the transfer payable to Axis Holdings. An' maybe we'll be seeing ya.' The line went dead.

That pretty much left me at a loose end, stuck waiting for someone to contact me. Still, I had plenty of faith that Slinky would be in touch about the van Meyer situation before long. He was one of my most reliable contacts, particularly when his bones started to ache. My own bones were more than a little weary but I felt too wired from the speed to sleep - a situation quickly remedied by a night cap of brandy with a couple of downers mixed in. The next twenty-two hours of my life passed in the much sought after oblivion of sleep. Poe may have loathed "those little slices of death" but I certainly didn't harbour a grudge against them.

Sajer badged the uniform outside the door of the ICU. The officer nodded curtly and pushed open the swing door to admit him. Sajer made his way over to where a tall blonde woman in hospital scrubs stood reading a chart. She looked up at his approach and then returned to the chart, making hurried annotations with a light pen. Sensing her disapproval, he moved to the head of the bed.

Brecht looked smaller than he remembered, but then people in hospital beds often did, particularly when hooked up to a ventilator and surrounded by monitors. For some unknown reason his head was swathed in bandages that, together with the breathing tube, gave him an alien look.

'We had to perform an emergency craniotomy during surgery after he suffered an intracerebral haemorrhage.'

'A stroke?'

Doctor Nystrom nodded. 'Were you aware Sergeant Brecht is an addict?'

'It's not uncommon for officers working undercover to find themselves in situations where it may be necessary to take drugs to preserve their cover.'

'I'd say his use went far beyond the line of duty. Tox screen tested positive for milspec stimulants and street quality methamphetamines. It required almost double the amount anaesthetic to sedate him during surgery. The combination probably contributed to the ICH. A fighter, I'll give him that. Technically dead for three minutes on the table, but he came back.'

'The surgery went well then?'

'We recovered four bullets – three from his abdomen and one from his right shoulder, the latter an earlier and already infected wound. I had to remove the spleen and perform a resection of the large intestine, stopping short of a proctocolectomy, which means the colostomy is only temporary.'

'I guess that's something Kurt can be grateful for.'

The left corner of Nystrom's mouth twitched downwards. Sajer recognised it as a tell. 'You disagree?'

'His recovery from those injuries is secondary to his regaining consciousness. He has a GCS score of six – a coma of such severity could continue almost indefinitely.'

'But he could regain consciousness?'

'It's possible. But probably best that you prepare yourself for the worst – severe disability requiring constant nursing care and attention. Whatever Sergeant Brecht was investigating, I hope it was worth the cost.'

CHAPTER 5

The Heidelman Psychiatric Foundation specialised in the recovery of those subjected to sexual abuse. It was to these pastel coloured corridors that the ECPD sent Rachel, John and Timothy Buscato for rehabilitation. The twins responded well to the treatment, their scarred minds only too willing to forget the harrowing abuse they had suffered. They quickly suppressed their parents' murder and accepted the implanted memories of a car crash.

Rachel proved to be an entirely harder proposition. Her mind steadfastly refused to accept the new version of events carefully constructed by the psychologists at the Foundation, and they were at a loss to explain her ability to reinforce the original version of events over those implanted by hypnosis, laser surgery and chemical therapy.

Brecht was informed of the situation when, prompted by Rachel's repeated requests to see him, he called the Foundation to arrange a visit. He would have come sooner but the doctors advised against it, fearing Brecht's presence would serve to undermine their work. They only relented when it became obvious that their efforts had failed and the consensus shifted to believing that the girl needed to confront her rescuer as a form of self-exorcism before she could begin the process of healing.

Brecht paused in the open doorway of the bright, airy bedroom decorated in a mixture of pale pinks and yellows, psychological feel-good colours that matched the bedding and curtains. He saw Rachel lying on the bed with a couple of soft toys beside her, doodling on a piece of paper.

Brecht walked towards her, 'Hello, Rachel.'

'Kurt!' Rachel threw her arms around his neck and hugged him. The two doctors watching by means of a concealed camera nodded approvingly at one another.

'I knew you'd come.' Rachel patted the bed beside her and Brecht, pausing to move a floppy white rabbit dressed in a waistcoat and gloves, sat beside her. 'They keep telling me lies. They want me to believe their stories but the pretty lady always reminds me what happened.'

'The pretty lady?' Brecht tried to keep the anxiety from his voice.

'Yes.' Rachel handed him the paper she had been drawing on when he arrived. She had drawn a surprisingly sophisticated sketch of a willowy looking woman with long dark hair, wearing a white dress. It resembled Lady Methedrine far too closely to be coincidence.

Brecht cleared his throat. 'That's a very good picture, Rachel. She's beautiful. What do the doctors think of your pretty lady?'

'You're such a silly. They can't see her, of course. She's my special friend. Yours, too, she told me. That's how I knew you'd come. She promised you would.'

'Er… that's right. She asked me to see you specially. So what do you and she talk about?'

'She tells me how she's helping you find the men who killed Mummy and Daddy. And that I'm her darling girl and she'd like to be my new Mummy. And, and she helps me remember every time they take me away and make me forget things.'

Brecht floundered as he searched for something suitable to say. He caught himself stroking the toy rabbit and put it out of his reach. A tiny pocket watch slipped from its waistcoat as he moved it. Rachel stared intently at him, waiting for him to continue. 'Wouldn't you be happier if you forgot what happened?'

'No, I'd be sad. I don't want to forget you. And the pretty lady won't be able to visit if I let them make me forget.'

'That's what she told you?'

'Uh-huh. You're being awful serious, Kurt.' She threw a stuffed dormouse at him and giggled when it bounced off his nose. 'Are you mad at me?'

'Of course not. It's just that I saw the pretty lady earlier today and she said to tell you that you should let the doctors help you. I'll still come and visit and that way you won't forget me.'

'And will she still come?'

'I,' Brecht paused, not wanting to lie outright. 'I'm sure she will, but she's very busy and it might be a while. Now what else have you been doing? Have you seen your brothers?'

'Yes. We play together every day.'

'And they're happy? You haven't told them about the pretty lady or anything else?'

'Oh no,' her voice dropped to a whisper, 'She's our secret, Kurt. She said I'd only upset them, and I don't want to upset John and Timmy. I love them. Mummy always said I had to look after them because I'm older than them.'

'Your Mummy was right. And she, just like the pretty lady and me, wants you to be happy. So I want you to make me a promise, okay?' Rachel nodded. 'All right. I want you to promise me that you'll let the doctors help you to get better.'

Rachel chewed her bottom lip. 'But she said…'

'I know what she said, but you trust me, don't you? You know I wouldn't lie to you?'

Brecht felt a wrenching sensation in his chest as she subjected him to a long studious look far too old for her years. She hung her head and said in a small voice, 'Okay. I promise. You're going to go away now, aren't you?'

'Yeah,' Brecht swallowed, finding his throat suddenly tight. 'That's right. I've work to do. But I'll be back. That's my promise to you.' He stood up and crossed to the door, where he paused in the threshold. 'Bye, now.'

Rachel, already intent once more on her sketching, didn't look up as she said, 'Bub-bye.' Brecht closed the door and walked away.

Brecht shifted uneasily in his chair as he stared at the clinically white walls of Doctor Wilsdorf's office. The doctor sat opposite behind an expansive desk littered with desktop toys and files. Wilsdorf was a man of middle years, almost skeletal in his thinness, and completely bald except for a fringe of brown hair behind his ears.

Brecht treated him to an inane smile, making a concerted effort to act as though he were behaving normally. It was a defensive action experienced by many in the presence of a trained psychologist, made all the worse by the fact that Brecht did have something to hide.

Wilsdorf noticed his behaviour and, having witnessed it many times, ignored it. He addressed Brecht using a form of pronounced reticulation currently in vogue with the city's elite. 'Quite remarkable, Mr Brecht. Not only is that the first inclination the Buscato girl has shown towards physical contact with another human being, but you also managed to get her to explain what is going on in her mind. Remarkable. It would appear that her id has constructed a surrogate mother figure - this pretty lady she keeps referring to. She is somehow using this construct to lock away events in a section of her mind we have so far been unable to reach. It would further appear that she has attached this mother figure to yourself, perhaps in a bid to create foster parents. Do you agree, Mr Brecht?'

'No I don't, actually. Mainly because I've met the pretty lady, which tends to blow a big hole in your hypothesis, wouldn't you say?'

Wilsdorf's eyes narrowed. 'I beg your pardon. Did you say you have met this imaginary woman? Please, Mr Brecht, do not insult my intelligence

- not even in jest.'

'I wasn't trying to be funny. I've met the woman in Rachel's drawing on several occasions. She calls herself Lady Methedrine.'

'And I suppose you are going to tell me that this woman has been floating in and out of my institution undetected, harassing one of my patients. It is no secret that I was against your admittance to the Foundation from the very beginning, but for a moment there I thought I had been mistaken. That was before you came out with this ridiculous fairy tale. Perhaps you require some therapy yourself? If so, I could recommend several eminent professionals and institutions.'

Brecht sighed; this was exactly the kind of situation he had been trying to avoid. Weill already had enough ammunition to use against him without a qualified professional voicing the opinion that he was mentally disturbed. 'Look, I think I've given you the wrong impression. I was simply trying to point out that it's a rather strange coincidence that I should have recently met a woman of similar appearance to this pretty lady of Rachel's. Especially when you consider her claims that the pretty lady knows me.'

'Hmph.' Doctor Wilsdorf glowered at Brecht. 'Well, whatever else you may like to think one fact remains unaltered - you can rest assured that no woman resembling the girl's description has entered this institution, let alone visited her. I'm sorry if that dismisses any Jungian theories of synchronicity you may have been constructing, Mr Brecht. But when all is said and done we are both rational beings, are we not?'

Brecht thought, *smug bastard*, and smiled. It was time to do some serious back-pedalling. 'Of course. Please excuse me, messing with people gets to be a habit in my line of work. Part of the interview technique, I'm afraid. You might call it an occupational hazard.'

'Do not concern yourself.' Wilsdorf assumed his most patronising tone of voice, 'It is nothing to worry about, so to speak. We all have our little foibles. Now, we really must press on. You came, after all, to hear my prognosis, not to debate a little girl's fantasies.'

'Quite correct. Please continue, Doctor.'

Wilsdorf sat up straight, assuming a more professional attitude. 'I am pleased to say that it is very good. With what we have learned from your conversation with the girl we should be able to take positive steps towards eliminating her trauma.'

'I see. And how soon do you think it would be safe for me to visit her again? After her treatment, naturally.'

The doctor took a deep breath and slowly released it as he regarded Brecht. 'You must understand that this is a transitional period for the girl. She has suffered severe emotional trauma. Once we have successfully concluded her treatment, it would be best if she were kept isolated from all associations with past events. There is always the danger of regression, flashbacks and so on.'

'In other words,' Brecht ground his teeth together, 'you're saying that in your professional,' he spat the word out, 'opinion it would be best if I never saw her again?'

'No, not never. Forgive me if I am being overly candid here, but I have read your case history. I know you must identify with the girl. No doubt as her rescuer you see a similarity between your relationship with her and that of your own with Guyon Sajer. What you must understand is that psychiatry has changed over the last twenty-five years. We have all sorts of new technology available for the treatment of such cases. You must trust me when I tell you that these treatments will give the girl her best chance of leading a normal, well adjusted life.'

Brecht rose angrily to his feet. 'Fine. You know all the answers, all of the angles. You have me figured out exactly. I'll go and take my emotional transference, or whatever it's called these days, elsewhere.'

'Calm yourself, Mr Brecht. I can assure you that I did not mean to cast dispersions on your motives. If you had let me finish, I was going to add that eventually it might be good for the girl if we introduced you again. However, right now I am sure you would agree that the important matter is that Rachel be made well again.'

'Yes, of course. You're quite correct. I must apologise. You should understand that my mother's death remains a painful subject for me to discuss. Even after all these years.'

'Of course, and I am sorry I had to raise those events again. This is only a suggestion, but if it still troubles you so much you might want to consider some further therapy. As I said, there have been many advances over the last two decades.'

Brecht shook his hand. 'Perhaps I'll do just that, Doctor Wilsdorf,' adding to himself, the fuck I will.

Doctor Wilsdorf pumped his arm enthusiastically. 'Glad to hear it. You may rest assured that we will do everything possible for the girl. Now, you must excuse me, I have rounds to make.'

'Of course. I mustn't take up any more of your time. I'll be in touch later.'

Wilsdorf reached for the phone as the door closed behind Brecht. 'This is Doctor Wilsdorf at the Heidelman Foundation. I wish to speak with Captain Weill, please. He is expecting my call.'

Brecht discovered a parcel waiting for him when he returned home. The sender had addressed it to his John Dumas identity, which meant the Vice squad mail drop must have forwarded it. He examined the package, a cardboard carton measuring half a metre square, sealed with masking tape.

The only other marking and clue as to its origin was a Naples district postal frank.

Brecht pulled out a stiletto from his hip pocket, triggered the blade and sliced open the carton, secure in the knowledge that it the Vice squad boffins would have scanned for explosive devices and other booby traps on receipt. A faint smell of perfume wafted upwards as he lifted the lid and discovered his trench coat lying inside. A single sheet of writing paper rested on top of the coat on which a neat hand had written in violet ink:

Dear Mr Dumas,

I just wanted to thank you for your kindness the other evening and to return your coat. Mr van Meyer liked your idea so much that he's bought me one of my own - a fur. I don't get to wear anything at all under it now, but I guess that's how it goes. A girl's got to earn a living somehow, after all.

Love,

Anastasia

P.S. Your secret's safe with me!

Brecht frowned as he picked up the trench coat, curious as to what his secret might be. He shook the creases out and threw it across his shoulders - cape fashion. While he had given it to the girl in good faith, he felt pleased she'd returned it, having grown attached to it over the years. His good mood evaporated when he slipped a hand into one of the pockets and discovered what Anastasia had referred to as his "secret". A look of pained disbelief settled on his features as he pulled the flat rectangle of plastic from the pocket. He stared at his Vice squad ID card, traces of white powder still clinging to its edges.

Brecht read the letter again, searching between the lines for any indication that Anastasia had informed van Meyer of his identity, but found nothing. He had no choice except to trust his gut feeling that the girl was on the level and go ahead with the operation. He crumpled the letter into a ball and threw it across the room. The trench coat followed it a second later in a feeble effort to vent his anger at his own stupidity. 'Fuck it,' he swore. 'What's done is done.'

A raid on his drinks cabinet turned up a half full bottle of brandy among the empties. He poured a generous measure and sat down to figure out his next move, the obvious answer being to press on regardless. Van Meyer was no fool. If he'd discovered that John Dumas was really Kurt Brecht he would be more inclined to pull out of the deal and cut his losses, rather than having Brecht killed. Van Meyer rarely took such overtly violent action. His avoidance of such being the main reason the Department had so far failed to convict him.

'Kurt, my man, you are looking bitchin' and awesome today.'

'And you, Slinky, look like the sorry piece of shit you always have been,' Brecht replied to the image on the vidphone. In a fit of brooding the previous evening he'd finished the half bottle of brandy and gone on to drink another. He was in the process of sleeping it off when Slinky's call woke him to the delights of a monster hangover. 'Cut the crap and tell me what's happening with the van Meyer situation.'

'You are so hostile, Kurt. But I just know you're gonna feel love and warmth towards me when I tell you Mr Paedophile wants to see you Friday night - as in the twenty-third of October.' He folded his arms behind his head. 'Happy?'

Brecht stopped massaging his temples and looked up. 'Well, I probably won't kick your skinny arse next time I see you. Now, where and when does he want to hand over the goods?'

'Twenty-two hundred. He has a warehouse in the Naples Industrial Estate - Vine Street. There'll be four trucks waiting for you to transport the merchandise to Amsterdam. Once you take delivery the responsibility of getting it there safely is your own.'

'Fine by me. It's going nowhere except the evidence room. And van Meyer's going straight to prison - hopefully after a beating. You got anything else for me?'

'Not me, personally, but van Meyer has an info-fix for you. He said to tell you Chromium Oxide is distributing the neuro-link torture discs - it's a subsidiary of the Tessler Corporation. Not that you'd have any luck proving it in a court of law. It's a no-go, Kurt. The distributors will react with extreme prejudice to anyone attempting to cut themselves a piece of the action.'

'Tessler again. There's a pattern emerging here. Isaac Vaughan definitely isn't the golden boy he's made out to be.'

'Sorry. You want to come again?'

'Just thinking aloud, Slinky. Thanks. Shit, no, wait. I've just remembered something I want you to look into for me. See if you can find anything out about a woman calling herself Lady Methedrine. Her real name would be a good start. She's about five foot seven or eight, mid twenties, long black hair and slim build. She always dresses in white and hangs out at the Docks and the Paradiso. Somebody's bound to know her. Crazy as they come.'

'Shouldn't be too hard to locate a chic chick like that.' Slinky grinned, revealing the rotting stumps of his teeth. 'What's this hot lady done to merit the attentions of the Brecht beast?'

'Given me the ultimate cold-cock for a start, but that's neither here nor there. Let's just say I want her to help me with my investigation and leave it at that. But while you're at it, see if you can get me the address of a girl called Anastasia. Don't know if that's her real name - probably not - but she works the door of Maximilians for van Meyer.'

'I thought you'd be staying clear of the chicks for a while after what happened between you and Hannah.'

Brecht flipped him the finger. 'Don't push it, Slinky. This one's strictly business.'

Slinky shrugged. 'Whatever way you want to tell it, that's fine by me. Just remember, payment in the usual manner. I'll see you around.'

CHAPTER 6

B recht hurried through the streets of the Naples Industrial Zone. Rising on either side, its towering factory skyscrapers made him feel dwarfed and insignificant. They were active even at this time of night, working twenty-four hours a day to provide consumer goods for the city's forty million inhabitants. Flashes of discharged energy from the automated machines produced a stroboscopic effect to the accompaniment of a low sonic rumble. Radio controlled cargo trolleys flitted back and forth, bearing raw materials in one direction and finished goods in the opposite. The few human workers ignored the detective as they loaded and unloaded the trolleys, appearing only a fraction less mindless than the automatons they worked alongside.

Here lay the dark underbelly of the city, faceless people slaving away in the bowels of factories. The poorly educated, or simply poor, who had no hope of finding a position among the city's scientific elite, those who would never work alongside the genetic engineers, cyberneticists and software engineers that were the life's blood of the city's technologies. These unfortunates were condemned to perform any task no matter how menial to escape the growing unemployment and poverty sweeping the city.

Every year the population swelled while the jobs grew fewer as automatons and machines took over the city's civic construction programs. The Cyber Age was dawning and humanity had designed itself out of a future. They had ravished the planet and now must cling to the few inhabitable pieces of land available. And so the city expanded in the only way possible, upwards, in a series of giant multi-storey blocks whose cramped living conditions bred violence and civil unrest. This in turn provided the city with its only growth human industry - the forces of law and order.

Brecht, like so many others, thought little about these conditions as he passed between the towering factory blocks. The factory workers could not afford the vices he fought against and therefore were of no importance to him. In his opinion it was the job of the uniforms, the SPF, to deal with the proletariat when they stepped out of line. He hunted bigger game.

Brecht had spent the previous two hours in a squalid motel room rehearsing the evening's plan of action while he lay on the stained sheets of the bed, the stench of sweat and cheap perfume conjuring the ghosts of whores and their tricks. The bodies of strangers to begin with, on to which he painted faces after visualising a familiar mole, birthmark or scar. Hannah, Marian, Lady Methedrine, separate and the same. Brecht pushed the images from his head and concentrated on the mission: meet with van Meyer at ten o'clock that evening as agreed, wired with a concealed mini-cam to record details of the transaction for evidence. Backup team would move in and make their arrests on completion of the credit transfer. A textbook operation that he'd followed many times.

Brecht swung his legs off the bed and padded across the threadbare carpet to a dressing table made from cheap extruded plastics that, like the rest of the furniture, had already been recycled half a dozen times in its brief lifetime. The gun resting on its surface was a different matter altogether. The Walther PP10 (Police Pistol), a recoilless semi-automatic capable of firing single shots or three round bursts, fitted with a staggered fifteen round magazine. Developed for the city's Police Department, its standard ammunition was the Richter 10mm depleted uranium high velocity shell. The impact shock from a single round was capable of killing a man, stopping power having become the prime requisite for all firearms in a city filled with designer stimulants.

The room's feeble illumination glinted malevolently from the gun's machined surface as Brecht picked it up. He pulled back the slide, checked the action and made sure he had a round chambered in the breach. Satisfied, he checked the safety before thrusting the pistol into a spring-loaded holster beneath his left armpit.

Sajer's warning echoed inside his skull. 'You're not to discharge your firearm during this arrest unless there is a clear and present danger. Unfriendly eyes will be watching. I trust I have made myself clear?'

Brecht felt very clear. Regardless of Sajer's wishes, he would bring van Meyer to justice for his crimes one way or another. He had made a promise and he always kept his promises.

He picked up his trench coat and examined the mini-cam, a device 25mm in diameter mocked up to resemble a coat button. Essentially a sound and vision transmitter, it utilised a satellite up-link to transmit signals to data storage equipment in the Halls of Justice. The discs were then sealed to prevent accusations of tampering when presented as evidence at trial.

Brecht pulled on the coat and examined his reflection in the cracked mirror above the sink. No tell-tale bulge or other sign of the gun; the coat having been tailored to hide them. Another reason for being grateful that Anastasia had returned it. Her name produced a surge of impotent fury as he remembered his stupidity concerning the ID card. He would never forgive himself if van Meyer escaped justice because of it.

The fear and guilt of two hours ago vanished as Brecht turned the corner into Vine Street. Years of training took over as he donned the mantle of the cool professional about his person. Ahead of him, four giant container trucks stood highlighted in the arc-lights of the warehouse. He paused, partially shielded by the wall of the corner building, and spoke quietly into his com-unit, 'Brecht, I'm about to meet with van Meyer. You'd better be set at your end.' He thrust the com-unit into his pocket and proceeded towards the trucks.

Van Meyer stood in front of the lead truck, flanked on either side by Simone and Anton. The two bodyguards were dressed as before in impeccably tailored suits, the only difference being that they were now armed with the latest flechette machine-pistols. Four truck drivers, bearing similar weapons, were visible behind the trio. To their left one other figure sat at a folding table in front of a workstation terminal, waiting to establish the up-link for the credit transfer.

Van Meyer nodded to him as he walked across the forecourt. 'Good evening, Mr Dumas, I trust you'll find everything in order.'

Brecht smiled back at him. 'I hope so,' he said casually. He cast a professional eye over the group taking in every detail about the three men. The scar faced man, Anton, and his silent partner, Simone, appeared to pose the greatest danger. An aura of violence emanated from the pair; too tense, and too eager for an excuse to use their weapons. He would need to watch them closely when the bust went down. Van Meyer appeared to be unarmed, relying solely on the efficiency of his two guards for protection.

'Good. I take it you'd like to see the merchandise before finalising the deal?'

'Yeah, I think that would be best.'

Van Meyer snapped his fingers, 'Simone, Anton, come.'

He gestured to Brecht that he should make his way to the rear of the trucks, which were drawn up in a diagonal line, each parked seven metres in front of the previous one. As they moved, Brecht got his first good look at the drivers. They were dressed in identical grey overalls and presumably selected for their lack of distinguishing features. Faceless servants easily forgotten after the delivery. Unlike the two bodyguards, these men handled their weapons with the kind of sloppy indifference that suggested they would be more of a danger to each other than anyone else in a gun battle.

Anton slung his machine-pistol across his chest, reached up and slid back the locking bars fitted to the rear of the trailer. He pulled out a flashlight, climbed the metal rungs fixed to the rear of the trailer and made his way inside. Brecht shifted nervously on his feet, acutely aware of the barrel of Simone's gun pointing at him as the bodyguard covered him. Simone moved the barrel aside as Anton signalled for them to join him. He ushered Brecht and van Meyer into the trailer and then followed. A fear inspired rush of adrenaline surged through Brecht's body as he stepped into the trailer. This would be an ideal opportunity for van Meyer to dispose of him if Anastasia had betrayed him. His only defence being to remain as alert as possible.

'Anton, show Mr Dumas his property.'

Brecht let out an appreciative whistle as Anton played the beam of the flashlight up and down a row of secured neuro-link chairs.

'You like?' van Meyer asked.

'John likes them very much. What about the discs?'

Van Meyer pointed to three cardboard cartons, similar to the ones Brecht had discovered in the warehouse on Ostenstrasse, secured to the side of the trailer by cargo netting. 'Over there, my friend. Would you like Simone to open one for you?' Brecht heard the whisper of steel on leather as Simone unsheathed a wicked looking combat knife.

'No, that won't be necessary. You could show me a handful of discs and I'd have no way of knowing for sure if your product was on them. There has to be an element of trust somewhere down the line.'

Van Meyer chuckled, 'Glad to hear it,' and slapped him on the back. 'Let's examine the other trailers and then we can close this deal.'

They went through the same procedure with the remaining trailers, with the drivers climbing into the cab of the rig after Brecht finished his examination. All four were sitting with their engines idling as Brecht, van Meyer and the hired muscle made their way towards the man sitting at the workstation. He looked up nervously as they approached. Up close Brecht could see that he was little more than a skinny kid, eighteen or nineteen years old at most. The boy swept his lank fringe out of his eyes. 'All of the links are complete, Father. I just need Mr Dumas' credit card and his authorisation codes to complete the transfer.'

'Some kid, eh?' van Meyer asked proudly. 'Two years at university and he's already found a dozen ways to improve the running of my organisation. At this rate I'll be able to retire in another couple of years knowing the family business is in secure hands.'

Brecht felt some of the tension drain out of him during this exchange. It being unlikely that van Meyer would have brought his son along if he were expecting trouble. Simone and Anton tensed almost imperceptibly as he reached inside his coat; they seemed disappointed when he produced nothing more sinister than a credit card. He handed the card to van Meyer's son. 'The code's Othila, Sol, Rune, Nine. It's set up for a straight credit transfer.'

The boy swiped the card through a reader attached to one of the ports and keyed in the password. Thirty seconds later the words "Transaction Completed" flashed up on the screen. Van Meyer turned to Brecht and shook his hand. 'I guess we're partners, Dumas.'

The roar of engines drowned out Brecht's reply as two armoured personnel carriers sped round the corner and drew up on the forecourt in front of the warehouse. They disgorged a squad of kevlar armoured SPF officers.

Sajer's amplified voice boomed, 'Europa City Vice. Lay down your weapons, switch off your engines and surrender immediately. We are authorised to use deadly force if you fail to comply.'

A sullen silence descended over van Meyer's men as they considered the ultimatum. Van Meyer stared accusingly at Brecht, causing Anton and Simone to tense as they waited for the command to act. Brecht opened his mouth to protest his innocence and then chaos broke loose as the driver of the lead truck decided to make a bid for freedom.

The truck's engine roared as he slammed it into gear and floored the accelerator. The SPF uniforms replied with a hail of fire that blew out the truck's windshield and tyres as it lumbered towards them. Their assault on the truck was curtailed as the other drivers began laying down covering fire, forcing them to take cover.

Anton made his move. He cocked his gun, swung it in Brecht's direction and screamed, 'You lousy fucker! You've sold us out.' He loosed a long, rolling burst of fire.

Brecht dived to the side to avoid the deadly stream of high velocity darts. The flechettes dug up clouds of tarmac around him as he rolled to one knee and loosed a three round burst. Fired on a rising trajectory, the first two rounds whistled between Anton's legs, leaving the final one to castrate him as it passed through his scrotum. At the same moment ribbons of pain lashed across Brecht's back as a burst of fire from Simone grazed him. Throwing himself into another diving roll, he fired two bursts at his new aggressor. The second salvo caught Simone in the chest, blowing his ribs through his lungs, causing them to burst from his back like so many groping fingers. Another flurry of flechettes lacerated Brecht's thigh as Anton re-entered the fight, one hand thrust between his legs to stem the flow of blood from his emasculated manhood. Brecht took him out with a head shot and rolled on to his knees to take stock of the situation.

During the fire fight the truck had rumbled on to ram the personnel carriers, scattering the SPF officers. Having failed to shove the vehicles aside, the driver had gone into reverse in an attempt to gain space to manoeuvre. Brecht looked up in time to see the truck jack-knife, its trailer swinging round to form a barrier between him and Sajer's forces, who were still trading sporadic shots with the remaining three drivers. He heard a low chuckle and turned to find van Meyer and his son behind him. The boy no longer looked quite as young as he raised his arm to aim one of the deadly flechette machine-pistols. Van Meyer sighed, 'I'm very disappointed in you, Mr Dumas, if that is your real name. You've cost me a great deal of money and I'm probably going to find it very difficult to evade prosecution. Even if I do escape, I shall have to spend the rest of my life in hiding. My one consolation is that I'll never see you again. Erwin, kill him.'

Brecht, unable to bring his gun to bear, braced himself for the impact of the killing shot. Instead, he found himself thrown through the air as two of the trucks erupted into incandescent fireballs. Brecht raised his gun as van Meyer scrambled to his feet and made a run for the warehouse. Erwin staggered in front of him as Brecht pulled the trigger, taking the bullets meant for his father in the left shoulder. The impact at such close range tore off his arm. The boy folded to the ground, staring in disbelief at the severed limb. He bled out fast, gouts of blood spurting from a severed artery in his shoulder. Van Meyer, who had stopped his flight at the sound of the shots, turned to witness his son's demise. A fit of rage seized him and he ran back towards Brecht. 'Erwin! You lousy pig bastard, you've fucking killed my boy!'

Brecht raised his gun to shoot van Meyer, only to discover it was out of ammunition. Having no time to reload, he threw it aside as van Meyer leapt at him, grabbing for his neck. The older man's fingers tightened around his throat in an implacable grip as grief and rage lent him inhuman strength. Unable to free himself, Brecht released his grip on van Meyer's wrists and flexed the muscles in his right forearm, firing the spring-loaded blade. Van Meyer rocked back in agony as the knife buried itself in his thigh, causing him to relinquish his hold. Brecht followed up on the advantage by smashing van Meyer in the face with an elbow strike that sent him rolling on to his back. Panting heavily, he staggered to his feet and ended the fight by delivering a kick to van Meyer's head. As he staggered back, his left foot skidded on something soft, sending him tumbling to the ground. Brecht stared at the glob of flesh lying inches from his nose and started to laugh. He had survived a gun battle and beaten off van Meyer only to slip on one of Anton's testicles.

Brecht winced as the medic pulled another of the tiny flechettes from his thigh. The impact of the high velocity darts had turned the surface tissue to jelly for an area of two centimetres around each of the entry wounds, the effect known as tissue quake. Brecht had been lucky in that he had only received three actual hits from Simone's burst; a number of quakes acting in concert could liquefy flesh entirely, making it almost impossible to save the limb. The medic dropped the last of the darts into a plastic dish and sprayed an antiseptic containing a combined painkiller and coagulant over the wounds. He concluded the procedure by wrapping a pressure bandage about the injury.

'I'm afraid you'll have to lie down while I attend to your back, Sergeant Brecht,' he said, pointing to a stretcher.

Brecht moved to comply, gritting his teeth as he pulled off his trench coat, noting ruefully that it would require a new back panel. The medic glanced up to see what the delay was and caught him in the process of trying to unbutton his shirt.

'I wouldn't bother with that. The blood has already stuck it to your back. I'll need to cut it off. Now get your arse on this stretcher before I have to kick it for you. You're not the only cunt with holes in him.'

'You've got a great bedside manner, you know that?' Brecht grumbled as he climbed on to the stretcher and lay on his stomach.

'I find it encourages my patients to get better quicker.' There was a shearing noise as he snipped away Brecht's shirt. 'This may sting a little.'

'Jesus fucking Christ!'

'No, Brecht,' said a familiar voice, 'merely your commanding officer. Is he giving you a hard time, Wallace?'

The medic grinned. 'No more than most.'

'What do you expect if you go about pouring napalm on people's backs?'

'This?' He showed Brecht a small aerosol device. 'It's merely an antiseptic. None of those flechettes may have penetrated your back but between them they've damn near flayed the skin right off. Skinned you like a rabbit. You're damned lucky they weren't poisoned.'

'That's me, luckiest bastard in the world.' Brecht turned to Sajer, 'So, what's the official verdict on the arrest?'

'Far from good. I have three dead SPF officers, another seven with various wounds, two of which are on the critical list, and half of our evidence is merrily burning behind you. The whole operation is a bloody fiasco.' Brecht mumbled something under his breath, prompting Sajer to say, 'Sorry, I didn't quite catch that remark.'

'I said you can't blame me for this one. Well, not all of it.'

'No, I can't. This is a case of the old military maxim of the Seven P's - poor planning and preparation produces piss poor performance. The truck drivers should have been neutralised the moment we moved in for the arrest.'

'How's van Meyer?' Brecht asked, hoping to change the subject.

'Alive, in spite of your best efforts. Although I'm sure that it will warm your heart to know that in addition to fracturing his jaw in three places you also succeeded in knocking out four of his teeth and in breaking his nose and right cheekbone. Quite restrained by your usual standards. I suppose one should be thankful for small mercies.'

'I suppose you should.' Brecht glanced over his shoulder. 'So, Doc, how long before I'm fit for active duty again?'

Wallace glanced at Sajer, who nodded almost imperceptibly. 'At least four weeks, I'm afraid. Tissue quakes are slow and awkward to heal.'

'No way! I've a hot lead on that locked box case you gave me. I can't sit on it for a month.'

'I'm sorry, Kurt, but that's how it is. You can either take four weeks sick leave or I'll simply suspend you for four weeks. It is one and the same whichever you choose. At least on sick leave you'll be allowed to retain your shield and your gun. I'm not going to lie to you, Kurt. There will have to be an official enquiry into this debacle and it will be better for all concerned if you're kept away from Captain Weill. Out of sight, out of mind, no?'

'Oh yeah, I get the picture.' Brecht got up from the stretcher. 'Now, if you would excuse me, I think I'll get started on that sick leave right now. Wallace take note, I commenced my sick leave at zero-oh-three ay-em, Saturday the twenty-fourth of October. Four weeks to the second, not a moment longer, that's how long I'm on leave for. I hope that satisfies everyone.'

'Noted,' Wallace addressed Brecht's back. 'And remember to stay off that leg.' Brecht replied by extending his middle finger as he limped away.

'Thank you, Wallace.' Sajer patted the medic on the shoulder.

'No problem. May I ask why? That's a far from happy man.'

'Brecht is on the edge, heading for burnout. If he doesn't rest there's every chance that he'll destroy himself. You could say that his wounding has proved most fortuitous, as I was looking for an excuse to remove him from his current case.'

'I see. Total bullshit, of course. You don't believe for one second that he'll sit idle for four weeks.'

'No,' Sajer turned away, 'more is the pity. But I tried and surely that is all any man can hope to do?'

27/10/85: Can't figure Sajer's game plan. Knows damn well that my injuries aren't that serious. But if he really wanted me off the case why point out that I'd still have my badge and gun on sick leave? As open an invitation to carry out a little freelance work as ever I've heard. He's playing some sort of game of his own and whatever it is I don't intend to become a sacrificial pawn.

Elsewhere there's nothing but dead ends - no Lady Methedrine and no appointment with the Shifting House. Three days of sitting idle, waiting for Lady Methedrine or Isaac Vaughan to make a move. Something has to break soon before I do!

29/10/85: Progress on many fronts. I have the current address of the Shifting House and I'm due to go there this evening. Met with Lady Methedrine last night and she answered several questions. I no longer fear for Rachel's safety.

According to Slinky no one had seen my mystery woman so I decided to go down the Paradiso in van Helsing mode and do a little vamp hunting. Having visited a "doctor" of my acquaintance earlier that day to obtain some suitable medication, I shot myself full of morphine to prevent my leg troubling me. To be honest, I think I overdid it on the morphine a little. But what the hell, life's a learning curve, right?

I arrived at the Paradiso feeling more than a little detached from reality, and with no better plan of action than to wait and see what developed. I set up station in what was rapidly becoming my regular corner booth, got myself a large whisky and baited my trap with a vodka Martini. The alcohol and morphine proved a bad combination and I found myself drifting off into a mild delirium, content to listen to the pounding back-beat of the music while nestled in the warm embrace of the booth's padded leather furnishing. A rough shake to the shoulder wakened me some time later. Lady Methedrine had arrived - only she hadn't, if you follow. The woman sitting opposite me certainly looked like her at first glance, but I began to notice subtle differences. This woman was younger and had warm, honey coloured eyes that seemed to draw the soul from your body. Her hair, still long and black, was mussed and disarrayed. Her style of dress also differed, the pure white forsaken for off-white with hints of pink; long streamers of jewel embroidered cloth trailed from the sleeves and bodice.

'Who are you?' I asked through parched lips.

'Surely you know me?'

True enough there was no mistaking that voice, although I thought it a little mellower than usual.

'What have you done to yourself? Your mind is so unfocussed. I can't concentrate. You're all primitive urges and desire. Your body cries for love and mine responds. It's so warm in here.' She leaned closer and unlaced the bodice of her dress, exposing the cream coloured flesh of her breasts.

I put out a hand to stop her. 'Enough. I came here to talk, not be hustled by some cheap slut. Get a grip on yourself, woman,' I spat, my anger clearing the fog from my mind.

She grew increasingly focussed, as though she were feeding off my new coherence, or perhaps my drug-induced vision of her was simply returning to normal. Whatever the explanation, a far more typical Lady Methedrine addressed me next.

'Slut?' She drew the lacing of her bodice tight. 'No more than some of the women you've chosen to lie with, and I didn't hear you complaining about my behaviour the other evening.'

I muttered a half-hearted apology before addressing the subject uppermost in my thoughts. 'I want you to leave the girl alone. I don't know how you got into the Heidelman Foundation without them observing you and I don't care. What I do care about is that you're tormenting Rachel, twisting her head with your warped notions. It's unnecessary. What's a twelve year old girl to you anyway? You some kind of lesbian with a taste for children?'

Her eyes flashed with rage, now blue and cold. 'Hardly. If you must know, she has a talent not dissimilar to your own. Coupled with her pain, that talent became a vital source of energy for me. It has allowed me to define the finer aspects of my form. My long birthing process is almost complete. Soon I will become an entity in my own right. I require only a single sacrifice more. The child's energy is no longer of importance to me. Soon I will be free of our ties, and I won't have it said that I owe you or any other man. So if it makes you happy, I'll free the girl. Call it my gift to you, Kurt. It cancels out what I owe you. Just beware of the cost.'

'I guess that's a risk I'm gonna have to take,' I challenged her.

By way of response, she picked up her Martini and fished out the cocktail stick. Holding it delicately between thumb and forefinger, she licked at the olive. Her eyes locked with mine and she breathed, 'Your choice.'

I wondered what new game we were playing. True to form, Lady Methedrine had gone from predatory cat to sex kitten in an instant. I realised that the usual Lady Methedrine now sat opposite me, long dark hair spilling across the white leather of her catsuit. Had the honey eyed girl merely been a delusion of drink and drugs, or was all that she claimed true? It seemed impossible and insane, but what other explanation was there? How else, except that she was all that she claimed, could she pass through locks and barriers unseen?

These questions tore through my mind as I watched her devour that olive in the Paradiso. Thoughts came to me, bordering dangerously close to madness, and I might have dismissed them as poppy fuelled dreams had she not turned to me and said, 'Why do you torment yourself with these questions when in your heart you already know the truth? I am Lady Methedrine. I am here, in your head, reading you like a book. What more proof do you need of my power?'

'None,' I whispered and bowed my head in submission. From that moment I knew I was lost to her, body and soul. I had created a monster, and fate always demands that the monster should turn on its creator.

My doom rose to her feet. 'Good. Many things will be easier now that you have accepted the truth. Go home, Kurt. Your contact, Georgio, has left a message for you. It's the information you seek. Others, too, are looking for you, to reveal the face of the King of Swords.' She stared deep into my eyes and then blew me a kiss. 'Farewell, Kurt. We will of course meet again, though by then your circumstances will be much altered.'

Lost for words, I watched Lady Methedrine's slender figure vanish into the crowd before making my exit. I walked slowly through the Paradiso's dark interior, taking note of its familiar features and examining those things familiarity had made common place. The long glass and stainless steel bar, the two oval dance floors with their enormous spider-like overhead lighting gantries, the people who stood below those rigs, their bodies gyrating to the beats and flashing lights like a form of pagan worship. I recognised many a familiar face in that crowd, the disaffected and disowned, fringe members of society, who were in many respects my brothers and sisters. I took in all of these sights as I left, for something deep inside told me that I would never see them again, at least not in the same light.

After two hours of sitting in my apartment waiting for the vidphone to ring, I stared to have serious doubts about the accuracy of Lady Methedrine's information. In fact, I began to doubt everything that had happened previously. Psychic entity indeed! The woman was obviously no more than a drug-addled bint.

Satisfied that I now had a rational grip on the situation, I relaxed into the sofa and let my mind drift. I became aware of the subtle scent of cherry blossom in the air, an absurd and impossible odour.

A woman's voice whispered in my ear, 'Shame on you, Kurt. Backsliding already.'

I looked behind and saw only empty space. Perhaps I'd been dreaming? Before I could consider it further the incoming call light on the vidphone flashed to life. I grabbed the handset from the table and stabbed the receive button. The fractal-patterned screen of a voice only link flickered into existence and the privacy conscious Georgio started to speak.

'Congratulations, buddy, you've passed the test. I'm pleased to extend to ya the pleasures of the Shifting House. If you're still interested, be at the Hotel Metropolis in the Rue Lang tomorrow evening at nine o'clock. There'll be someone waiting for ya in the hotel lobby.

'I take it these arrangements are acceptable?'

'Fine. Tomorrow evening. Hotel Metropolis at nine o'clock.'

'Ya got it, buddy.' Georgio broke the connection and the screen went blank.

I had just started to consider how to handle the Shifting House when I heard a knock at the door. Less than half a dozen people knew the address of my John Dumas safe house and none of them were stupid enough to risk blowing my cover by coming round. I grabbed my gun from the table and crept to the door. Having psyched myself up, I threw back the bolts and yanked it open. A dark figure tumbled forward and I slammed the door shut and ordered the illumination to full. I recognised Slinky immediately. A small man, about five foot six, his rail thin body topped with a mop of long, greasy, dark hair.

He rolled on to his back with a groan and stared up at me, his eyes widened when he saw the gun. 'Kurt, baby, lose the hostile hardware, man. I came here in person to give you some very vital dope.'

I lowered the gun and he stood up, brushing imaginary flecks of dust from his clothing. Why he bothered, considering its general state of grubby disrepair was a mystery.

'This better be good,' I warned him, 'because I don't much care for house guests, especially the uninvited kind.'

'Max and relax, bro,' he oozed.

'I'm not your brother,' I spat and raised the gun again. 'Now quit stalling and tell me what's so important that you feel you have to start making house calls? If someone sees you we'll both be in the shit.'

'You, or should I say John Dumas, is attracting some serious attention from an enforcer named Georgio. He's checking out your credibility and then some. He probably knows which hand you use to wipe your arse with by now. I hope your cover's good because this man's associates are terminally dangerous.'

'Not as dangerous as I am, believe me. That's the big bad secret? You came running to see me just because somebody's asking a few questions?'

'You're not listening, Kurt. These people are big, as in Corporate. They have access to everything, and I mean everything. Comms records. The lot. I just couldn't risk it. They find out you're Vice and it'll be multiple disappearance time. They won't just burn you, baby. They'll burn everyone you've spoken to in the last six months to be safe. Is any of this reaching you?'

'All of it but don't sweat it. Georgio just called me so I guess my cover must be good. I'm to meet with his terminal associates tomorrow in the Paris district. So you can go home, get yourself a change of underwear and breathe easy.'

Slinky relaxed. 'That's something, I guess. Hey, I got something else to tell you!'

'You trying for the Gunther Rosenstein Award for Industry, or are your bones aching so much that you're getting desperate?'

'Hey, baby, chill out and cut the abuse. I came here as a favour, man.'

'To yourself, perhaps. Spill it.'

'Remember you asked me about that Anastasia chick?' He rubbed at his pointed nose, reminding me of some kind of rodent. A sewer rat to be precise. 'I checked her out like you asked. She used to live in an apartment in the Naples district.' He twitched nervously. 'Hey, Kurt, since you mentioned it, I'm starting to feel a little anxious. You got any stuff?'

'Later.' I noticed that he'd used the past tense. 'You said used to live. Where is she now?'

'That's the whole point, man, nobody knows. Disappeared a couple of days after that business with van Meyer. But you'd know more about that than I would.'

'Don't push it, Slinky.' I smiled maliciously. 'Are you hurting real bad?'

His voice took on a snotty, pleading tone, 'C'mon, Kurt. Please don't fuck us around. You holding or not? I had to pass up a good score to come here. Please?'

'All right already. Quit grovelling. I got some morph if that's any good to you.'

'That's fine, baby. Just hurry.'

I fetched two ampoules and the compressed air hypodermic from the kitchen and handed it to him. He snatched the gear from my hand and worked quickly, his hands trembling as he tied a tourniquet about his upper arm and tapped up a vein. He loaded an ampoule into the hypo and I heard the hiss as he triggered it. A blissful look transformed his mean, rodenty features and he slumped back on the couch.

As I watched him nodding out in my living room I wondered how far I was from being him. In some ways I was already way past him. At least he wasn't making pacts with psychic entities! Slinky's only real problem was that he loved junk more than he loved himself. He'd been on a dozen programs, any one of which could have got him off it. The only thing keeping Slinky on junk was Slinky. His decision though. Who was I to interfere? I slipped a disposable credit card into his pocket and went to bed. He would be gone by the morning.

CHAPTER 7

Kurt groaned as he threw the tumbled sheets from his bed. A jackhammer pulse thundered inside his skull, reminding him of the previous evening's excesses. He inspected the pressure bandage on his thigh, relieved to discover no signs of bleeding. A glance at the clock informed him it was time to eat, so he limped through to the kitchen. While he waited for the kettle to boil, he rummaged through the refrigerator for food. The search yielded a couple of chocolate bars, which he called breakfast. Kurt poured the coffee, added a wrap of speed and went through to the living room to check his e-mail. Several new messages were waiting, including one marked with a departmental priority flag; the dossier he had requested on Isaac Vaughan. Kurt swallowed a bite of chocolate and started to read:

Born: 10/11/43, Surrey, England.
Following the death of his parents in the Great Flood of 2049, Vaughan was relocated to Europa City from Refugee Camp 27 in March 2052. Graduated from New Oxford University in 2064 with a First Class Honours degree in psychology. Refused a position at the Heidelman Foundation and immigrated to the Religious States of America.
Entered the RSA Templar officer's training academy in 2066. Graduated in 2068 with the rank of Lieutenant. Assigned to the Middle East following the American annexation of Kuwait in 2069. Subsequently served four tours of duty in Iran, Iraq and Jordan between 2069 and 2075. Promoted to Captain in December 2070 after completing his first tour of duty in Iraq. He subsequently transferred to Major Wilson P. Brodie's 107th Covert Operations Unit in February 2071. Vaughan spent the next two years operating behind enemy lines in Iran and Jordan. Also thought

to have taken part in clandestine operations in Saudi Arabia and Syria during this period. Twice wounded in action during this time, he received a third wound in March 2073 in a disastrous raid on Baghdad, during which Major Brodie was killed in action. Awarded the Congressional Medal of Honour for successfully leading the four remaining members of the COU platoon through enemy lines to safety in Kuwait.

Shipped back to the RSA in April 2073 to receive his decoration and to convalesce from his wounds. Assigned to the presidential staff as a strategic military advisor and promoted to Major in August 2073. Transferred back to the Middle East in September 2074 at his own request to fight insurrectionists in Kuwait. It took Vaughan less than three months to put down the uprising, at the end of which its leaders were publicly executed on live television. His actions during this period saw him promoted to Colonel in December 2074.

Dubbed "Vicious Vaughan" and "Colonel Killcrazy" by the tabloid press for authorising the use of soft ordinance and fuel-air strikes against the civilian populations of Iran and Iraq. Recalled to Richmond in August 2075 following an official complaint by the United Nations, Vaughan was asked to account for his actions before a Senate inquiry in September 2075. After the inquiry he resigned his commission on the twenty-first of that month, issuing the following statement:

"This once great nation has been betrayed by bleeding heart liberals and the weak and feeble minded. I was instructed by my superiors to win this conflict by any means necessary. We were, and still are, engaged in total war with the nations of Islam, who selfishly hoard their oil. In such a war there can be no place for outmoded concepts such as civilians. This is a war of survival - total attrition - the very fate of our race hangs in the balance. Those who will not submit to our will must be destroyed. I have no regrets and I give no apologies for my actions in this conflict. I did my duty both as a soldier and to my adopted fatherland. I expected to be treated better in return for my services. It is a deeply saddened man who turns his back on this Administration."

Following his resignation, Vaughan embarked on a public speaking tour of the RSA to promote his best selling book "The Enemy Within", which condemned those he perceived as the "weak liberals" responsible for undermining the authority of the RSA.

Dropping out of sight in May 2077, he returned to Europa City on January 14, 2079 to assume the position of Chairman of the Board of the Tessler Corporation. The corporation, largely by means of Vaughan's contacts in the military, subsequently secured a contract to supply experimental cyber-ware to the RSA in 2081. Its profits tripled over the next financial quarter, allowing Tessler to acquire several other arms manufacturers (including Ingram, Walther and Heckler & Koch).

Vaughan, in the interim, became politically active. Standing for the Europa Nationalist Party, he won the London seat by a landslide majority in the local elections of June 21, 2081. Though he was an active force in the General Election of 2083, which returned the Europa Nationalist Party to a third term in office, he later refused the offer of a place on the city's governing council.

The Tessler Corporation and Vaughan have since been linked to accusations of insider trading, arms smuggling to the Middle East and numerous black market activities within Europa City. None of the above allegations have been proven to date and Vaughan has strenuously denied any links with criminal activities or organisations.

Charismatic and respected, he successfully retained his seat, despite a press smear campaign by the Europa Socialist Party, in the local elections of May this year.

Addendum: The Tessler Corporation submitted a tender to secure the rights to supply arms to the Europa City Police Department on September 17, 2085. The tender is due to be reviewed by a Joint Departmental Committee at the end of October.

A brief physical description of Vaughan followed the biography:

Height: 186 cm
Weight: 96 Kg
Hair: Brown
Eyes: Green
Dist. Features: RSA Templar tattoo on upper right arm. Bullet scars on right pectoral, right arm and left shoulder.

Kurt downloaded the file and sat back with his hands clasped behind his head. He felt uneasy. Vaughan, as Lady Methedrine had predicted, was an intelligent and powerful man. Not the type to let a casual customer get close enough to bring him down after one visit to his - if indeed it was his - underground prostitution racket. Kurt would have to find some means of penetrating his organisation if he wanted to catch old "Colonel Killcrazy".

The lift doors slid open and Weill stepped out on to the roof top patio. A gentle breeze stirred the foliage of the potted trees and shrubbery arranged as a privacy screen around the perimeter of the building. From this vantage point, a hundred stories high, the building's occupant could survey the contours of the surrounding city. A maze of towering glass and concrete blocks by day, a thousand winking lights by night. Weill remained oblivious to these sights as he stood there, his attention riveted firmly on the back of the man who stood before him.

A tall and muscular figure, its clothing tailored to accentuate rather than hide the wearer's physical bulk. He stood in a stiff military posture with his hands clasped behind his back as he gazed at the blood red sunset. Vaughan spoke in a well-modulated tone, his eyes fixed on the horizon, 'Beauty from pollution. How ironic. Eh, Weill?'

Weill shifted uneasily; unsure whether the question was rhetorical or if a response was expected. He decided to risk a reply. 'Is it?'

Vaughan pointed at the clouds. 'Those vibrant red, orange and gold hues are caused by the sun's rays filtering through layers of pollutants suspended in the atmosphere. Men such as you observe it and say, if they bother to comment at all, magnificent or splendid. Few, even at this late hour, think of the wider implications. The planet has become hostile to us and only the strongest, the most ruthless, will survive. The weak must perish as nature demands.

'What month is it, Weill?'

'Er,' Weill floundered, taken aback by such an obvious question, 'October.'

'And what was the temperature today?'

'About average - eighty-three degrees.'

'Sixty years ago a good day might have been sixty-five for this season in this area. Do you understand what I'm saying?'

'I think so, Colonel.' Weill, growing impatient with Vaughan's prosaic questions, sought to change the subject. 'You wished to see me?'

Vaughan turned to face him. His features were strong and even, etched here and there with a few lines of worry or concentration. The first grey was starting to creep through his hair at the temples. In another man the effect would have been quite handsome, but in Vaughan's case the cold stare of his eyes offset such aesthetic considerations. They were the eyes of a man who had seen and done too much evil in life. Eyes that stared straight through Weill as if focused on another place, a different time.

'Colonel?'

Vaughan snapped back from wherever he had been. 'The arms contract, Weill, can you secure it for me? Why is that fool of a Commissioner dragging his heels? We are the best - the only arms manufacturer - for the contract. The name Tessler is synonymous with cutting-edge military hardware.'

'I think you expect too much of me, I'm only a captain. I can't be expected to sway the entire Council.'

'You led me to believe that you had the Commissioner's ear because of your ties to Damocles. Is that not so, or have you been lying to me?'

'Of course not, but unfortunately in this case Haynes doesn't appear to be applying his usual autocratic power. He's convened an inter-departmental committee to debate the issue rather than deciding unilaterally. I can sway him a little and make sure IAD is seen to favour your tender, but we're going to have problems with Sajer. He thinks you're dirty and he'll argue that the public will take it as a sign of corruption if we give the contract to Tessler.'

'Which is precisely why I want this contract - to force the ECPD to give Tessler a clean bill of health. Exonerate the corporation from any accusations of criminal wrongdoing. To do anything less would appear to be an endorsement of organised crime.'

Weill frowned. 'And what if they choose to award it to someone else. Had you considered that?'

Vaughan snorted, 'Of course I've considered it. Why do you think I bought up those other companies? Tessler is now the only option. We supply arms to the Religious States of America, what more of a reference do they need?' He gestured at the surrounding tower blocks. 'Look around you, Weill. Out there, on the streets, there is nothing but chaos and disorder. A tide of rising violence and civil disobedience that only a military state can hope to contain. The Police Department is hopelessly outdated, its methods archaic. Once Tessler, and by extension myself, have been washed clean, I will ascend to a seat on the Council from whence I can bring my plans to fruition. I will cleanse Europa City and make it a state to be reckoned with. The world is going to hell and I for one don't intend to go with it. The conflict in the Middle East is now into its third decade. How long do you think it will be before both sides finally lose patience and wheel out the big nukes? But if we are prepared for that day we can rise above the ashes of the RSA and Islamic Caliphate and become the leading power in the world.'

'Mad, quite gloriously mad,' Weill breathed.

Vaughan lunged at him and grabbed him by his lapels. 'Is that what you think?'

Weill swallowed nervously; he had not meant to speak aloud. He licked dry lips, suddenly aware of the other man's crushing strength. 'I didn't mean to sound as though I doubted you. It just kind of came out like that.'

'Worm,' snarled Vaughan, throwing Weill to the ground. 'What do I care for your opinions? Just remember you are in this up to your neck. After all, you were the one who authorised Costello's assassination. All it would take is for me to make one call and you'd be finished.' Vaughan paused and his eyes took on the glazed look Weill had observed earlier. He started to speak again, almost as if to himself. 'True men of vision have always been ridiculed throughout the ages. Yet who can deny the military achievements of Napoleon, Hitler or St Clair?'

Weill, who had taken the opportunity to regain his feet, was acutely aware that he was on dangerous ground. 'No one, I would guess,' he replied, hoping to placate Vaughan. Inwardly his thoughts ran toward having Sword pay the colonel a visit. First, he had to survive this interview.

Vaughan nodded gravely. 'Only the weak, Weill. Not strong men, men of courage like us. For we are not afraid to look into our own hearts and see the darkness therein. Now tell me how Sajer's investigations into my affairs progress. It would be unfortunate if he, too, had to be removed.'

Weill blanched at the suggestion. 'You can't just kill the Commander of the city's Vice squad.'

'Can't I?'

Weill stared into his eyes and realised that Vaughan was capable of doing that and more. 'The question is academic anyway. I can assure you that it will never come to that. I've been gathering material on Sergeant Brecht - the detective he has assigned to your case. Even as we speak Sajer will be reading my report recommending that Brecht - what's the military jargon?' Weill clicked his fingers. 'Be section-eighted out of the force. Sajer will have no choice but to shut down the investigation.' He laughed ingratiatingly.

'Are you absolutely certain of this?'

Weill shrugged. 'If not, I'll drop the Sword on him; detectives working undercover get wasted all the time. No one is going to mourn the loss of a psycho like Brecht.'

Vaughan wrapped an arm about Weill's shoulders in an exaggerated display of camaraderie. 'Excellent work, Weill. I knew my investment in you was justified. Come inside and have a night cap. I've just acquired a rather passable cognac, which I'm sure you'll appreciate.'

CHAPTER 8

As Brecht stood in the white tiled room listening to the screams, he wondered how it had gone so wrong. Was it his choice of the John Dumas identity, finding Anastasia in that hotel room, or simply Sajer's maxim of the Seven P's coming into effect? He couldn't say for sure and before he had time to dwell on it further he found his attention drawn back to the brutal charade being enacted before him.

The naked man screamed in agony as his torturers threw him to the floor, jarring the razor wire inserted into his anus. Desperate to escape the pain, he rolled on to his knees and shrieked as the impact drove the bullet casings hammered into his kneecaps deeper into his flesh. He finally found some measure of relief by rolling on to his side and curling into a foetal position.

Vaughan nodded to his swarthy skinned assistant who casually kicked his victim over on to his back. Ignoring the fresh burst of screaming, he turned to Brecht and said, 'I learnt this out in the Middle East when my unit was captured in Baghdad. The rag-heads took twenty-two of us alive. Eighteen hours later there were only five of us left who were fit enough to make our escape during an air raid. We had to watch those sand-niggers torture each of our comrades in turn, knowing it would soon be our own screams disturbing the dogs.' He pointed at the figure writhing on the blood splattered tiles. 'They did that to Major Brodie, hardest man I ever knew. Made him scream like a bloody woman to be put out of his misery. I'd give this poor wanker another two minutes at most before he's begging to tell me everything, from how he used to steal money from his mother's purse to which position his wife prefers to be shagged in.'

'That a fact?' Brecht said, struggling to keep his voice level. 'I assume there's some point to my witnessing this little display?'

'I just wanted to make sure you know where you stand, Dumas. I

71

checked up on you. You're a ruthless bastard – connections to the Sciarrone Family, not that you openly advertise that fact. I could use a man of your talents, but if you ever try and fuck with me what I do to you will make it look like we've been tickling this bastard with a feather. I hope I'm making myself clear, son?'

'Emphatically. People who try and fuck with you can expect to get fucked up in return.'

Vaughan laughed. 'I think we're going to get along just fine, Johnny. Now, let's finish this off - then we can negotiate how much I'm going to sell you that little gym-slip slut for.'

The dark skinned man spoke to Vaughan. 'He's ready to talk now, Colonel.'

'Thank you, Hassan.' Vaughan squatted down to hear his victim's confession.

The blood splattered figure coughed up a mouthful of bloody phlegm. 'You… you're right, I'm with the Police Department. I was assigned to penetrate your organisation.'

'I know all that, Officer Conroy. My men found your badge, after all.'

Conroy stared at him wild-eyed. 'Then,' he spat out a mouthful of blood, 'then why did you torture me? What do you want to know?'

'Nothing. I merely wished to emphasise a point to my new associate. I find visual aids to be most effective in such matters.' He stood up, retrieved Brecht's gun from the table and handed it to him.

'Game's over, son.' Vaughan drew his own gun and pressed it against Brecht's temple. 'Time to prove your commitment to the cause. You've got five seconds to kill this fucker before I kill you instead. It's your call.'

Brecht levelled the pistol at Conroy's head; it was a malignant weight in his hand. He tried to convince himself that the boy was as good as dead - if he did not pull the trigger someone else would. Conroy stared at him with imploring eyes. Brecht had recognised him as soon as he had entered the room. The kid had only been awarded his detective's shield three weeks ago, transferring from the SPF. Vaughan's count reached four and Conroy closed his eyes and looked away. A trigger squeeze later, fragments of the same face were staring back at Brecht from the blood soaked tiles.

Brecht let Vaughan guide him from the room. 'Hell, son, you had me going there. I thought you'd gone soft on me. Hassan, clean up this mess.'

After much deliberation, Brecht decided on the simplest plan of action available to him. He would approach the operators of the Shifting House as a potential investor, relying on Georgio's vetting of his John Dumas personality to have revealed his links to several underground prostitution rackets. From there, once he had identified who was running the Shifting

House, he would contact Sajer and call in the necessary backup to close down the operation. The only real flaw in the plan being that he had used the scenario of John Dumas, mobbed up criminal looking to invest big, once too often. He thought it highly probable, especially after the van Meyer bust, that others besides Anastasia knew that John Dumas and Kurt Brecht were one and the same. But with no official backing, he had no choice except to use an existing persona, even though he might be walking into a bullet in the back of the head. It was a risk that he had to take. The memory of Sajer kneeling over his mother's blood soaked body wouldn't let him walk away. Its spectre had haunted him for over twenty-six years and the threat of death couldn't exorcise it. The child was truly the father of the man.

The lights of the Hotel Metropolis beckoned through the early evening gloom, welcoming Brecht's approach. Walking along the Rue Lang lost in thought, head down, hands thrust deep into his pockets, he drew up short, surprised to find himself at his destination. The Metropolis' doorman halted him with a meaty hand on his chest. 'Hold it, sir. I'm afraid I have to search you before you enter. Just routine, you understand?' Brecht nodded and rough, practised hands proceeded to pat him down. Pausing below his left armpit, the doorman slipped a hand inside his coat and pulled out the Walther. 'Now what would you be needing this for?'

'Vermin control.' Brecht said, his face deadpan.

'You must get big rats back home.'

'Huge. They wear black suits with little bronze badges and are forever poking their snouts in where they're not wanted.'

The doorman chuckled, 'That's good. I like that one. But I'm still going to have to keep this until you leave. It's hotel policy. You can reclaim it at reception when you're done.' He slid the gun into the waistband at the rear of his trousers and pulled open the door. 'Welcome to the Hotel Metropolis, sir. Rates are by the hour. I hope you enjoy your stay.'

A cramped and cheaply decorated lobby greeted him inside. A reception desk occupied the left wall; a low table surrounded by half a dozen moulded plastic chairs took up most of the remaining floor space. On the opposite side of the lobby a series of artificial plants were attempting to lend an atmosphere of hospitality to the entrance of the lift. The room's sole occupant sat with one leg draped elegantly over the other at the table. Female, mid twenties with dark, bobbed hair and a good figure. She stood and greeted Brecht in a low and husky voice as he entered, smoothing the creases from her black evening dress. 'Mr Dumas.' A statement of fact, not a question. 'I'm Georgio.'

Brecht gave her a hard stare as he tried to reconcile the image of femininity with the gruff male voice he had heard on the vidphone. 'I take it the operation was a success then?'

Georgio looked puzzled for a moment and then smiled wryly. 'Oh, you mean the voice on the phone. A simple security measure, we must protect our clients and ourselves. If you would like to follow me upstairs, we can discuss your needs and select an appropriate girl and scenario to maximise your pleasure. And we do want you to enjoy yourself, because a happy customer is a returning customer.'

'Yeah, I guess they just come, come again, and keep on wanting to come.'

'Very droll, Mr Dumas. And it was actually funny the first two or three times I heard it. Please do hurry along.'

Brecht followed Georgio to the lifts, hanging back slightly to admire her figure as she walked across the floor with an unstudied grace. 'You know, I'm beginning to believe my needs involve a tight black evening dress.'

Georgio turned as the lift door slid open. 'You couldn't afford it.'

'I wouldn't be too sure of that. I'm a wealthy man. But you checked up on me, so you know that already.'

'I wasn't talking about money. Believe me, you couldn't afford me.'

The lift travelled up to the fourth floor with the soft hum of servomotors and disgorged its two passengers into a scarlet carpeted hallway. From there Georgio led Brecht some twenty metres down the corridor to a door numbered 416. The room showed signs of recent redecoration, converting it to a hospitality suite. Modern steel and leather couches formed a bizarre counterpoint to the antique mahogany of the bar and writing bureau. But the grey plastic computer terminal sat on top of the rich wood of the bureau provided the real incongruity.

Georgio indicated that Brecht should take a seat at the console. 'Images of all of our current girls are stored on-line for you to browse. There is also a list of their vital statistics and any... specialist skills they have. Once you've made your selection insert your credit card and key in the girl's code. After that the ball, so to speak, is in your court. Any questions?'

Brecht idly tapped at the keyboard, giving the succession of faces no more than a cursory glance. 'To be honest,' he said, 'I didn't really come here for the girls.'

Georgio pursed her lips, her forehead puckering into a frown. 'Well, we have one or two boys, but this sort of thing is most irregular. We like to know in advance if our client's tastes are non-hetero.'

Brecht smiled, 'I think you've misunderstood me. I didn't come here for sex. I wanted to meet your employer. I'm looking to make an investment and this was the easiest way of getting into the Shifting House.'

'I really don't think I can help you. I don't have that kind of authority.' She picked up a pack of cigarettes and a table lighter from the bar, shook one loose and lit it with shaking hands. 'Smoke?' she offered.

'No thanks,' Brecht declined. 'Don't give up the day job, 'cause you're a lousy actress, Georgio. We both know you're not the kind of woman who gets that nervous - not over a simple request that she can block with a "no". You already told me I couldn't afford you, so stop playing games and go and get me somebody that can authorise a meeting with your boss.'

Georgio exhaled a long stream of blue tobacco smoke and then crushed out the cigarette. 'Tough bastard, eh Dumas?'

'Yeah, I am.' Brecht's features hardened. 'But it's not the social handicap it used to be. Now, can I see your boss?'

'It's your funeral.' She turned to leave. 'By the way, you're going to get charged regardless, so you may as well see if any of the girls takes your fancy. You're a lousy actor, too, Dumas, if you expect me to believe you're not interested in sex. You've stripped me naked with your eyes about a dozen times since we met. Unfortunately, your imagination's not nearly good enough to even come close.'

Brecht laughed. 'You don't have a sister called Marian do you?'

'Not that I'm aware of. But you may rest assured that she's not in my class.'

The door closed and Brecht resumed his examination of the Shifting House's stock of girls, more as a means to kill time than from any prurient interest. He read through eight or nine, growing increasingly bored, and was just about to switch off when a familiar face caught his eye. No mistaking that bright red hair and baby doll dimples, which he had last seen under the sodium glare of a street light outside Maximilians. Anastasia. Inexplicably caught up once more in his affairs. The words of her letter came back to him as he speculated on how she had found herself in the Shifting House, "a girl's got to make a living, after all," she had written. Brecht realised that he was at least partially responsible for her present predicament. Anastasia would have been just desperate enough after van Meyer's arrest to approach an organisation like the Shifting House. Cursing yet another unexpected turn of events, he quickly formulated a plan to extricate her. He inserted his credit card and keyed in the appropriate code, putting everything in place by the time Georgio returned.

The major-domo radiated her usual cool elegance. 'I've discussed your request with my principal and he's in favour of it. Return to Hotel Metropolis tomorrow evening at twenty-one hundred hours and there will be transport waiting to take you to your destination.'

'Good.' Brecht nodded his acceptance. 'By the way, I've decided to take you up on your offer. I've selected the girl in five-oh-eight. I'm prepared to wait, if she's currently engaged.'

Georgio moved over to the console. 'Flesh and blood after all, Mr Dumas? I knew you were no different. Hmm, a little younger than I would have expected. You don't strike me as the sort of man who would be interested in young girls.'

'Let's just say I'm making an exception, unless you're willing to offer your services in her place?'

'No. The Madam of the House is not for sale.'

'Who said I was offering to pay? We're both old enough to recognise where we stand on this.'

'Don't,' Georgio protested, the pulse in her throat quickening. 'That kind of talk could get you crippled or even killed. I'm a corporate asset, Mr Dumas, as much as this building is, and the men that own me guard their investments zealously. You don't strike me as the kind of man who takes advice but I'm going to give you some. Enjoy the girl and go home. If you have any common sense at all, be anywhere but here tomorrow evening.'

'Thanks for the warning but I'm afraid I'm the stupid, stubborn type. Let's go. Floor five, room eight.'

Georgio locked the room and ushered Brecht down the corridor and past the lifts to a stairwell at the far end. She climbed the stairs swiftly without speaking and held open the door to the fifth floor for him. It opened on to a corridor carpeted in electric blue. Brecht stepped through and turned to face Georgio. 'Thanks for all the help and advice, asked for or otherwise. Perhaps we'll meet again tomorrow?'

'I doubt that we'll meet again, Mr Dumas, my employer keeps me very busy.' She became brusque and business like. 'Her room is the fourth door on your right. The entry code has been set to seven-eight-zero-one. Try and be gentle with her. She's just had her medication and may be a little confused.' Georgio shook his hand before closing the door, the sound of her heels on the stairs echoed sharply as she descended.

Turning his back on the closed door, Brecht made his way to room 508. He typed in the first two numbers and then hesitated as a vision of his mother's blood splattered body flashed before him. Forcing the image from his mind, he keyed in the final numbers and entered the room.

The room was humid, windowless, and furnished only with a bed. Something stirred amidst the tangle of sheets and the pink gleam of flesh caught Brecht's eye. The naked figure struggled on to its hands and knees. Brecht barely recognised the glassy eyed, slack featured, giggling girl as Anastasia. Welts and bruises covered her body, evidence of several beatings. He sat beside her cautiously, gripped her shoulders and shook her gently.

'Anastasia? Can you hear me? Snap out of it, girl.'

The girl's eyes cleared for a moment. 'Kurt? What are you doing here? Dangerous. Bad people. Kill you dead.' She moaned and slid back into her drug-induced delirium. 'It's raining and I'm cold. You give me your coat. Look at my face when you speak. Not body. I'm a people. Not animal.'

Brecht held her close. 'Hush now. I'm going to get you out of here.

76

Don't sweat it, kitten. Every thing's going to be okay.'

He stayed with her for about an hour before leaving, sponging her down with a cloth he found in the room's shower unit. Jacked up too high to speak coherently, she writhed languorously and screamed at him to take her. Brecht would draw the sheets up over her only for Anastasia to throw them off again in a fit of giggling. He won through in the end and the cold soothed her enough for her to relax into a light doze.

Brecht settled the sheets about Anastasia once more and gently smoothed away the tangled strands of hair that clung to her sweat drenched skin. Asleep, her features softened, reminding him of how young and vulnerable she had looked in the rain that night when he had given her his coat. He sighed as he rose from her bedside, cursing himself for being foolish enough to get involved in the girl's problems. Deep down, he had a feeling in his gut that it would cost him dearly.

The sound of a sharp knock at his office door brought Sajer back to the present. He placed Brecht's com-unit on the desk and slid a file across it. 'Enter.'

One of the Hall's secretaries peered round the door. 'I'm sorry to disturb you, Commander,' she apologised, 'but Captain Weill sent me. He said I was to give you the report on the Tessler bid. He was most insistent that I should give it to you this evening.'

Sajer's eyes narrowed as he took the datakey from her. 'He would be.'

'Sorry?'

'Nothing of consequence, Miss Petersen. Merely thinking aloud. Thank you. You may go.'

Sajer tossed the datakey down on his desk and picked up Brecht's com-unit. He turned it over his hand, unwilling to continue reading for fear of what he would discover next. Too late for regrets. No one had forced Brecht to become an addict. Plenty of deepcover agents played out their role without getting hooked. Blockers and system purges were available for exactly that reason. Brecht had willingly flaunted the regs and paid for it. Doctor Nystrom refused to commit herself but the unspoken prognosis of permanent brain damage had been clear. They would know more when Brecht regained consciousness. An event that remained far from certain. It would be better for all concerned if Brecht remained in a vegetative state. Doctor Nystrom's last report indicated that they had taken Brecht off the ventilator and he was breathing without assistance, although there remained little sign of higher brain activity.

Shrugging off his concerns, Sajer flipped open the com-unit and recommenced reading.

31/10/85: I am so royally fucked! I've got a sixteen year old girl on my sofa smacked out of her head on some form of bio-engineered derivative of MDMA and I've just blown Marcus Conroy's fucking brains out - a detective from my own squad! Losing it BIG time. I'm on my own with no hope of help from Sajer and to cap it all there's no sign of that leather clad bint, Lady Methedrine. So much for her bloody help.

Guess I should write down what happened as a form of testimony or confession.

It started last night when I went to the Hotel Metropolis, the current location of the locked box prostitution case I'd been working on. Posing as John Dumas, I decided to approach the Shifting House's operators as a potential investor and identify those responsible for running it. With this in mind, I arrived at the Hotel Metropolis and met with my contact, Georgio (who incidentally turned out to be a woman), and persuaded her to get me an interview with the House's owner at nine o'clock the following evening. The smooth running of my plan had been interrupted by the discovery that Anastasia, the girl whom I'd first met outside Maximilians, was now an unwilling internee of the House. Now I had to worry about getting her out of the Shifting House as well as bringing down the operators.

To cut to the chase, I arrived back at the hotel the following night at nine on the dot to discover the same goon at the door. Reaching into my jacket, I pulled out my gun and gave it to him. 'Thought I'd save you the bother of searching me this time.'

He accepted it without smiling. 'Thank you, Mr Dumas, but don't worry, you won't be going inside the hotel this evening. There's a car waiting to take you to your meeting. Follow me.'

He grabbed my left arm in a light but firm grip that suggested he could apply a lot more pressure if necessary and steered me a couple of hundred yards down the street to the corner. We stood in silence for a full five minutes before a black limousine pulled up. Its license plates and sleek lines proclaimed it the latest model, while the mirrored glass assured the anonymity of the occupants. I was still admiring the car when the rear door opened and the ever-helpful doorman thrust me inside. I heard an ominous click as the doors locked and then a soft hum as the motor kicked in and we glided into the flow of traffic. I peeled my face away from the upholstery and took stock of my surroundings. A minimal view to say the least, the rear window having been polarised too dark to see through, while an opaque privacy screen separated me from the driver. On the positive side, it had very comfortable leather upholstery and the small bar, unlike the rear doors, proved to be unlocked and well stocked, the latter presumably a gesture of goodwill on behalf of my mysterious host to compensate for my inability to see any of the sights on my journey. I shrugged and poured myself a generous whisky and settled back to await my host's pleasure.

At this stage in the narrative it would be nice to say that I sat there concentrating, committing to memory every turn, every speed bump, the time we travelled for, sounds of nearby monorails et cetera, using all of my carefully honed detective skills to their full advantage in determining the location of my secret meeting. Yeah, it would be nice to say that, it would also be a fucking lie. Instead, I kicked back and relaxed with a couple of drinks, figuring that if I walked away from the meeting it wouldn't matter a damn where my captors held it. And if I didn't walk away, it was hardly going to be of much consolation on my way to hell that I knew where I'd been snuffed.

Four whiskies later on the Brecht drinks consumption time-scale, the limousine drew to a halt and the door opened. I stepped from the car to discover myself in the dimly lit basement parking lot of one of the city's many high-rise blocks. Grey pre-cast concrete blocks and pillars surrounded me on all sides offering no clue as to my whereabouts. The faceless anonymity no doubt a deliberate ploy to keep me off balance. Casting a final glance around the lot, I turned to face the car and discovered two men standing behind me. The first, who I assumed to be the chauffeur, was short with a wiry build and the kind of swarthy complexion suggestive of Middle Eastern extraction. I recognised the other, tall, muscular and distinguished looking, from the photograph in the dossier and his many television appearances. It took all of my self control to restrain my smile of triumph as I addressed him: 'Colonel Vaughan, an unexpected pleasure. It would appear that your corporate enterprises encompass areas hitherto unknown by the voting public.'

He subjected me to a smile that had no warmth in it whatsoever. 'Perhaps, son, but I wouldn't try and use that to your advantage if I were you.'

I feigned insult and growled back, 'I'm a businessman, not some petty extortionist. I came here to make you a proposition, two of them, actually - no more no less. And I must assume you're interested or else you wouldn't be here. Am I right or am I right?' I was fronting it big time and we both knew it but Vaughan was the kind of man who expected such behaviour from his associates. A man's man - I could picture him sipping brandy while propping up a bar next to Hemingway.

'If that's the case you'd best speak fast, son, while you still can.'

I gave my surroundings a derisive glance. 'Here, in a parking lot? Hardly the business suite at the Sheraton, is it?'

'I conduct all of my preliminary interviews down here. That way if I decide you're wasting my time I don't have to worry about replacing the carpets.' He gestured the chauffeur over and the Arab handed him my piece, which he pointed meaningfully in my direction. The look in his eyes suggested I might have taken my smart-arse act too far.

I spoke fast; 'I'm offering money here - away to expand both of our business profits. You run the Shifting House as a kind of select club for your rich associates, a dark playground where anything goes. Trouble is you have to keep moving venues and keep recruiting fresh girls because they fade fast from the drugs you got them whacked out on. I, on the other hand, know the true underground prostitution business. That gives me access to buildings and to a steady supply of girls. Now it's no secret that I've been known to dabble in a little arms trading as well - hell, anything I can turn a profit from. What I'm proposing here is a simple trade. I give you the girls and locations for the Shifting House and in return you give me the names of some contacts that might be willing to buy my weapons - maybe even sneak me a little new technology. What do you say?'

Vaughan flicked off the Walther's safety. 'Why should I bother? I'm doing all right finding girls as it is. I don't really see that you're offering me anything I haven't already got, son.'

I have to admit it sounded rather weak to me when I thought about it, but being the only plan I had I ran with it. 'Because it isn't going to cost you anything apart from a little goodwill and in return it'll save you a load of hassle and administration costs. Not to mention the increase in profit from the expanded customer base I'm going to provide you with.'

Vaughan lowered the gun. 'You might have something there. Enough to keep your breathing privileges for the moment. Right, what's this other proposition of yours?'

'I want to buy the girl in room five-oh-eight of the current Shifting House. Reckon she's about perfect for a little enterprise I'm planning. Kind of a hostess service with added extras.'

'I thought you had a steady supply of girls, what's so special about our little whore?'

I shrugged. 'She caught my interest. As soon as I saw her I knew I had a position for the girl.'

'A little missionary work, no doubt.' Vaughan nudged me in the ribs with the muzzle of my gun. I leered and let him think what he wanted, my plan too full of holes to risk arguing. Despite the thinness of my cover story, the colonel seemed satisfied with my credentials. At least that was the impression I got when he slipped a friendly arm round my shoulders and said, 'We'll discuss the girl later. Right now, I want to show you something important. Something you're going to have to understand if we're going to do business with one another.'

With that oblique statement Vaughan led me across the lot, Hassan bringing up the rear, to a service lift marked with an "Out of Order" sign. We disembarked at the bottom level and Vaughan and his henchman escorted me through a maze of plant equipment to a concealed door disguised as a section of wall panelling. Vaughan opened it by running an electronic keycard between the vertical seams and gestured me inside.

The white tiled room was approximately five metres square, illuminated by a single overhead fluorescent strip. A plastic table had been bolted to the floor in the near left hand corner. The room's sole occupant huddled in the opposite diagonal corner. A young man in his early twenties, stripped naked, with his hands cuffed in front of him. I recognised him at once as Marcus Conroy, he'd made detective a few weeks earlier. I hate to admit it, but I felt more concerned that he was going to blow my cover than for his safety. Initially, at least.

Vaughan placed my gun on the table beside an assortment of worrying items that didn't bode well for Conroy. Two other men, clad in rubber aprons, entered the room. They were a strange, mismatched pair. One was a typical looking heavy, big and muscular, with the kind of scowl that must have taken hours of posing in front of the bedroom mirror to perfect. Just the kind of man you would expect to find working as an enforcer for Vaughan. The other proved more of an enigma. Of medium height and build, he wore a pin-stripe shirt with a pocket handkerchief and tie beneath his apron, giving the impression he'd wandered in from the accounts department by mistake. At Vaughan's command, they picked Conroy up off the floor and suspended him just above ground level by placing the centre link of the handcuffs through a hook fixed to the wall. They secured his legs by snapping a pair of wall mounted brackets about his ankles.

'This little turd thought that he could fuck with me, Johnny,' Vaughan stated, fitting an impressive degree of menace into his pronunciation of the informal version of my name. 'Hassan is now going to show him the error of his ways.' The Arab picked up two shell casings and a wooden mallet from the table. Placing one of the casings between his teeth, he held the other against Conroy's left kneecap and struck it with the mallet. I turned away as the poor bastard started screaming, and kept on screaming as Hassan struck the casing twice more, the final blow accompanied by the sound of splintering bone. Ignoring his victim's cries and writhing, he repeated the procedure on Conroy's other knee.

Vaughan turned and asked, 'Enjoying the show so far?' I looked away again, and he started issuing further instructions. 'Okay, boys, you can turn him round now.'

The heavy and his accountant buddy unclipped Conroy's ankles and spun his body to face the wall. They had just finished securing his blood-spattered ankles when Hassan, now wearing padded gauntlets, returned from the table. He held a length of lubricated plastic tubing, which he inserted into Conroy's anus. Once he had it in place, he shoved a length of razor wire up the inside before withdrawing the pipe, being careful to ensure the wire remained in place.

I didn't think a human being was capable of screaming as loud as

Conroy did when that little bastard tugged the wire from side to side to make sure the blades had caught. I think he must have bitten through his tongue at that point because a stream of blood frothed from his mouth and he started making gagging noises. Hassan nodded his satisfaction to Vaughan and he instructed "Brains" and "Brawn", as I had christened the strange duo, to release Conroy. Removing his handcuffs, they placed him on the blood soaked tiles and quit the room as silently as they had entered.

I stood there numb as Vaughan had Hassan throw Conroy from his side on to his back or on to his knees as the mood took him, causing either the razor wire or the bullet casings to send fresh surges of pain through his body. He didn't want any information from Conroy; he just wanted to prove a point to me. That's what he told me, anyway.

Bad enough that I just stood by and let him torture a fellow officer, let alone what happened next. God help me, I swear I don't know how it happened. Vaughan gave me back my piece and drew his own, ordering me at gunpoint to prove I was with him by executing Conroy. Me or him, and Conroy was already fucked while I still had a chance. That's what I'm trying to ask you to understand. All I remember is Conroy giving me a look that seemed to say he understood and the next thing I know I'm standing there with my gun smoking and Conroy's brains plastered over the walls. The deed done, Vaughan led me from the room and back to the lift.

The lift travelled all the way up to the penthouse apartment on the hundredth floor where I followed Vaughan into a luxuriously furnished sitting room. I sat down on the couch of a low-slung suite while Vaughan busied himself mixing drinks. Still trembling with adrenaline when he returned with the drinks, I accepted mine gratefully and downed it in two gulps. Vaughan, meantime, sat there taking measured sips of his own, avoiding eye contact. I got the impression my apparent lack of stomach for killing disappointed him. He had brought the bottle over with him and he poured me another drink before initiating the talks.

'That's the way I do business, Johnny, and if you want to be in my gang you'll have to learn to do things my way. As for the girl - you might have gathered I'm hardly short of cash, Tessler being one of the largest corporations in this god forsaken city - what say I just give her to you as a token of my good faith? A down payment on all of those services you're going to offer me. After this evening I feel sure that you're not the kind of man who would try and fuck me over. Are you, Johnny?'

Threat implicit in his words, I hurried to agree with him and head off any doubts he might have already started to formulate. Another reason for my swift agreement being that there was no way I could approach Sajer for money to buy Anastasia's freedom. This way all I had to worry about was whether Vaughan would kill me for not coming through with my end of the deal before Sajer caught me for wasting Conroy. My mistakes were mounting rapidly - I possessed several unregistered handguns and yet I'd brought my service weapon with me tonight. Luckily there were enough on the black market for a police issue special not to draw comment. A number of petty gangsters liked the irony of "offing the pigs with their own weapons", but that was the only break I'd caught this evening. I'd got myself in the classic situation of being between a rock and a hard place. I seriously considered killing Vaughan there and then but was enough of a realist to know it would accomplish very little. The Tessler Corporation would continue without him and Anastasia would still be a prisoner in the Shifting House.

So I went along with him. 'That sounds fair,' I said, taking a more measured drink this time. 'All right if I pick her up tonight?'

Vaughan shrugged. 'If that's what you wish. I'll have Hassan take you back to the Metropolis later, which, incidentally, is becoming rather well known.'

The final line obviously added for my benefit, the none too subtle hint that we were dealing quid pro quo here. 'No problem. I can have a new place and a couple of more girls organised for you by the end of the week. Give me a contact number and I'll be in touch with the details.'

'You still have Georgio's number?' I nodded. 'Good. Use that. You have five days, Johnny. Don't disappoint me.'

And that more or less concluded my first meeting with Isaac Vaughan. We sat finishing our drinks while he talked a little about Tessler's cybernetic research: hard-wired reflexes and neuro-links capable of downloading information directly into the human brain. Nothing ground breaking - these kinds of ideas had been around for over a century, but the military implications were obvious. I gathered they even had a couple of operational test subjects - science fiction becoming science fact.

I listened politely without taking any real interest in what he told me. Tessler's legitimate business dealings were no concern of mine. I wanted evidence of narcotics and arms trafficking, but Vaughan didn't give anything away. I left an hour and a half later with blood on my hands and no further evidence against him.

To sum up the situation, I'm up to my neck in shit with no easy way out.

'Four friggin' weeks,' Duvall cursed. That was how long he'd been working in Records. He thumped the desktop and rubbed at eyes blurred by relentless hours spent staring at a monitor. He had long since decided it was all Sajer's fault, or more accurately that bastard Sajer's fault. Turning back to his work, he idly tapped a few characters on the keyboard, causing a fresh set of figures to scroll down the screen. He picked up a light pen and began methodically checking the rows and columns of numbers.

Duvall had been there for three days, searching for the source of a seven hundred and fifty thousand euro-dollar discrepancy in the financial records of the Vice squad. The big question being whether it was a genuine accounting error or some form of embezzlement. He was entertaining the warming thought that Sajer might have been skimming money off the squad's slush fund. A flag caught his eye; Sajer had requested a credit transfer of one million on the 13th of October last year. He scanned down the list only to discover it had been returned in full on the 21st of the same month. Changing tactics, he checked the list of payments to informers. One name appeared repetitively, Slinky, Kurt Brecht's main player, unfortunately it all appeared to be routine. Duvall leaned forward and paused, his finger hovering over the erase button, his attention caught by an anomaly concerning Slinky. The file indicated that the Department had closed his account the day after Brecht's shooting yet someone had authorised an inter-department transfer of ten thousand into that same account on the 25th of December - four days later. Duvall keyed up the transfer details and discovered it had been authorised by Sergeant Horrowitz from Internal Affairs. He pulled up Horrowitz's file and keyed it again in case he'd made a mistake. The same flashing message glared back at him, Horrowitz had died six months ago. A chill swept up and down his spine. Something was very wrong.

Duvall copied the relevant files on to datakey and set about hacking his way into IAD's financial records. The fact that he had been entrusted with the security codes for the Halls of Justice servers made the task considerably easier. A quick trawl through the records confirmed this as the only posthumous transaction made by Horrowitz. The remainder of the records appeared to be in order, assuming someone had not already doctored them. Finding it impossible to identify who had really authorised the transaction, Duvall paused to consider his next course of action.

Three quarters of a million was a lot of money, therefore it made sense that he was looking for either a large transfer or, more likely, a series of smaller ones. He keyed in a search for all credit transfers exceeding fifty thousand. The screen went blank for a few seconds before producing a single line of text. A payment of one million euro-dollars authorised to the Damocles Project. Duvall had never heard of it but he was certain that any operation requiring such a large clandestine transfer of funds had to be suspect in some manner.

Duvall's suspicion increased when he tried to access the files on the Damocles Project and discovered them protected by an unknown password. He sat back, idly rubbing at the stubble on his chin as he considered how to crack the code. The password was five characters long, producing thousands of possible permutations from a standard alphanumeric keyboard. It was reasonable to assume that repeated wrong entries would trigger a lockout or an alarm indicating his unauthorised presence in the system. Humans being lazy and to a certain extent predictable, people often used the simplest and most unimaginative passwords. If he could get his mind in synch with the designer's then he might stand a chance of figuring out the most likely option, the obvious assumption being that of a name or date associated with Damocles. Duvall cast his mind back over the fragments of Greek mythology he remembered from school. Damocles was an ancient noble whose king had forced him to eat a sumptuous banquet with a sword suspended above his head by a single horse hair. The knowledge that the sword could fall at any moment rendered even the greatest of delicacies bland and inedible. A lesson in humility, intended to illustrate the constant peril faced by powerful men.

Duvall smiled, wondering if the password could really be that simple. Only one way to find out. He typed in 'sword' and a pop up warning appeared: Invalid Password. Long seconds passed with no alarm or other indication that his activity had been discovered. Deciding to try again, he turned a few other options over in his mind but sword remained the most likely. He retyped the password with a capital. Beads of perspiration broke from his pores as he waited for it to clear. Just as his nerves reached breaking point, the monitor gave a single beep and filled with text.

'Holy Shit,' Duvall muttered under his breath. His sense of disbelief increased with every word as he scanned the text. The ramifications of the Damocles Project were almost unimaginable. At the very least they would guarantee him a transfer back to the Sector Patrol Force, probably with a promotion. His fingers trembled as he inserted a fresh datakey and initiated download.

If someone else had told him what he'd just discovered he would have dismissed him or her as crazy. IAD were running an assassination bureau from within the Department. Meticulous to a fault, they had kept records of all their "sanctions". They were responsible for the deaths of over twenty people, ranging from political dissidents to suspected criminals that had escaped prosecution. Most chilling of all was the final name on the list - Kurt Brecht! Duvall wondered if Sajer was aware that Weill had authorised the attempted assassination of one of his men. Sajer might well have approved it, which meant he couldn't be trusted. Bypassing the chain of command and going straight to the Council was the only sure method of exposing the conspiracy.

'Congratulations, Duvall, I must admit that I never credited you as having enough intelligence to unmask Damocles. You might have gone far, if your career had not ended so swiftly. C'est la vie.'

Duvall turned at the sound of Weill's voice and found himself staring down the barrel of a pistol. The sound of two gunshots fired in quick succession reverberated round the room.

CHAPTER 9

3 1/10/85 (cont.): Hassan drove back to the Hotel Metropolis where I
guess word must have got round that I was on the payroll. This time
when I offered the doorman my gun he indicated for me to keep it. I
hurried on into the lobby where I encountered the delectable Georgio, who
greeted me with a rather unbecoming sneer.

'One of the boys now are we? You move quickly, I'll give you that,
Dumas. Your first pay off is still in room five-oh-eight. I guess you
discovered you had more of a taste for young flesh than you thought?'

'Kind of late to be developing a conscience isn't it? You've been
running girls like her for God knows how long. What's the sudden interest
in the girl's well-being? Discovered your door swings both ways?'

She tensed with barely restrained rage and then grabbed my right arm.
Her nails dug into my flesh as she dragged me towards the lifts. Her voice
low and menacing, she said, 'Don't you dare judge me. Not a low-life shit
like you, Dumas. You don't know the who, why or what about me. I, on
the other hand, know everything about your "business". Whatever has
happened to the girl here won't come close to the kind of horrors the meat-
markets you run are going to expose her to.'

The lift arrived and I shoved her inside. Now it was my turn to give a
self-righteous speech. 'I don't care what you or Vaughan want to think, but
believe it or not I'm doing this for the girl, not myself. The why, as you put
it, doesn't concern you. But if it makes you sleep any easier you can rest
assured she's not destined to become some sado-masochist plaything or the
slave of some Middle Eastern warlord. And before you suggest it, I'm not
interested in fucking her physically or metaphorically either. I just want to
give the kid a break.'

Having finished my spiel I stood there breathing heavily and glaring at
Georgio, daring her to contradict me. She took an involuntary step away

from me and found herself against the side of the lift carriage. You can quote all the jargon you want about sexual equality and the modern woman, but it would be a rare female indeed who, when confronted by a large and powerful man in an enclosed space, didn't feel threatened in some measure. To give her her due she rallied pretty well. Her voice hardly cracked when she asked, 'Why? You say it doesn't concern me but what you've said doesn't fit with what I know about you.'

A good question. What was I doing attempting to explain my motives to one of Vaughan's minions? My cover was thin enough without this lapse in character. Surely it was to my advantage to let this woman believe I was as big a bastard as Vaughan? The answer, of course, was guilt. I'd just killed Conroy to protect myself, to allow myself to continue with my crusade against Vaughan. Now here I stood screaming to the world that I wasn't all bad, that I was capable of being a positive force as well as a destructive one. All the while digging a deeper hole for myself.

Meanwhile, Georgio was still waiting for my answer. Having nothing better to tell her, I decided to opt for an old cliché. 'She reminds me of somebody I knew a long time ago. Someone who wasn't so lucky.'

Georgio subjected me to a look that defied interpretation - perhaps she believed me, perhaps she didn't. Perhaps my explanation sounded so much like bullshit she reckoned it had to be true. The strange thing being that in a way it was true. I did remember another woman, older and with blonde hair, who had been caught in a similar situation, only her knight in shining armour had arrived too late to save her.

Anastasia was out cold, doped up to the eyeballs, when we entered the room. Standing at her bedside, staring at her features so calm in repose, a strange thing happened. Her image oscillated before my eyes, she would age and her hair changed from auburn to blonde, the bed to a mortuary slab. Funny how you never seen to get warm and fuzzy flashbacks.

I flinched visibly when Georgio touched me on the shoulder, her voice sounded harsh in the silence. 'Stop gawking and give me a hand getting her dressed. You can slake your unnatural desires later.' We were back to the old accusation. I decided to let it slide this time.

Working between us, we managed to manoeuvre Anastasia into a loose fitting blouse, worn jeans and stiletto ankle boots - the clothes she had apparently arrived in. She was still no nearer consciousness by the time we finished and I asked, 'What now? Am I supposed to sling her across my shoulder and casually stroll past reception?'

'Only if you really want to. Alternatively, you could take her down to the basement garage in the service lift and I'll have Hassan pick you up.'

'I think we should go with Plan B, don't you?'

I was about to bend down and pick up the girl when Georgio moved in close. 'Look, I don't know if the BS you fed me earlier about wanting to help her is true, but if it is you're going to need these.' She handed me a small phial of tablets. I pulled the stopper loose and shook one on to the palm of my hand. A small pink tablet, it smelled vaguely of strawberries. Replacing it in the phial, I shot Georgio a questioning glance and she explained, 'It's an engineered derivative of MDMA. It relaxes the girls, removes their inhibitions and radically increases their sex drive - their need for physical human contact. It's also highly physically and psychologically addictive, producing the most horrendous withdrawal symptoms. You'll have to wean her off gradually unless you want to kill her.'

I found it a strange gesture on her part and let her know. 'Tit for tat, my dear. You've already questioned my motives for wanting to help the girl, what about your own? I don't see she's any different from any of your other charges.'

She smiled enigmatically. 'Let's just say you're not the only person who's not what they appear to be; Vaughan's girls may not be burning out quite as fast as he thinks they are.'

'Den Mother to the world and whore with a heart of gold, eh? I don't suppose old Vaughan would be too pleased to find out that you're spiriting his girls away, would he?'

My first comment must have struck a raw nerve because her lips drew tight, white with rage, and there was pure venom in her voice. 'I'm many things, Mr Dumas, but I'm not a whore. Don't think you can threaten me, you've a lot more to hide from Vaughan than I have.'

'Touché,' I replied, subjecting her to my most boyish grin. 'Look, all this crap is getting us nowhere. Let's just agree to disagree about each other's morals and leave it there. 'Cause standing arguing like this isn't going to help Anastasia at all.' Without waiting for a reply, I picked Anastasia up and made for the door. Georgio, gathering that the conversation was at an end, followed mutely behind me. Her eyes bored into my back like daggers all the way along the corridor. Some people are such poor losers.

Georgio sulked all the way to the basement. I placed Anastasia on the back seat of the limousine and attempted to make peace with her. 'Look, thanks for the pills. I know you didn't have to give them to me, and that you were taking a risk telling me the other stuff. I'm certain you don't want to hear any more of my opinions but if you ask me, you want to take your own advice and get as far away from Vaughan as you can. And you want to do it now while you still can.'

'You're a bit of an idealist at heart, aren't you, Dumas? Don't bother replying, we both know the answer. For what it's worth, you needn't worry about me. I have everything sorted, believe me. Now get out of here.'

'Certainly, Madam.' I gave her a theatrical bow before opening the front passenger door and climbing in beside Hassan. I didn't bother to look as we drove away, knowing Georgio would have already turned away.

'You trying to make it with Georgio?' the little Arab asked. 'Don't bother. Colonel Vaughan, he snap your spine. She his woman.'

That one is nobody's woman, I thought to myself.

The night time streets of Amsterdam were awash with the red-orange glow of flames. The acrid smell of smoke caused Sajer's nostrils to twitch as it penetrated the cruiser's overloaded filtering system. Sirens and rumbling explosions rent the air as police and civilians clashed in the streets. Rioting had become common place with two or three skirmishes erupting every week. Spotting an obstruction, he slammed on the brakes, causing the cruiser to skid sideways past the wreckage of a SPF squad car. Changing down and accelerating, he crashed through a makeshift barrier of rubbish that marked the beginning of the territory thought, at least nominally, to be under police control. He spied a cluster of SPF vehicles up ahead and pulled to a halt opposite an alley entrance between two of the older housing blocks.

An armoured SPF officer opened the door of the cruiser and saluted sharply as his superior alighted. Sajer returned the younger man's salute and surveyed him speculatively.

'Full kevlar? I take it from your garb and the explosions that the reports of rioting in this district have not been exaggerated?'

'No, sir, they have not. Initial disturbances broke out at four ay-em this morning in the Kierkengrasse when riot troops were called in to deal with looters following a power cut. There have been sporadic clashes ever since with our situation becoming increasingly untenable. At last count, there were sixty-three officer casualties with forty-eight fatalities. Riot gas and water cannons have proved ineffective against the looters' heavy ordnance. But that's not why we called you in. Dispatch received an anonymous call detailing the location of a body.'

Sajer tutted impatiently. 'I am the Commander of Vice, not Homicide. What is this body to me?'

'Just coming to that, sir. The caller said the body was one of your men. He identified you by name and said,' the officer suddenly looked very uncomfortable, 'and I'm quoting directly now, sir. "Tell that worthless shit, Sajer, that it's going to take more than half trained boys to take me." That was it, just that and the location. Under the circumstances we decided it was best to call you in immediately.'

'Yes. Thank you for your unstintingly accurate report. Shall we proceed?'

The body lay draped across a pile of rubbish bags stacked against the wall of the alley. A naked, male, with wounds to both knees. The head, with the exception of the lower jaw, was missing.

A squatting figure greeted Sajer as he approached. 'Detective Peter Kurtzman,' he held up a polymer gloved and blood-stained hand, 'hope you don't mind if I don't shake. I'll be leading the investigation. An' this is...'

'Marcus Conroy - detective, third class,' Sajer interrupted.

Kurtzman's eyes narrowed. 'You recognise a mole or something? I needed a DNA print to identify him.'

'Nothing so scientific. I recognised the style of the call as belonging to that of the organisation that I'd assigned Conroy to infiltrate. It would appear he was less than successful in his attempt.' Sajer pointed to the body. 'What are those wounds on his knees?'

'Sadistic is what they are. Some prick hammered a couple of ten millimetre bullet casings through his kneecaps just before or after they'd jammed razor-wire up his ass. I've seen a lot on the job but I don't mind telling you this one ain't for the faint-hearted.'

'He was tortured?'

Kurtzman nodded. 'I'd say so. Actual cause of death appears to be a large calibre gunshot wound to the head. We'll know more when we get the pathology reports. You said you recognised the style, you want to clue me in on who you think did this?'

'Isaac Vaughan.'

'This the same Colonel Vaughan we're talking about here? Decorated war hero, rising star of the Nationalist Party and all-round corporate sleaze ball. You telling me the guy's dirty?'

'Utterly corrupt would be my choice of description. Unfortunately, he is also very adept at covering his tracks, which makes it rather difficult to prove my allegations. Worse still, I don't have much time left to do so.'

'How's that? I'd have thought the Council would have been a hundred-percent behind you, it being an election year.'

'The Tessler Corporation is about to secure the Police Department arms contract. You can imagine how embarrassing it would be if I were then to arrest Vaughan. I must make a case against him before then or else forget about him.' He added to himself, *Now that Conroy's dead my only hope is that Brecht is being as reckless as usual and flagrantly flaunting my orders. Machiavelli could have learnt a thing or two working for the police in this city.*

'That's a bitch, but internal politics don't concern me. My work starts when the body's called in an' it ends when I get a confession. If Vaughan's responsible for killing your man I'll see he goes down for it, even if I have to beat it out of him. In the meantime we should get out of here before the real fighting starts.'

Sajer looked around at the burning vehicles. 'The real fighting?'

'Yeah, this is just skirmishing. Cumberland's waiting for the authorisation to use deadly force against the rioters. Thirty seconds after that he'll have the tanks rolling, on account of him being a first class human being an' all.'

A nearby explosion shook the alley and seconds later an armoured head appeared round the corner. Its owner paused and shouted at the uniform who had accompanied Sajer from his cruiser, 'Duvall, get your arse up to the barricade on the double, the riot tanks need back up,' before disappearing into the smoke.

As he watched the young officer's retreat, Sajer inquired, 'Are forensics about ready to bag the body?'

'Yeah, they're just coming towards us now. Time we followed the kid's example an' beat a retreat. We can catch the results on tomorrow's newscast.'

'Kurtzman, did anyone ever tell you that you are the most appalling cynic?'

'Only everybody I ever met.'

01/11/85: I'm writing this entry as a kind of therapy, or perhaps more accurately a work in progress to aid me in planning my next move. I might as well start by listing the known facts.

Fact: I need departmental assistance to have any chance of bringing down Vaughan and the Tessler Corporation, therefore must approach Sajer.

Fact: only Vaughan and Hassan know who shot Conroy.

Supposition: (sop for a guilty conscience): Vaughan would have wasted Conroy whether I'd been present or not. He was raw and inexperienced and paid the price for it. I'm the real victim of circumstance here.

Fact: the above is pure bullshit and I know it.

Fact: Should Vaughan and Hassan die, for the sake of argument let's say resisting arrest, the knowledge that I killed Conroy will die with them.

Fact: I have a sixteen year old girl doing cold turkey on my sofa who would seriously benefit from professional medical supervision - another good reason to contact Sajer.

Fact: Sajer expressly told me that I was to drop the case under risk of suspension, and will not be best pleased to learn that I've been pursuing Vaughan regardless. A major reason not to contact him.

Fact: Vaughan is expecting me to supply him with a new location and some girls within four days time. He will doubtless react with extreme prejudice if I fail to come through with the aforementioned merchandise. Sajer can supply said merchandise and save both my cover and my worthless hide. Good reason number three to contact him.

Well I guess that about...

The entry ended abruptly and Sajer leaned back in his chair as he considered the import of the last few pages. He recalled how Weill had burst into his office waving a hard copy of the pathology report on Conroy. His expression had bordered on the grimly satisfied as he informed Sajer of its contents. 'Bullet fragments match those of a standard Department issue ten millimetre depleted uranium slug. It appears that another officer snuffed out your boy. Is there anything that you'd like to tell me, Commander?'

Weill pronounced the last word a distinct sneer - the veiled threat that Sajer might not be in possession of his rank for much longer. Weill's entire body seemed to radiate a sense of triumph, giving Sajer the impression that he was waiting to deliver some form of verbal coup de grace. In the meantime, whatever Weill had up his sleeve, and regardless of their history, he remained a commander and he would be damned before he submitted to badgering from a lower ranking officer. He rose to his full height and barked, 'Yes, I have something to say, though I doubt you will be particularly pleased to hear it. You have overstepped your authority, Captain Weill, barging in here, making obscure accusations. What is more, am I now to take it that you're in the habit of intercepting my internal e-mail? Pathology should have sent that report directly to my office terminal. I don't recall placing a request for it to be routed via Internal Affairs.'

Weill's smile did not even slip a fraction as he replied in a sly tone of voice. 'I apologise if my manner seemed a little brusque but I, like everyone else in the Department, have been under enormous pressure lately, what with all the civil unrest in the city. And for the record, I didn't intercept your mail, the pathology department sent me a copy after processing the results; results, I might add, which they felt warranted the attention of Internal Affairs.'

'I see,' Sajer conceded, deflating slightly. 'Well, do not keep me in suspense, Weill, continue.'

'The bullet fragments have been identified as being consistent with those removed from Anton Bergman and Simone Bacall. In other words, your pet rottweiler has finally turned rabid. I trust you read the psychological report and profile Doctor Wilsdorf submitted? It warned that Brecht is living in a fantasy world, dangerously close to a full scale mental breakdown.'

Sajer cleared his throat awkwardly. 'The use of Brecht's sidearm does not automatically imply that he is our shooter. Someone else could just as easily have fired the killing shot.' He was clutching at straws and he knew it. His attempt to play Brecht off against his own agenda had backfired and Marcus Conroy had paid the ultimate price for his arrogance.

'Do you honestly believe that? Please, we're both adults. I don't enjoy bringing down a fellow officer any more than you do, but as regrettable as it is, it has to be done on occasion.'

'So you work for IAD as a kind of self-purgatory, do you?'

'You're well aware of the circumstance of my original transfer. I was hardly willing,' growled Weill, his thin veneer of civility slipping.

'Perhaps, but you do seem to have taken to it quite readily.'

'In your opinion, yes. But that is not the topic under discussion. Has Brecht reported his weapon stolen? Have you received any communications from him since he went on sick leave?' Sajer was about to answer when Weill held up his hand to silence him. 'The answer to those questions is no, and we both know it. On the other hand, did you not receive a report from Conroy identifying Brecht entering the Hotel Metropolis on the night of the twenty-ninth of October? The very location of a locked box prostitution racket that you had ordered him to cease investigating. Furthermore, you appear to have turned a blind eye when Brecht authorised a transfer of ten thousand euro-dollars through his John Dumas identity whilst on sick leave. I put it to you that you have been guilty of complacency in this matter at the very least. Have you anything at all to say in your defence?'

'No. I can't deny any of the points that you have so clearly illustrated. You may not read my mail but you certainly appear to read my squad's classified files.'

Weill stiffened. 'That's quite within my rights when conducting an investigation.'

'Hmph. That's beside the point. The real question is what do you want from me? Because that is the only rational explanation as to why you have approached me before showing your superior this information, who, I imagine, would presumably process it through the normal channels.'

'Correct as always, Sajer. What I want is your signature,' Weill's eyes glittered malevolently, 'on a Damocles Sanction. In return, I'm willing to assume that you were giving Brecht the benefit of the doubt based on his previous record. Otherwise I may feel compelled to state that I believe you to be guilty of complicity in Conroy's death.'

'God, Weill, I always suspected you were a thorough going bastard and now I know. My career or a man's life, what sort of choice is that to offer anyone?'

'I don't know, perhaps Conroy's widow could help you choose? Come on, give him up. He's beyond help, and every second you procrastinate increases the chances of him killing another innocent.'

Sajer sat down again. Suddenly he felt very old. He decided to make one last effort to spare Brecht's life. 'Perhaps he can still be persuaded to come in of his own freewill?'

'Damn it, man!' Weill shouted. 'Think with your head, not your heart. It's over. You gave him every break you could and now it's time to end the matter. We can't have another of our men on trial. The people have little enough faith in the ECPD as it is. It would be the final nail in the coffin of our credibility. Christ, it is not as if this is the first sanction you've authorised, is it?'

'All right,' Sajer's shoulders sagged in defeat, 'give it here.' Weill passed him a plain looking document, which he read through quickly before signing. 'There. Now take the damn thing and get yourself out of my sight.'

Weill flashed him a debonair smile. 'Don't be such a sore loser, Sajer. Consider this a learning experience.' He picked up the document and carefully scrutinised the signature. 'Well, this all appears to be in order, so I'll leave you in peace.' He paused at the door. 'In my opinion you've made the right decision, whatever your reasons.'

Sajer fixed him with a steely glare. 'Perhaps. But I sincerely hope that you come to rue this day's work, Captain Weill.'

'Well everybody's got a right to hope, just don't hold your breath.'

Now more than a month later, as much as it galled him, Sajer had to admit that Weill had been correct. Brecht had been out of control and he had his written testimony to prove it. Yet in spite of all the evidence, he still could not accept that Brecht had snapped. There had to be something more, something that had so far escaped him. With nowhere else to look for answers he queued up the next page of Brecht's journal and began to read.

CHAPTER 10

O 1/11/85 (cont.): An unexpected visitor interrupted me and the now familiar voice of Lady Methedrine said, 'I suppose she's kind of cute in a baby-doll sort of way.'

I looked round to discover her perched on the edge of the sofa examining Anastasia with a kind of detached interest. There was a time in our acquaintance when I would have been curious as to how she had entered my apartment unannounced, but not now. Far too much had gone down for me to worry about such little details. I cut straight to the chase. 'So what brings you here? We had a deal - you promised to help me. Where the fuck were you when I needed you? Surely you could have saved Conroy? Or is getting me up to my neck in shit some new definition of help I wasn't previously aware of?'

'You should know it doesn't work like that,' Lady Methedrine replied. Losing interest in Anastasia, she rose, accompanied by the whispering rustle of her dress. 'As for Conroy, all the most powerful goddesses demand sacrifice.' She winked. 'You were warned my services don't come cheap.'

Suddenly lost, I shook my head. 'What have you done to me?'

'I've made you all that you've ever wanted to be. I've given you strength enough in your convictions to carry them out whatever the cost.'

'You've made me a killer,' I snarled. 'That's what you've done.'

She threw back her head and laughed like some baying animal. 'You were always a killer, Kurt. It's just that you believe it's okay to kill the so-called bad guys.'

I tried to think of some suitable retort but failed. What is there to say when faced with the truth? I watched her stand there as she played with a long curl of hair, twisting it around her index finger and then slowly letting it go. Her gaze shifted and I found myself lost in the bottomless depths of those sapphire blue eyes.

'Primitive man made sacrifice to the White Goddess when he wished to petition her favours,' she informed me in a sulky tone of voice. 'Don't you think it only good manners to accept yours?'

I backed away as she moved towards me; the curves of her body delineated through her dress by the harsh light of the room. I wanted to tell her - to say - 'Your favours come at too high a price. I'm no longer willing to pay it!' but the words froze unspoken in my throat. For the first time the roles in our master / servant relationship became clear to me - that I would serve her well. I knew what Faust must have felt when he first came to regret his pact, though he at least had known he was getting involved with the Devil. I'd merely thought myself to be humouring the whims of a mad woman, albeit an extremely attractive one. Then, the time for rational thought was gone as she enfolded me in her embrace. Her body moulded around me, cool but never cold. The thumping rhythm of that indomitable heart beat against my chest. At that moment it occurred to me that she was a true vamp, if not an actual vampire. Like all beautiful women down through the ages, she had the power to subjugate and destroy those men that fell for her charms. Hopelessly ensnared, I crushed her to me and kissed her. Her tongue was like fire in my mouth, suffusing me with unholy energy. I felt its power wash over me as it blew apart the twisted demons I had constructed in my mind. It washed me clean of sin as it burned through every fibre, leaving me cleansed. This, then, was my reward and I took it as gladly as I took her body. Lost in the flow of my base animal instinct, I revelled in our union, and when it was over and the sweat had finally dried, I found myself forced to concede that she was not a hard mistress to serve.

I stared at my front room with fresh sight, seeing it for the first time as it really was, a collection of bric-a-brac that meant nothing in real terms. Nothing more than the consumerist detritus we surround ourselves with to kill time as we pass blindly through our lives. Distractions for those that could not accept the truth of the brief burst of light bounded on either side by eternal darkness that was existence. My streamlined thought process concluded this almost instantaneously as I experienced that feeling of calm, cerebral logic that often comes with the extended use of amphetamines. But this was no drug-induced psychosis; it was now my permanent state of being.

Staring at my vampiric lover in wonderment I asked, 'What... have... you... done... to... me?' pausing between each word as I suddenly found the process of speech alien to me.

'I've given you what you've always wanted.' She threw a languorous arm about my neck and drew me close to whisper, 'I've killed you, Kurt. You're dead; you just haven't stopped moving yet. That will be your power, for who can stand against that which does not live? Vaughan and Tessler will fall before you and then you'll be mine.'

'A harsh price,' I said, bending to kiss the hollow of her throat.

'Is it so harsh, Kurt?' It's not how long you live for but what you accomplish with your time that is important. Would you rather live for seventy or eighty years, achieving nothing, or die tomorrow having fulfilled your ambition? The brightest flame burns for the shortest time and I can assure you that you will burn very brightly. But first there are preparations to be made.'

Lady Methedrine rolled away from me and was suddenly fully clothed again. 'You must move quickly for those closest to you seek to betray you. Your mentor, Sajer, will have no choice but to join them. After this night you will no longer be in a position to help the girl, and this place shall no longer be safe. You must place her in safe hands and flee underground before your nemesis finds you.'

'Must it always be riddles with you?'

'It's the nature of my being to speak as I do. Put simply, tonight you are still Detective Sergeant Kurt Brecht; tomorrow you will be a hunted fugitive. I must go now.'

She shimmered and began to fade to transparency, a trick she hadn't performed previously. I called out, 'Wait. How do you know what Sajer will do?' but I spoke to empty air. Shrugging, I picked up the vidphone and started calling in favours.

Sword sat down opposite Weill with the creak of oiled leather. His features set in a permanent sneer, he glared across the desk at the policeman. 'You have work for me,' he stated in a tone that was as dead and impassive as his eyes.

Weill nodded, not trusting himself to speak, and handed Sword two colour photographs. Finding his voice he said, 'The first is your target, Kurt Brecht. You are to terminate him with extreme prejudice. The woman is his girlfriend, Hannah Schade.'

The assassin flipped over the top photograph to reveal the image of a young woman with blonde hair and green eyes.

Weill continued with his briefing. 'Brecht has gone to ground. We suspect he may be staying with her. The address is in the file along with a list of other known associates. Pay particular attention to Marian Dupree, a prostitute of Brecht's acquaintance, and Andreas Rosenstein; he's a full time junkie and some time informant. His street name is Slinky. Beyond that, Brecht's known to frequent the Amsterdam Paradiso, Hamburg Docks and the Berlin Loft Club. It is imperative that you carry out this sanction as quickly as possible.'

'Relax. I've never failed to carry out a sanction.' His hand and arm blurred into motion as he reached across the desk and snatched Weill's gun from its holster. A sardonic smile twisted his lips. 'For who in this city is equal to the Damocles Assassin? No one. The ECPD has made certain of that. Kurt Brecht is a dead man. He just hasn't stopped moving yet.'

'I'm glad you feel so confident. But I'll warn you, be careful with Brecht. He's completely psychotic, and a genuine hard man.'

'Brecht is just a piece of meat like all the rest. I was killing his sort before he was born.'

'That's what's worrying me.'

'Don't trouble yourself, Weill. I've the heart and lungs of a sixteen year old. Not to mention his spleen, liver, kidneys and eyes.'

The assassin smiled maliciously and Weill blanched. Recovering his composure he said, 'Yes, very good. That will be all. You may go now.'

Sword rose to his full height, a little over six feet, and leaned forward, resting the palms of his hands on the desktop. Staring into Weill's eyes he said, 'Don't make the mistake of thinking you control me.'

'Perhaps you'd like to explain this mistake to me?'

'Oh I think you know.' Sword turned smartly on his heel and left the room, his threat hanging in the air.

Sitting on his own, Weill muttered, 'Arrogant bastard. I must have words with Doctor Erlicht and see how his replacement is proceeding.'

Brecht stared vacantly at the vidphone as he considered his next words. The image on the screen showed a middle-aged woman of Afro-Caribbean descent. She had a strong, attractive face, with fine traces of laughter lines around the eyes and corners of the mouth. The woman tossed her head, causing her braids to dance about her shoulders.

'C'mon, Kurt, don't be shy. I'm your doctor. You can tell me anything.'

Brecht shook his head in a far more negative gesture. 'It's not that simple,' he explained, obviously uncomfortable. 'I need a favour, Claudia. As much as I hate to cast up the past, you do owe me. You'd be doing a twenty stretch if I hadn't misplaced that disc.'

'Guess I should count myself lucky for being struck off and having to spend the last five years running an underground surgery for petty criminals. Where would I be without my good friend Kurt Brecht?' Claudia scoffed, her voice laden with sarcasm.

'Shit. Look, I didn't mean it to sound like that. Anyway, it's more of a favour to someone else. There's this girl...'

Claudia interrupted him with an angry outburst, 'My God, Kurt, what do you take me for, some back street abortionist? If you've knocked up some trollop you can damn well take her somewhere else!'

Brecht became indignant, 'Have I got a reputation or something? It's nothing like that, I barely know her. She's linked to a case I'm working. I freed her from the Shifting House but she's hooked on rapture. Trouble is that I've got myself in some pretty deep shit and I'm about to make the most wanted list. So all I'm asking is for you to keep her somewhere safe while she's kicking.'

Claudia's voice dropped in pitch, 'Is it really as bad as that? I was just mouthing off earlier, I'm grateful I'm not in prison. I know you took a risk reaching out like that for me. Hell, I'm making more money now than I ever did when I was legit. So you want a favour, you've got it.'

'Thanks. You know it's appreciated, Claudia. Don't worry, I won't ask for another. I'm not likely to be around after this.'

'You know I don't like to pry, but is it really as bad as you're making out?'

'Worse. I wasted a cop. Sajer will have no choice but to throw me to the wolves. It's my own fault. I've got myself in too deep this time.'

The doctor's eyes widened in disbelief. 'Lord Almighty, you don't do things by half when you mess up, do you?'

'Guess not.' Brecht hurriedly changed the subject. 'You still at the Berlin address?' Claudia nodded. 'Good. I'll bring her round in a couple of hours. I've some more calls to make.' Brecht hesitated, unsure of what to say next. Long seconds passed as he stared at the image on the screen. 'Thanks, Claudia. You don't know how much this means. I'll see you're not forgotten.' He paused again before adding, 'I guess this is goodbye, Aunt Claudia.'

The corners of the doctor's mouth curved upwards in a smile. 'That takes me back a few years. I'm surprised you remember. You had such a lot of "Aunts" when you were little.' She sniffed and brushed at the corner of her eye with a knuckle. 'Excuse me. I think I've got a lash in my eye.'

Brecht smiled kindly at her and for a moment all of his cares lifted from him, erasing the harsh lines from his face. He looked almost boyish again. 'You know what the funny thing is? I used to lie awake at night worrying my aunts would catch cold because they were always so scantily dressed.'

'Most of them came to a worse end than that I'm afraid.'

Brecht broke eye contact. He looked down at his feet and replied, 'I know. I checked up on them. But you, you were always the smart one. You had a brain and enough common sense to quit the game before it started playing you.' He looked up, meeting her eyes again. 'This really is goodbye now. I must make those calls.'

'Wait,' Claudia called out as he reached to break the connection, 'you should never say goodbye, Kurt. It's unlucky. You'll be fine and I'll see you soon.'

'I hope not. Not where I'm going,' Brecht replied, terminating the call.

Claudia stared at the blank screen for a moment before burying her face in her hands. A short while later she whispered, 'Please forgive me, Kurt,' and reached for the vidphone handset.

The black clad figure stepped back into the shadows beneath the fire escape as the headlights of a passing vehicle swept across the wall of the building. Crouching down, he tensed himself, bunching powerful muscles, gathering energy for a vertical spring. He leapt the moment darkness returned, his fingers finding purchase on the grilled flooring of the fire escape ten feet above. Locking his legs together, he swung his body forward, once, twice, gathering momentum on each successive back-swing. On the third pass, the assassin released his grip and somersaulted over the rail of the fire escape to land silently on the grilled flooring. Sword paused briefly to glance at the street below to ensure no one had observed him and then started to climb. He agilely shinned his way up the series of metal rungs that connected each of the caged balconies of the fire escape and arrived on the eighteenth floor. Removing the slim case strapped to his back, he began to assemble a compact sniper rifle. Each component slotted into place with practised ease, the operation concluded by the insertion of three cartridges into the rifle's magazine. The well greased bolt slid silently as he pulled it back to chamber the first round. Satisfied, the assassin trained the rifle on the window of the apartment block on the opposite side of the Nichtstrasse.

In apartment 1804 of the Cannaris tenement block, Hannah Schade rolled over and ran her fingers down her partner's spine. 'Honey,' she whispered, 'I want some more wine. Would you get it for me?' The man grunted, fought briefly to stay submerged in his warm drowse and then gave up. Disentangling himself from the dishevelled bedding, he yawned and stretched as he sat up.

'Sure, Hannah, no problem,' he said and reached for the light switch.

On the opposite side of the street Sword observed the man's heat signature through the rifle's night scope. He breathed in and held his breath as he slowly squeezed back on the trigger. It bit home an instant after the light illuminated the bedroom, giving the assassin his first clear look at his target at precisely the moment he fired. 'Fuck!' he cursed. The man in bed with Hannah Schade was not Brecht. He pulled the rifle to the side. Too late. The first bullet detonated inside the man's skull, splattering blood and brain tissue across the bed and rear wall of the room. The impact left his eyeballs adhering almost comically to the wall above the headboard. Bullet number two kicked up a cloud of foam insulation from the mattress, while the third buried itself in soft flesh. Hannah screamed and rolled on to the floor dragging the sheets with her.

Sword slid down the vertical ladders of the fire escape, gripping the outsides with his insteps. He released his grip on reaching the first floor and dropped to the ground. A length of polymer sheeting slipped back to reveal the sleek black and chrome lines of a motorcycle. Mounting the bike, he pressed the ignition, kicked it into gear and shot out of Nichtstrasse into the path of an oncoming freight truck. With no time to brake or go around the truck, he made the decision to go under it. Heeling the bike over almost ninety degrees, he slid below the bed of the trailer accompanied by a shower of sparks and the screech of tortured metal. With almost preternatural strength, Sword kicked himself upright and roared up an exit ramp on to a fly-over, scraps of leather and skin trailing from his thigh in the slipstream.

Hannah grabbed the vidphone from her bedside table and thumbed it to vocal command mode. Clutching at her abdomen, she moaned, 'Triple Zero, emergency services,' and waited for the reply.

A tinny voice burst from the cheap speaker, relayed from the main screens in the apartment's front room. 'You have dialled Triple Zero, what service do you require?'

Hannah struggled to think through the waves of pain that were now surging through her body as the initial shock wore off. She grunted through gritted teeth, 'Been shot. Need help. Oh God, please don't let me die.'

The voice on the other end of the line remained cold and unemotional; its owner desensitised by years of experience. 'What is your location, Madam?'

'Home - in the bedroom.' Hannah slipped into unconsciousness.

'I meant your address,' replied the voice, a hint of exasperation creeping in at the edges.

A new voice interjected, 'Forget it, the line's still open. Run a trace and dispatch the nearest SPF unit and paramedics.'

Duvall drew his gun and looked at his partner, 'Eighteen-o-four. This is it.' He tried the handle and said. 'Locked. How do you want to play this? The shooter could still be inside.'

Falconer lowered the visor of his helmet. 'Carefully: I'll count three and you bust the door. Ready?'

Duvall nodded and stepped back, raising his leg. The flat of his foot smashed against the door opposite the main locks. A splintering crack sounded as the door frame split and screws tore lose from their hinges. Duvall pushed open the door and shone his flashlight inside. The beam played over the still interior of the room, highlighting the neatly arranged furniture, tasteful paintings and expensive ornamentation. Something caught his eye on the far side of the room and he swept the beam back.

There, the bedroom door was ajar; the narrow beam of light shining out allowed him to make out the slim fingers of a woman's hand gripping at the deep pile of the carpet. He drew his gun and inched towards the bedroom.

Falconer followed closely behind him, his weapon darted from side to side as he passed every point of concealment. He noticed Duvall waiting beside the bedroom door and motioned for him to open it. That's it, rookie, you take all the risks. Your kevlar will stop a bullet just as well as mine. And if they're using armour-piercing rounds, they'll damn well near be spent by the time they punch through you.

The expected attack never came. 'It's clear!' Duvall called. 'Get the paramedics in here quick, she's hurt real bad.'

Falconer paged the two medics who had been waiting a safe distance down the corridor to come forward with their gurney. On entering the bedroom, he discovered Duvall kneeling beside Hannah, gripping her left wrist as he felt for a pulse. He observed the blood soaked sheets gripped between her thighs and commented, 'That sure is one heavy period.'

Duvall shot him a venomous glance. 'Anyone ever tell you that you're an insensitive bastard, Sam?'

'Yeah, often, but I'm too thick skinned to take any notice. She still with us?'

'She's got a pulse and she's breathing, but I can't tell how bad she's injured. She won't let go of the goddamn sheets.'

The paramedics entered and another voice said, 'Then why don't you leave it to the experts and go and look for whoever did this?'

Duvall shuffled out of the way. 'Sorry. Just trying to help,' he mumbled.

'I know,' the other medic said, not unkindly. 'But right now the most help you can give this woman is to let us get on with our job.'

Falconer diverted Duvall's attention from the medic. 'I hope you ain't had supper yet, 'cause you should see the state of this other poor bastard.' He pointed to the remains of Hannah's lover on the bed.

'Shit!' Duvall exclaimed, 'How are we going to get an ID on that?'

'Guess we could hunt about the room for his teeth. They've got to be around here somewhere.' He jerked a thumb above the bed. 'We know he had blue eyes. Least an iris scan ain't gonna be a problem.'

'There's something seriously wrong with your sense of humour, Sam,' Duvall said, stepping towards him.

The older man held up his hand to stop his partner. 'Woah. Don't step on that glass in front of you; forensics will want to check it out.' He pointed to the shattered window. My guess is our shooter was a sniper from the opposite building. But we'd better call in the boys from homicide and let them nose around. They like to decide these things for themselves.'

The paramedic who had asked Duvall to move aside came over. He was a short, dark haired man, about the same age as Falconer. 'We've got her stabilised now and I'd say her chances are good. That's one lucky woman there, I can tell you. The odds against an explosive round like that failing to detonate are over a thousand to one. Mind you, I wouldn't recommend it as the best way of getting a hysterectomy.'

'Damn straight,' Falconer replied. 'Anything else you can tell us?'

The medic shrugged. 'She's a natural blonde if that's any help,' he said, prompting a snigger from Falconer.

Duvall stared at the two older men before bursting out angrily, 'What the fuck is it with you people? A man's been killed and a woman's seriously injured and you're standing around making jokes.'

Falconer laid a hand on his shoulder. 'It's like this,' he explained. 'When you've seen two or three murders six days a week for over ten years you learn to stop taking it personally. If you don't you'll find yourself in a rubber room wearing a jacket that laces up the back. I don't find that woman's pain funny - not that she's in any state to give a damn - but laughing is the only way to cope with all the shit you're going to see everyday. You'd do well to remember that.'

Duvall shrugged off his hand. 'Maybe you're right but, no offence, I hope I never wind up that insensitive.'

'The way your heart's bleeding you won't live long enough. Come on, let's get back on patrol where we belong.'

CHAPTER 11

Poorly lit, wreathed in cigarette smoke and populated by men anxious to avoid eye contact, the sex club conferred anonymity on its patrons. Brecht could think of no better place for his rendezvous with the Quartermaster, the old line about Vegas holding true. What happened here stayed here. A topless waitress sidled over as he examined his watch for the fifth time in as many minutes and he irritably waved her away.

'Sorry, sir, I'm afraid there's a three drink minimum. What would you like?'

'I'd like to be left alone,' he grumbled, smiling to take some of the edge off his words. 'But since you ask and you're only trying to do your job, make it three cognacs - large ones.' He fished in his wallet for his card and tossed it on to the girl's tray. 'Buy yourself one too,' he winked at her, 'and make sure no one else disturbs me for at least thirty minutes after you bring the drinks.'

The waitress squeaked as a bulky figure loomed up behind her and pinched her bottom. A heavy baritone rumbled, 'And I'll have a Good Hard Fuck,' - one of the club's more risqué titled cocktails. The newcomer squeezed his bulk into the booth beside Brecht, placed a matt grey attaché case on the table, and introduced himself. 'I am the Quartermaster and I assume that you are Kurt Brecht and that you have my money. Otherwise this little meeting is going to go downhill very rapidly.' He held out a meaty hand that Brecht shook while carefully examining the man attached to it.

The Quartermaster was a grossly overweight man in his late fifties, his skin pink and florid with a bald pate offset by the bushy growth of his silver-grey beard. He wore a white linen three-piece suit, the waistcoat of which looked particularly stressed by his massive girth. A heavy gold chain trailed from one of its buttonholes and disappeared into a pocket where it presumably attached to an old fashioned fob watch.

Brecht released the Quartermaster's rather damp hand. 'Yeah, I'm Brecht. And, yes, I have your money. So I hope you and I are going to be friends. That's providing you live up to your reputation.'

'My good fellow, you may safely rest assured that in this cesspool of a city there is no better procurer of illicit arms and prohibited substances than myself, although I must admit that some of the items on your list presented quite a challenge even to me.' He removed a small palmtop from the inside pocket of his suit and snapped it open. 'Now, if I could just check your credit?'

Brecht removed another card from his wallet and was about to hand it over when the waitress returned. She set a tall, frosted glass down in front of the Quartermaster. 'Your fuck, sir,' she said before turning to Brecht and adding, 'your cognacs.' The waitress placed the three balloon glasses in front of him and handed back his card. A leer from the Quartermaster sent her scurrying off into the crowds surrounding the bar.

The fat man laughed as he took Brecht's card from his unresisting fingers. He slid the card into a suitable port, tapped a few keys and waited. A short time later a synthesised voice whistled the first three bars of "The Sun Has Got His Hat On" and the Quartermaster said, 'That will do nicely, sir.' He removed Brecht's card, folded away the palmtop and reached for the attaché case. Opening a small panel next to the lock, he pressed his thumb against the exposed sensor. The case gave a loud click as the locking mechanism responded to his DNA. As he pulled back the lid he spun the case round to face Brecht with a theatrical flourish.

Brecht stared at the items stored in the foam rubber compartments with grim satisfaction. He removed a roll of coloured metal discs. He looked up at the Quartermaster who explained, 'Micro-grenades. Red is high explosive, silver – fragmentation and blue - hallucinogenic nerve gas. Gives a whole new meaning to the term death trip, I can assure you. It's absorbed through the skin, so be very careful where you use it. The pink phial is the antidote. It must be taken at least two hours before exposure to the gas and provides immunity for seventy-two hours.'

'Nasty,' Brecht commented as he carefully replaced the grenade. He turned his attention to a compact machine-pistol similar in design to a scaled down version of the twentieth century Uzi, with a long ammunition clip slotted inside the pistol grip.

'Now that baby,' the Quartermaster beamed proudly, 'is a Heckler & Koch FD20 flechette pistol. One hundred and fifty round magazine, each dart coated in a fast acting curare derivative. It comes fully loaded and I've supplied you with four additional clips. You'd have to be one very unpopular fellow to have any enemies left after that.'

'Just the one, but the hired help may have to be forcibly laid off.' Brecht removed the three remaining items from the case, an electronic smart-card, a computer datakey and a bubble pack containing three ampoules of some unknown drug. He waved the card at his fat associate. 'My new identity?'

'Correct. Gunnar Leith, age thirty-two, software engineer grade triple "A" at Chromium Oxide. As far as their records are concerned you've worked there for the past five years and are currently on a three week vacation. The identity is completely watertight, right down to a social security number and complete financial records of regular salary payments into your account. As far as the Europa City databases are concerned Gunnar Leith is as real as you or I. Actually, that's where most of your money went. That kind of system wide hacking doesn't come cheap.'

Brecht slipped the card into his wallet. 'And the datakey?'

'A cyber-mole. You can infiltrate any information net or web in this city just by inserting it into a workstation and running a virus sweep. Pretty ironic really. It immediately infects the hard drive and proceeds to worm its way on to the servers where it can delete or introduce data of your choice, including viruses. Afterwards it removes all trace of its presence before consuming itself.

'And that,' the Quartermaster continued, pointing to the bubble pack, 'is a little bonus for you: frenzy - the latest in milspec combat enhancement stimulants. It's engineered round a basic methamphetamine and increases physical strength and reaction times by up to twenty-five-percent and includes a built in pain-blocker. You could break every bone in your body and you wouldn't feel a thing for hours. In layman's terms, it works by preventing all pain stimuli from the central nervous system from reaching the user's brain.'

'I take it you are satisfied with the merchandise, Herr Leith?'

'Very,' Brecht replied. He picked up the flechette pistol and made as if to place it in his inside coat pocket.

The Quartermaster stopped him with a shocked outburst. 'No, no, no! There's no need for that. You may keep the case with my compliments. I have my reputation to think of. It would be inconceivable for me to send a customer away with bulging pockets, as it were. You'll find the case contains a full electronics countermeasure suite capable of allowing its contents to pass through most standard security systems undetected. I'll change the thumbprint ID for you.' He took out a keycard and swiped it through a slot mounted above the sensor pad, causing it to turn red. 'If you'd just press your thumb against the pad you'll be in business.' Brecht did as the fat man instructed and the sensor pad faded back to an opaque grey. The Quartermaster sighed contentedly and handed over the keycard. 'There. That's everything settled. It was a pleasure doing business with you, sir. Please feel free to contact me the next time you get an urge to start a small war.'

'I don't think so. My pockets aren't deep enough for one thing, and I'm told this will be my final battle.' Brecht finished packing away the contents of the case and snapped it shut. 'Now, if you'll excuse me, I still have a few calls to make before the evening is out.'

The Quartermaster saluted him with his glass, took a large swallow and said, 'Of course. Me, I still have a minimum of two drinks to go, and I'd wager that young filly will soon realise that an old man with a bulging wallet can be as equally attractive as a young one with bulging muscles. Good night to you, sir. I'm certain I will be reading your press cuttings in the not too distant future.'

'Right.' Brecht grinned and walked away.

Weill sat straight-backed and pensive as he resisted his natural inclination to relax into the heavily cushioned chair. His eyes darted nervously round the expensive furnishings of Vaughan's penthouse suite, alighting one moment on a surrealist painting, the next on an Art Nouveau sculpture, all arranged in a chaotic jumble, regardless of period or movement. Dali sat next to Rennie-Macintosh, who in turn nestled beside Dürer, kept company by Warhol. The entire room reeked of the peculiar brand of crass ostentation that so often stemmed from newly acquired money. A vulgar display of wealth by one who previously had little in life and now wished to announce his success at every opportunity, the home of a looting barbarian. Weill reflected that Hitler might well have furnished his own residence in such a fashion, or perhaps more aptly Mistah Kurtz, had he made it out of the jungle and back to that "White Sepulchre".

The owner of this eclectic selection of art treasures had meanwhile risen to his feet, whisky tumbler in hand. He subjected Weill to a baleful glare and violently stabbed a finger in his direction. 'You've let me down, Weill. You screwed up. You promised me this Brecht character wouldn't be a problem. Not only do you let him penetrate my organisation and have it away on his toes with one of my girls, you have to compound your error by giving Sword out of date information.'

Weill stiffened. 'With all due respect, it's hardly my fault if Brecht's strumpet starts screwing around with other guys. How was I supposed to know she'd dumped him?'

'That's precisely my point, you retard. You're supposed to be a policeman - a detective. I pay you an exceedingly generous retainer to know such things.'

'Don't give me that hire 'em and fire 'em crap,' Weill snapped. 'You know damn well that sort of personal information isn't always standard for Internal Affairs, and not without cause. And quit bitching. It all worked out rather well for you. You got Brecht to snuff one of Sajer's men without even knowing he was the man you were after in the first place. A very neat if unintentional frame, making him fair game for a sanction. If all that isn't enough, the homicide detectives investigating Reiss's murder think Brecht killed him in a fit of jealousy over his ex. The manhunt for him is intensifying as we speak. As such, Brecht is in no position to endanger your operation. It's a cakewalk. You simply have to sit back and wait for that arms contract to be delivered right to your door.'

Vaughan slammed his glass down on an antique rosewood table and grabbed Weill by his lapels. He lifted the smaller man off his feet and raised him until their eyes were level. Flecks of saliva spattered against Weill's face as Vaughan snarled, 'You'd better pray you're right about that, you cunt lapping motherfucker! Because if Brecht damages my organisation or my plans in any way yours will be the first arsehole I tear myself a piece of. I want that contract secured and I want Kurt Brecht - dead!' Veins throbbed in his temples as he shook Weill like a rag doll to give his next statement added emphasis. 'Do I make myself clear, Weill? I do hope so because I hate having to repeat myself, though not as much as you'll hate it.' He flung the now terrified Weill across the room, where he crashed into a display cabinet dislodging a Laliqué car mascot which fell to the floor and shattered. Rising to one knee amidst the glass fragments, Weill dabbed a trace of blood from his bottom lip with the back of his hand and spat out a glob of bloody phlegm. His voice shook, not with fear but anger, as he said, 'I think we understand one another. Brecht's a dead man, I promise you that.'

Vaughan brushed an imaginary speck of dust from his suit and proceeded to mix himself a fresh drink. Keeping his back turned to Weill, he said, 'Don't talk - act. Now get the fuck out of my sight before you make me really angry.'

Duvall shone the flashlight back and forth across the alley, highlighting a mass of torn refuse sacks, empty bottles, boxes and cans. The sharp odour of stale urine rose to greet him as he prodded a sack with his night-stick. Behind him, Falconer grunted impatiently.

'Come on, kid, give it up. Our shift was over five minutes ago. I need to hit a bar.'

'Gimme a couple of seconds, Sam. The caller said she heard some kind of disturbance.'

'So what if she did? There's nothing but winos and junkies hang out here. They're always fighting amongst themselves. Who cares about them?'

'I do. We're supposed to protect everybody, regardless of class or background.'

'What did I do to deserve you? Damn Holtz for retiring and lumbering me with Mr Do-it-by-the-book-social-conscience! I'll tell you, you've got a lot to learn about how we actually police this city. But fine, go ahead and knock yourself out. I'm gonna wait in the car. Don't blame me if you get a needle-stick or worse. God only knows what a guy could catch poking around here.'

'Shut it for moment, will you?' Duvall hissed as he spotted something further down the alley. 'Shit! I think we've got us a body.'

'What?' Falconer asked, suddenly interested. He took out his own flashlight and shone it along the same path as his partner. No doubt about it, at the end of the beam he could see an arm sticking out from beneath a pile of boxes. 'Fuck. I guess that drink is gonna have to wait.'

'Should I call it in to homicide?'

'Nah. We'd better check in case we've still got ourselves a live one.' When Duvall hesitated he added, 'Come on, hotshot. You wanted to check it out, so now it's time to get your hands dirty.'

Duvall moved forward reluctantly, he had already seen enough death for one day. Pale and stiff, the hand lay in a pool of blood and Duvall knew what he was going to find even before he lifted the boxes.

The victim was a white male adult. Judging by the state of his clothing, he had been living rough for some time. As Falconer said, probably a junkie or a wino. Only this one had become important because somebody had ripped his throat out and left him to bleed to death. And although no one had been prepared to stand up for him when he was alive, homicide would assign someone to speak for him in death. That was how it worked.

'Well?' Falconer prompted. 'Have you completely fucked up my night or what?'

'Yeah. Kinda looks that way. He's dead. You'd better call it in, Sam.'

The assassin unscrewed the cover-plate from the door's security lock and attached the electronic equivalent of a skeleton key across the memory chip. The key's infiltration program penetrated the microprocessor's software and sought out the hexadecimal values of the lock's six figure PIN number, which it then reproduced on its own LCD display. Sword removed the device and reattached the cover-plate before typing in the code. He moved on cat-silent feet as he slipped inside and locked the door behind him.

He now stood in a narrow hallway with a door at its far end, two doors on the right and one to the left. Having previously memorised the floor plans of the apartment, he ignored the doors on the right side and crept towards the one on the left, the bedroom. He slipped quietly inside and waited for his eyes to adjust to the darkness. Fuzzy grey shapes gradually became distinctive outlines, revealing the slumbering figure beneath the covers of the bed. The sheets rose and fell in a steady rhythm, synchronised with the sleeper's breathing. A shock of tousled peroxide blonde hair spread across the pillows.

Sword moved closer and sprang into action. Clamping one hand across the woman's mouth, he used his other arm and left knee to pin her to the bed. The woman started awake at his touch, struggling violently against her unknown attacker until he subdued her by jerking his knee into her abdominal muscles, while simultaneously lowering his elbow to apply pressure against her windpipe. Staring into her fear glazed eyes he whispered, 'That's a girl, Marian. Just behave nicely and answer my questions and this will all be over as painlessly as possible. On the other hand' - he dug his elbow into her throat - 'if you don't co-operate I shall have to teach you fresh meanings for pain. Nod if you understand.' A frantic bobbing of her head followed. 'Good. I'm going to remove my hand and you're not going to scream. You will lie calmly and answer my questions.'

He raised his hand and she gasped, 'Who are you? Aah!' her voice trailed off into a scream as he applied pressure to a sensitive nerve cluster in her inner elbow.

'I'm the one asking the questions. Where can I find Kurt Brecht?'

'Who?'

More pressure, another scream.

'Please don't play stupid with me.' He pulled out a knife and ran its point down her inner thigh in a lazy motion, drawing beads of blood. Marian shuddered, gasped and squirmed but she could not free herself from his grip. 'Y'know, short as you are, you have a beautiful body. But men can be kind of funny about a woman covered in scars.' The assassin gently ruffled her labia with the point of the blade. Marian whimpered and stopped struggling. 'Let me remind you. Kurt Brecht, about six feet, weighs a hundred and ninety pounds. Crew cut blonde hair, blue eyes, wears a leather trench coat. You've been seen with him on numerous occasions in the Paradiso. Sound familiar yet?'

'Garth! That's Garth you're speaking about,' Marian cried out desperately.

'Ah, now we're getting somewhere. So where can I find "Garth"?'

Tears streamed down Marian's cheeks as she sobbed, 'I don't know. Honestly, I don't know where he is. I just see him from time to time. Usually when he's hunting for a little sulph' or some coke. I swear to God that I don't know anything else.'

'God is dead, Marian. And that's not a good answer if you don't want to join Him.' He waved the knife in front of her eyes. 'Do you know there are still primitive tribes that practice female circumcision? Quite painful I should imagine.'

'No! Please don't do this to me.' She turned pleading eyes on Sword. 'Rape me if you want but don't cut me up. Just don't cut me up. I can't tell you any more than I've already done. Check the clubs in the German Quarter, that's where he hangs.'

The knife disappeared with a practised flick of the assassin's wrist. He bent close and whispered in her ear, 'Fortunately for you I believe you.'

Marian felt a brief sting as he pinched her carotid artery and then she slipped into welcome unconsciousness.

Brecht jerked the steering wheel and the car swung hard left as he took the exit ramp for the Berlin district at the last possible moment. He checked the rear view screen on the dashboard for signs of pursuit but found none. Relaxing slightly, he glanced over his shoulder to check on Anastasia. The girl still slept soundly, strapped into one of the rear passenger seats. With any luck she would remain that way until he reached Claudia's. Returning his attention to the road, he scanned the traffic. Lighter than he would have liked, making his vehicle more obvious. Two taxis laden with late night revellers occupied the lane in front, while a freight truck travelled towards him on the opposite side of the central reservation. A stab of panic lanced at his heart as it drew close enough for him to read the Tessler Corporation logos plastered across its bodywork. It could be coincidence, Tessler being a large corporation with a lot of city wide traffic, but Brecht didn't intend to take any chances.

He prepared for action as the two vehicles rapidly approached one another. At a distance of ten metres he reached for the flechette-auto sitting on the passenger seat beside him. Flicking off the safety, he operated the electric window and waited for the danger sign that would catalyse him into action. Five metres, two metres, then the truck roared past in a blast of air and noise - a false alarm. He checked its rapidly retreating form on the screen just to be certain before closing the window and laying the gun aside.

The remainder of the journey to Claudia's surgery proved uneventful except for a tense moment when he passed a squad car. The two officers gave his vehicle scant notice as they continued their patrol circuit, justifying his decision to travel in a vehicle not registered to any of his identities.

The surgery was located in a basement office of one of the district's commercial sectors. An area of wide avenues flanked on either side by towering shopping malls that opened twenty-four hours a day. A Mecca for the consumerists of the city who came to worship by spending their hard earned credit on the mass produced goods. Even at this late hour there were a number of insomniac shopaholics thronging zombie-like between the stores. Outside of his car the dark of the early morning blazed with the multicoloured glow of the neon and fluorescent signs of the shop fronts and advertisement hoardings. The eyes and limbs of the holographic figures beckoned to the casual passer-by, inviting them to enter this shop or that. Brecht ignored their enticements and made a right on to Mercy Boulevard, where he slowed to a halt in an area of darkness between two street lights.

Claudia leaned against a set of railings on the opposite side of the road. She wore a grey silk designer suit; the skirt and jacket of which hugged her figure in the series of sharp, crisp lines that only come from expensive tailoring. Brecht thought she looked nervous and gave her a reassuring wave as he stepped from the car. He opened the rear passenger door and unfastened the restraints holding Anastasia in place. The girl stirred and shrugged languidly in her sleep as he slipped one arm behind her shoulders, the other behind her knees, and lifted her from the car. After checking for traffic, he carried her across the road to where Claudia stood waiting.

The doctor said nothing as he approached. She swung open a gate in the railings and ushered him down a short flight of concrete steps at the bottom of which stood the door to her surgery. He followed her along the familiar, brightly lit corridor and entered the first room on the left. It was a standard doctor's consulting room with a large desk, two chairs and an examination table. Various medical charts decorated the walls and a screen stood a short distance from the wall adjacent to the desk.

Claudia pointed across the room. 'Put her on the table and I'll do an initial work-up to check on her condition,' she said in a voice raw edged with tension.

Brecht placed Anastasia on the couch and heard the soft whirr of servomotors as its surface automatically adjusted to provide maximum comfort. He turned to discover Claudia standing behind him biting a thumbnail in an uncharacteristic display of anxiety. Instincts sharpened by years spent undercover screamed their warning. In all the years he had known Claudia he had never seen her this ill at ease. Her eyes flicked from him to the screen and back again. Brecht held a finger to his lips to shush her, crossed the room and pulled back the screen to reveal the whipcord figure of Guyon Sajer.

His commanding officer smiled sardonically. 'Good evening, Kurt, enjoying a quiet period of sick leave?'

Brecht's gaze moved from Sajer to Claudia who, unable to meet his gaze, lowered her head. 'I'm sorry, Kurt,' she explained, 'I couldn't let you throw your life away, whatever trouble you're in, your mother would never have forgiven me. Guyon is a friend from the old days and I owe him like I owe you. You didn't really think losing that disc was enough to close the investigation, did you? It was Guyon's influence that buried the case.' Her voice grew smaller, even more fragile sounding. 'Please say that you understand.'

Brecht stared at Claudia who suddenly seemed to be every one of her forty-eight years and more. He reached out and gently caught her chin between thumb and forefinger and tilted her head up until she met his gaze. His voice soft, he told her, 'Yeah, I understand. Each of us must do what we think best, which is why I can't let Sajer take me in. I still have work to do. Take care of the girl like I asked while he and I try to resolve this mess.' He turned aside to let Claudia pass before stepping back to lean against the edge of the desk. With his arms folded across his chest he said, 'Well, Commander, what's it to be? Are you willing to shoot me if I refuse to come quietly?'

Sajer regarded him gravely. 'Do not even joke about it, Kurt. I swore an oath the same as you to uphold the law and that is precisely what I am going to do.'

'Even when those same laws permit injustice and suffering? When you know the system is riddled with corruption? I don't think so. I know for a fact that you believe in true justice, and that it isn't always the sort that's recorded in the statute books. I'm going to walk out of here this evening and we both know it. The only real issue is whether or not we'll still be friends afterwards.'

Sajer shook his head sadly. 'Is that truly what you believe? I will admit that the system has faults, but you can't run around like some dark Angel of Death dispensing the justice of the gun. Was Marcus Conroy corrupt, or simply in the wrong place at the wrong time?'

'Don't you dare throw that in my face! It wasn't my fault! Isaac Vaughan is the one responsible for his death. Did you see what those bastards did to him? If you were ever my friend, Guyon, you'll understand that I've got to make Vaughan pay for it.'

'Kurt, it's precisely because I am your friend that I'm here. I must warn you that you have been sanctioned. Weill left me no other choice. As we speak, the assassin is stalking the streets, hunting you like an animal. I came here to give you one last chance to turn yourself in. You can still walk away from this mess alive. But only if you come with me. Mark my words, if you walk out through that door you're a dead man. Collateral damage aside, the Sword of Damocles has never once missed his target.' He held out his hand. 'Come on, Kurt, give me your gun and badge and I'll give you your life. You will not get a better offer than that this day.'

'The Sword of Damocles - my life - how very dramatic,' Brecht sneered. 'I've got power on my side as well. I'm protected, so don't threaten me. You disappoint me, Sajer. I thought that you understood. How can you sit idly back while the likes of Vaughan and his corporation get away with destroying people's lives?'

'I don't like Vaughan any more than you but you have to look at the big picture. The city is on the brink of chaos. We need the weapons Tessler can supply to combat that tide of lawlessness. The alternative is to surrender to the anarchy of mob rule. But if it makes you feel any better, yes, I'm behind you, in your opinions at least if not your methodology. Vaughan is the type of filth that I would personally like to see burn in hell. I wanted to arrest him before Tessler got the contract and Vaughan got his get out of jail free card, but that was before word came down from on high. Law and order are breaking down. There are city wide riots, mass murder, looting and rape. Compared with that, what does it matter if Vaughan wants to run an illicit brothel for his friends or sell missiles to terrorists? In short, it does not. Not if he helps us cut down on the real human misery in this city. Why do you refuse to acknowledge the truth? There is a hurricane blowing through this city and those that do not bend will be broken.'

Brecht drew his gun and backed away from Sajer. Wide-eyed and sweating, a muscular spasm twitched the left side of his face. Suddenly his self-control snapped completely and he screamed irrationally, 'I don't believe it, they've fucking got to you as well, man. You're one of them now, spouting your "big picture" bullshit. You're a fucking hypocrite, Sajer, reminding me of my oath one minute and then telling me the next that I should let the small crimes go for the sake of keeping the lid on the big ones. Whatever happened to integrity, tell me that? I bet you can't, can you?'

Sajer stepped forward with his hands held high. His voice almost pleading as he attempted to calm Brecht. 'You are overreacting. You're sick, Kurt. You need help. Let me…'

Brecht interrupted him with another violent outburst, 'I'm sick? Fuck you! You want to see overreacting?' He raised the Walther and fired a couple of bursts into the wall behind Sajer, sending him diving for cover from the stinging shards of concrete. Claudia screamed as he backed away from Sajer, groping blindly for the door. His eyes flicked maniacally from the frightened Claudia to a grim-faced Sajer as his fingers scrabbled against the handle. He seemed confused and cocked his head to one side as if listening to someone. 'Yeah, that's right,' he agreed. 'She knows the truth, Sajer. She tells it like it is.'

'Who, Kurt? What is she telling you?' Sajer asked cautiously. He received no reply as Brecht slipped around the door post.

Sajer had just risen to his feet when Brecht appeared back in the doorway. Fearing another violent outbreak, he threw himself on the floor only to discover Brecht was no longer interested in him. He flashed a cocky grin at Claudia and said, 'Take good care of the kid and I'll see you around. This is au revoir, not goodbye.' Then he was gone, leaving behind only the echo of his boot heels striking the floor of the corridor.

He reached the top of the stairs, vaulted across the railings and paused. Something gnawing at his subconscious, a shape he had caught out of the corner of his eye when he first entered the street. It came to him as a form of pattern recognition, in much the same fashion as a rabbit may recognise the shadow of a hawk. Up ahead, in a pool of shadow similar to that where he'd parked his car, he saw the distinctive bulk of Sajer's personal SPF cruiser. A vehicle more than capable of pursuing his own, and outfitted with the necessary communication equipment to call further pursuit and interceptor units. He had to destroy it. A dreamy smile crossed his face as he pulled the red metallic disc of a high explosive micro-grenade from his pocket. 'Detonation five seconds from my mark,' he commanded, having previously programmed it to recognise his voice pattern and command phrase. He flipped it like a coin to land between the rear wheels of the cruiser and hurried across the road to his vehicle. Once inside, he shouted, 'Detonate,' and prepared to drive off.

As Brecht hammered the car into reverse, he noted with a certain satisfaction that Sajer had arrived at street level in time to witness the destruction of his cruiser. The windows of Brecht's car automatically polarised against the glare of the explosion as the cruiser disappeared in a blinding red-orange fireball. The shockwave hurled Sajer to the ground as the windows on either side of the boulevard shattered in a deadly hail of flying glass. The last thing Brecht saw as he turned the corner, still travelling in reverse, was a heavy black pall of smoke mushrooming above the wreckage as white-hot fragments of steel rained down.

CHAPTER 12

Sajer picked at one of the scabs that pockmarked his face, a legacy from the night two weeks ago when he had made a final attempt to persuade Brecht to give himself up. The whole incident had culminated in near disaster when Brecht destroyed his cruiser in an attempt to prevent Sajer from following. The shockwave and hail of shrapnel that accompanied the blast and caught Sajer more or less by accident, ironically saved his life by throwing him clear of the larger, more dangerous debris, although he still suffered numerous cuts, contusions and burns. All of which paled into insignificance when he considered the damage to his pride. He, the Commander of Vice, had not only allowed a known murder suspect to escape but had also allowed the suspect to destroy over two hundred thousand euro-dollars of state of the art police cruiser in the process. There was also the matter of a further estimated hundred thousand worth of damage to private property. But what really burned him up was Brecht being a member of his squad, a man to whom he'd been as good as a father. Worse still the fact that every word Brecht said in the consulting room was true. Inspired by paranoia and psychosis perhaps, but nonetheless true for all that. The Police Department was selling out to the Tesslet Corporation, giving Isaac Vaughan carte blanche to contravene the law so that they could keep the lid on the boiling pot of political dissent and racial violence Europa City had become. And Guyon Sajer, self-proclaimed man of principle, was going along with this so-called expediency without a single word of complaint.

And so it was with some reluctance that he forced himself to begin reading the latest progress report on the unofficial manhunt for his wayward officer and former protégé. Political expediency had once again dictated that it would further undermine the ECPD's already dented reputation to announce to the public that one of its officers had gone rogue. Better a degree of collateral damage among the civilian population than any further undermining of the Department's authority.

Sajer read the file briskly, pausing every so often to emit a sigh or to shake his head negatively. The report contained no evidence as to Brecht's present whereabouts. Not that he found that surprising. Brecht, through his years of undercover work, had forged many links within the city's criminal fraternity, making it easy for him to disappear if he so wished. No doubt he had many a dubious associate unknown to anyone but himself. The sort of people possessed of the necessary connections to arrange for him to vanish completely into the underground networks operated by the criminal classes.

The networks were descended from the old Mafia and run accordingly on similar principles. The foot soldiers' loyalty to the heads of these extended family units being absolute. A closed system with nothing going in and nothing coming out. Bitter experience had taught the Department that the networks were impenetrable. They operated on a system of cut-offs that used terminal methods to silence anyone suspected of leaking information.

Sajer held the opinion that such a group had adopted Brecht, making it a waste of police resources to continue searching for him on the streets. He had said as much to his superiors, who responded by stalling him with bureaucracy, ignoring his view that Vaughan was the key to apprehending Brecht. His obsession with revenge would inevitably draw him to Vaughan. They had wasted numerous man-hours hauling in all of Brecht's known associates, subjecting them to a series of interrogations and depredations that had ultimately yielded nothing. At least nothing pertinent to Brecht's present location. The prostitute, Marian, had revealed details of an armed assault on her person by someone who was also seeking Brecht. Her description of the assailant sounded suspiciously like the Damocles Assassin. A fact that appeared to confirm Sajer's suspicions about the real identity of the perpetrator responsible for the murder of Victor Reiss and the wounding of Hannah Schade. Weill had remained stubbornly silent on the subject when Sajer attempted to question him, a sure sign that he knew far more than he was willing to disclose.

The other citizen to whom they had granted the dubious pleasure of helping the police with their enquiries had even less to tell them. Largely because Brecht's main informant, Andreas Rosenstein, had spent most of his various interviews in the grip of massive withdrawal symptoms. Between the bouts of vomiting, fits of palsied shaking, profuse sweating and violent stomach cramps he had found it rather difficult to say anything remotely coherent. Judging from the sickness, Slinky did not appear long for this world.

Sajer's line of deductive reasoning came to an abrupt close when the intercom on his desk buzzed to demand his attention. Irritated, he stabbed down on the switch and enquired tersely, 'Yes, what is it?'

A female voice answered, 'You requested to be reminded that you have a meeting with the Commissioner and the Arms Contract Committee at fourteen hundred hours, sir. It's for the first approval of the Tessler bid.'

'Ah, yes. Thank you, Miss…' Sajer floundered as he attempted to recall her name.

'Petersen,' prompted the PA.

'Yes, of course. Thank you Miss Petersen. You may inform the Commissioner that I'll be with him presently.'

16/11/85: It feels strange to be writing again, especially after the events of the last two weeks, but I need to share my thoughts, even if it's only with a load of ones and zeroes.

I've seen the world in a fresh light since that evening when Lady Methedrine came to me and I took of her body, like some unholy communion. From that moment onwards my perception altered irrevocably. My mind became calm and focussed and my body charged with energy as the years of my emotional torment dissolved in the heat of her body. She revealed to me the weakness of the flesh and the lies on which this city is founded. I now know that for which I am destined.

Vaughan is a cancerous growth eating away at the heart of Lady Methedrine's city and it is up to me, the instrument of her will, to excise him. She remains constantly with me, offering guidance to me on my quest. Thus I am fully prepared for what is to come, armed by the Quartermaster, freed from dependants by Claudia's sheltering of Anastasia, and hidden from prying eyes by the Prinzi family. My only regret is that my friend and mentor, Guyon Sajer, has chosen to stand with those who side against me. Despite this betrayal, I was heartened to learn that he survived our confrontation on Mercy Boulevard.

Afterwards, I drove back to my apartment and put the final stages of my plan into motion. I had one last call to make. One final favour to call in, a favour owed to me by Emmanuel Prinzi, the Godfather of the Prinzi family. I'd attended the same University as his son, Robert, during which time I saved him from a beating when he'd run into some trouble with a local street gang. It had cost me three broken ribs and a back molar which, though painful at the time, now seemed a small price to pay for being able to rely on Emmanuel's protection.

Sajer paused in his reading of Brecht's journal to reflect on this latest piece in the puzzle of Brecht's final movements. He had been correct in assuming that Brecht had sought refuge with one of the city's crime families. But the reason for his failure to find conclusive proof at the time now became apparent. He had only thought to check possible links with Brecht's case files in his search for a connection. It never occurred to him that Brecht might have formed such an association before joining the force. A prime example, Sajer reflected, of sloppy thinking and a possible sign of old age. He snorted and resumed his reading of Brecht's increasingly schizoid journal entries.

Had the Prinzi Family been anything but the strictly anachronistic organisation that it was, I might well have chosen to forego their protection. But Emmanuel Prinzi was unique in the fact that he refused to have any dealings with those who dealt in drugs or human flesh. He made his money instead from the time-honoured traditions of smuggling, gambling and extortion, which seemed more in tune with the world of the 1930's than the present day. He held firmly, if erroneously, to the notion that he only took money (through gambling) from those that could afford it, and that for a small fee he was happy to protect the weak from the predatory advances of other organisations. The only other image he liked to maintain beyond that being the old family tradition of respect.

Anyway, that's how I came to be in my present location of a small basement apartment on the outskirts of the Rome district. Only Emmanuel, his son, and three of his most entrusted enforcers know of my presence here, Emmanuel Prinzi having personally escorted me here on the night I fled from my own apartment. Since then, Robert and the three enforcers have taken it in turns to supply me with food and street level news of any major events in the city. The most joyous of which being the death of that little bastard, Hassan, the victim of one of my departing preparations.

After contacting Emmanuel and arranging to meet him on the Cologne fly-over exit, I set about arranging a suitable reception for any curious visitors to the John Dumas apartment. In truth, I hoped to take out the so-called Sword of Damocles with my booby trap, as he was the man I considered the greatest threat to the successful completion of my mission. But it would be churlish to complain after I succeeded in extinguishing the life of a particularly sadistic and foul specimen of humanity.

I set in motion the circumstances of his demise as follows. On my return to my apartment, I performed a core memory dump of all my computer files, downloading them to a datakey before purging the hard drive. Names, addresses, contacts, anything that my enemies might use to trace me, swept away into the electronic ether. After that, I made double sure by burning all the hard copies as well, which was probably a little over cautious as I had no intention of allowing anyone who broke in seeking such information to live long enough to benefit from it. I'd constructed a booby trap from a micro-grenade and a motion detector to take care of that particular problem. Programmed to detonate after monitoring thirty seconds of continuous movement within the bounds of the front room, I'd concealed the device in one of the desk drawers beneath my workstation. I'd also tossed a fragmentation grenade and thirty rounds of live ammunition in beside the rigged high explosive grenade for good measure. A nasty surprise for anyone foolish enough to try ransacking my apartment.

Having left my welcome package, I set about packing some clothes and the few personal items I wanted to take with me. Books, holomovies, my mother's picture. The very presence of such items went against all my training, it being foolish and dangerous to possess anything not directly linked to my John Dumas identity. A sign of how sloppy I'd become over the last couple of months. With that sorted, I just needed my weapons.

All of my armaments were stored as per regulations in a steel security locker in the bedroom. It required a palm print and retina scan to confirm my identity, after which the door hissed open and I set about stowing its contents in a rucksack. The only exceptions were the attaché case of specialist equipment and a kevlar vest that I strapped on beneath my shirt. That done, I was ready to leave. I paused to have one last look around the room and spotted the familiar plush features of Blake, a toy tiger Hannah had given me in remembrance of my fondness for the poem. I threw him in the rucksack with the Walther and a combat shotgun, feeling more than a little juvenile. I guess sentimentality can make fools of us all.

I activated the motion detector and locked up. From what I have been able to gather from newscasts and from hacking into the ECPD forensic files, Hassan and the mismatched pair of heavies who assisted in Conroy's torture must have broken into my apartment three days later. The accountant type (identified as Paul Capaldi), sat at the desk when the grenade detonated, died instantly. The muscle (Lennie Niehaus) was less fortunate. The blast having torn off both his legs and his left arm, he managed to drag himself to the door before bleeding to death. I read the section of the report pertaining to Hassan's death three times. Coupled with the demise of Capaldi and Niehaus, his manner of dying almost made me believe that there might be some natural force of justice at work in the universe. Situated in the bedroom at the time of the explosion, the door shielded Hassan from the main force of the blast. Shrapnel, however, punctured both of his lungs and the coroner estimated that he subsequently spent the next ten to fifteen minutes slowly suffocating as he drowned in his own blood.

There were no additional casualties reported, the explosion contained by the apartment's blast proof walls and windows. A standard feature on all

Department safe houses intended to protect against small arms fire and rocket attacks. It also had the inadvertent effect of containing any explosion within itself.

And that was that. I suppose in some small way it felt like my first strike against Vaughan. A warning of what he could expect when I really got to grips with destroying his official and unofficial organisations. A small blow, true enough, and unlikely that finding replacement henchmen would present Vaughan with any difficulty. But it still gave me a warm glow to imagine his reaction on hearing about the explosion. The phrase "apoplectic fit of rage" springs to mind.

There were only two other pieces of news that were of interest to me in the following days. The first I read with more than a little anguish when it revealed that Hannah had been involved in a shooting incident. The details were sketchy but I managed to access Department files and discover that a sniper had fired into her apartment from the fire escape of the building on the opposite side of the road, wounding her and killing a man identified as Victor Reiss. It didn't require an IQ of a hundred and sixty to figure out the shooter had assumed me to be the man sharing Hannah's bed. From there a very small leap of logic identified the shooter as Weill's pet assassin, Sword. The quicker I managed to take that bastard out of the equation the safer everyone connected to me would be.

The second piece of news was far more widely publicised. Today being the day that the ACC (Arms Contract Committee) would convene a special meeting to award the contract for the supply of all arms, munitions and vehicular hardware to the ECPD. Vaughan's grinning countenance stared out at me from a host of vidzine and newspaper front pages. The accompanying text stated that the Tessler Corporation was widely tipped to be awarded the contract, ushering in a new era of law enforcement for the city. A Tessler spokesperson had been quoted stating that the police force could expect to be armed with the latest generation of "smart weapons" to aid them in the war against crime if the Tessler Corporation proved successful in its bid. All very rousing stuff and no doubt designed to generate positive publicity for Commissioner Haynes, currently running for re-election. The more cynically minded would call it blatant electioneering and I for one wouldn't have disagreed with them.

Other prominent members of the Committee listed in the press included Commander Oswald Tirpitz (Homicide), Commander Guyon Sajer (Vice) and Captain Bertold Weill (Internal Affairs). Weill would certainly be backing the Tessler bid and Sajer (or should that be Judas Iscariot?) had intimated to me that he would be more or less compelled to go with the general consensus of opinion, so it looked as though Vaughan had got it all sewn up.

Sajer winced as he read the latest segment of Brecht's journal. While he had said many of the things Brecht accused him of, in the end he had found it impossible to go against his principles by endorsing the Tessler bid for the contract. He felt somewhat aggrieved by Brecht's shout of treachery. The memory of the hush that had descended over the conference chamber when he voiced his objections remained vivid. His had been the one dissenting voice raised against the other four.

He recalled how he had sat staring at his reflection in the polished surface of the conference table, seeing the ghost of his former idealism. Above him, the star decorated vaulted ceiling concealed the layers of blast proof concrete and steel that protected the chamber from attack. Here, where all of the ECPD's high level meetings and conferences took place, Sajer experienced his epiphany. His eyes had swept around the circumference of the table examining each of the four men in turn. Commissioner Haynes, stooped and grey, gnarled and twisted by what Sajer viewed as nothing short of apostasy. Captain Weill, dark, brooding and treacherous as always. The red-headed, freckled, open features of Captain Miller from the motor pool, and the blonde, sharp eyed Commander of Homicide, Oswald Tirpitz. With the exception of Miller, they were a collection of uncompromising hard-liners, but all of them were one hundred-percent behind the Tessler bid. While the others had their own political agenda to further all Miller cared about was having enough funds to keep the vast fleet of SPF cruisers and interceptors running in the face of increasing fuel shortages. For him the contract represented nothing more than a means to an end.

The Commissioner, having made his case, put the matter to the vote. 'If there are no arguments against it, I propose that we award the ECPD arms contract to the Tessler Corporation.'

Sajer sighed as he locked eyes with the Commissioner. He knew his next words would probably drive the final nail into the coffin of his career but he could remain silent no longer. 'I'm sorry but I must object most strongly to that proposal.'

A murmur of surprise rippled around the table. 'Good grief, man!' spluttered Haynes. 'I thought our little chat had sorted this out once and for all. This meeting was intended to be a mere formality.'

'Perhaps you had, sir. But with all due respect, I can't sit calmly while you award the contract to a man whom we all know to be little more than a whoremongering fascist. Damn it! I have proof that the man is actively involved in illegal prostitution, narcotics, insider trading and arms dealing. Were that insufficient, his political ambitions clearly show a ruthless tendency to the extreme right, which his war record more than backs up. What more could you possibly need to hear?' He halted, out of breath, and glowered round the table, challenging the other four to meet his argument.

Weill, spoiling for a fight as always, picked up the gauntlet. 'So he's no Snow White - big deal! You know the reality of policing a city with a population in excess of forty million. There isn't a man at this table who doesn't have blood on his hands. Surely we agree that law and order must be maintained at all costs? The alternative is anarchy - mob rule. Your limp-wristed liberal crap would set us back a thousand years.'

'Is that what you honestly believe? You think the citizens of this city can be made to obey the law by giving our officers bigger guns? Forget the carrot and employ a great big stick that you can use to beat the poor bastards into submission. Perhaps we should usher in the new Dark Age you speak of and cast ourselves as the Church? If we ban anyone outside of the justice system from learning the proletariat will be too stupid to recognise that they have no rights. Is that your solution, Weill? Damn justice. Damn acting on the square or the level, and most importantly, damn their civil rights! Our New World Order will give them justice if it kills them.' Sajer snorted derisively. 'Well I for one do not wish to be a part of that. Both your policies and your person disgust me, Weill.'

Haynes sprang to his feet, his face red with fury. 'Commander Sajer, I will not tolerate foul language in this chamber or such blatant disrespect of a fellow officer. You have already made your feelings on Isaac Vaughan clear on numerous occasions without repeating yourself.'

'Have I?' Sajer rose from his seat. 'Well let me express one or two other feelings while I have your undivided attention.'

Miller interrupted him. 'Hey, Guyon, loosen up a little. We're all a little tense here. Let's just take a moment.' His statement clearly an attempt to prevent Sajer from saying anything else that might get him into further trouble.

Sajer smiled at him and shook his head sadly. 'It's too late for that. What I have to say must be said, regardless of the consequences. It's about time that someone told our good Commissioner that he is not fooling anybody. I'm right am I not, Wilson? You at least should know better.' The Commissioner answered the question with silence. He, like everyone else in the room, was waiting for Sajer to finish his denunciation.

Sensing he still held the floor, Sajer continued. 'You, him and him,' he jabbed a finger at Haynes, Weill and then Tirpitz. 'You are not interested in justice or in the well-being of the citizens you claim to serve. You're only interested in trying to hold on to your power. Consorting with the likes of Vaughan will serve only to further damage the Department's credibility. Having more heavily armed officers on the streets won't miraculously cut down on the incidents of murder, rape, looting and rioting. Fairer policies, better living conditions and employment, these are the things that help to reduce crime, not beating people to death for failing to toe the line. Are you all so blind that you cannot see that or do you simply choose not to see?'

Sajer slumped back down in his chair in an attitude of defeat, weighed down by the knowledge that he'd been wasting his breath on those present. Although the minutes clerk's horrified expression suggested that he'd at least made his point. Whether Haynes had it struck from the record remained to be seen.

'Your opinions have been noted, Captain Sajer,' Haynes said, smoothly glossing over every accusation that Sajer had made. 'Now, if there are no further objections?' he paused momentarily, 'I suggest we put the matter to the vote. Those in favour of awarding the ECPD arms supply contract to the Tessler Corporation raise their right hand.' He raised his own, closely followed by Weill, Tirpitz and Miller. 'Four,' he counted somewhat unnecessarily. 'Those against raise your left hand.' Sajer raised his arm in a half-hearted gesture. 'One. Thank you gentlemen. I think we can safely say that the issue has been decided.' Haynes addressed the stenographer, 'Please note the Arms Contract Committee awarded the contract for the supply of all ECPD ordnance to the Tessler Corporation at,' he examined his watch, 'fourteen-oh-three hours, by a vote of four in favour, one against. Since there appears to be no further business, I declare this special meeting closed.

'I'd like to thank you all for your time and careful deliberation on this matter,' he subjected Sajer to a disapproving glance, 'and to assure you that you have made the best possible decision for this city and its inhabitants. Now, I won't keep you any longer as I'm sure that you're all very busy with the running of your divisions.' He pointed to the door. 'Please feel free to leave whenever you are ready.'

Tirpitz and Weill rose rapidly and made for the door with Miller and the stenographer trailing in their wake. When Sajer made to follow the Commissioner caught him by the arm. 'Not you, Guyon, I feel we need to have a little chat. Strictly off the record, if you comprehend my meaning.'

'Oh, I think so,' Sajer replied as he sat in the chair next to Haynes. He added silently to himself, *Now here is the rub*. His face cracked into an insincere smile while he waited for the commissioner to say his piece.

'I expected better of you, Sajer. I had such high hopes for you, both within the Department and outside of it, but it would appear that your loyalty and dedication is in doubt. Have you anything to say in mitigation, Guyon? Anything at all to prove my trust in you has not been misguided?'

Sajer remained stoically quiet. He had expected such a lecture would follow his outburst.

'I see. That saddens me a great deal. As you know, I'm due to retire soon and I'd hoped to recommend you as my successor. It would have been a great comfort to leave the Department in hands I felt I could trust.'

The last proved too much for Sajer, who snorted, 'You mean amenable to your agenda!'

'There's no need to be so hostile. You know perfectly well that it's not my personal agenda. The Council is in agreement; it is for the good of all.'

'Your interpretation of always acting on the level with your fellow man clearly differs from mine. You may have forgotten the basic principles of justice, but I have not. I told you once before what I thought of your plan, and I do not think I need repeat myself. Nor should you need reminding that personal business should not interfere with professional affairs, especially where those affairs involve the laws of the state.'

'Maybe in times past, but no longer. If you're foolish enough not to be part of the New Order, that's your own affair. Just don't compound your error by trying to stand against it. No one, Guyon, is indispensable.'

CHAPTER 13

2 1/11/85: Yesterday, I put stage one of my plan against Vaughan into motion - the sabotage of Chromium Oxide - the front for his illegal neuro-link torture disks. Some might think this a touch hypocritical, considering the use I've made of these discs in the past. But I like to believe that the end justifies the means. Right and wrong might be a question of perspective for some people but for me it has always been black and white.

I decided that the time had come for Gunnar Leith to return to work fresh from his three week vacation. The security systems of Cronenberg House fortunately overlooked the fact that he hadn't existed four weeks previously and only existed now as a series of falsified computer records. I encountered no resistance of any form as I used my new ID card to enter the building, made my way through palm print and retina scans and arrived at Software R & D on the fourteenth floor. Proof that top quality hacking can still accomplish almost anything, given the time and money. The security guard on the door even gave me a cheerful wave as I entered, fresh from the commuter hell of an early morning underground ride. Just another faceless exec in a sharp suit, the latter of which one should never undervalue as part of the corporate spy's arsenal when embarking on a spot of industrial espionage. The high numbers of staff employed by a large corporation immunises other employees against their natural suspicion of an unknown face. This peculiar brand of myopia allowed me to sit down unnoticed at a vacant terminal in the R & D office. Anyone who had travelled this far into the building must be in possession of the appropriate security clearances, right?

An apparently nonchalant spin of my chair allowed me to take in the details of the room. Walls, ceiling and floor executed in a sterile shade of white to allow for maximum light reflection, it contained a dozen workstations. Only three others besides my own were in use, staffed by two females and one male. They were in their early twenties, dressed in smart suits covered by identical grey lab coats, typical products of corporate education and social moulding techniques; raised by Tessler Corporation to serve Tessler Corporation. As such they were no more interested in my presence than they were in the amoebas in their (fluorinated for better health) drinking water.

I logged into the terminal and removed the datakey with the cyber-mole from my attaché case. I'd already loaded it the previous evening with a particularly destructive virus that would destroy every single file stored on the Chromium Oxide network. I hoped to delete or corrupt everything from financial records to the sensor data used in the formatting of the torture scenarios. Unfortunately, this would be more a minor nuisance than a fatal blow to the subsidiary company. The big corporations all use the services of data storage specialists for their backup databases as protection against fire, terrorist attack or act of war. These vaults have nearly impenetrable security systems and are shielded against blast damage and EMP emissions. Still, my little virus would still cost Tessler a small fortune in lost revenues and production while they purged the network and repopulated it with the duplicate files. I hoped Vaughan would find the loss particularly painful, as he couldn't call in outside help to investigate without risking the respectable front that Chromium Oxide hid behind as a manufacturer of military simulation games.

All I had to do was insert the disc and run a virus check and I would be home free, so what possessed me to nose around the system I can't say. Curiosity as to what his software engineers were up to probably had as much to do with my decision as anything else. But idle curiosity or not, it yielded some rather interesting dividends. A number of combat simulations were currently under development for the Police Department, ones with a heavy emphasis on crowd control and pacification techniques. In fact, there were an alarming amount of paramilitary weapons training and manoeuvres included as part of the exercises. Just the sort of training required by anyone intending to prepare the force for the introduction of Martial Law. I had a sudden intimation as to why Vaughan wanted to procure the arms contract for the ECPD. Coupled with his rising political prominence, he was apparently putting all the machinery in place to turn Europa City into a Police State with himself as the figurehead. Not a pleasant thought when one considered that the man was a right-wing racist and misogynist, who considered the ramifications behind ethnic cleansing to be roughly akin to those of trimming his fingernails.

Working quickly, I inserted a blank datakey into the terminal and copied across the relevant files, praying all the while that no one had thought to protect the system against anyone "taking their work home". As there were no flashing lights, ringing bells or charging security guards, I felt it safe to assume that I had gotten away with it. I dropped the datakey inside my case, inserted the cyber-mole and activated it. Fives seconds later I received the all clear and removed my copy. Mission accomplished.

I was in the process of packing up when a voice behind me asked, 'What are you doing?'

I turned around and found myself staring into the face of an olive skinned girl. Her dark hair and slanting eyes marked her as being of Eurasian descent. Her expression, fortunately, appeared to be one of curiosity as opposed to anger. Recovering quickly from my surprise I replied, 'I'm just leaving, if that's okay with you?' with a gruff edge to my voice.

'Oh,' her eyes widened, 'I'm sorry. I must seem terribly rude. That wasn't what I meant at all. I only wanted to know what part of the project you're working on.' She held out a well-manicured hand for me to shake as she introduced herself. 'I'm Jade Courson, behavioural analyst. I'm working on simulating the crowd reactions for the new scenarios. Group response to police presence, the flight or fight instinct, those kinds of actions.'

'Uh,' I stalled as I tried to dredge what little I knew about Vaughan's operation from memory. 'Gunnar Leith, software engineer. I've been sent over from Tessler cybernetics division to run an analysis on the scenarios for compatibility with our new direct neuro-link interfaces.'

'That explains it.'

A moment of panic; 'Explains what?'

'Why I hadn't seen you here before. I felt sure I would have remembered a face like yours. But why didn't you just arrange a direct download over the net? Surely that would have been far more efficient than coming over here in person? Though not nearly so much fun.'

Even with the flirtation, it was exactly the sort of question I'd been dreading. A prime example of one of those occasions when opening your mouth got you into even more trouble. 'Ah, well, the main server is down and head office wanted this analysis urgently. So they decided to send me over rather than waiting for the network to be restored.' I could see her working her way through my explanation and knew I had to press on immediately before she thought it through in too much detail. 'That reminds me, I must get back and begin running my analysis.' I flashed my most debonair smile at her and made for the door. I could tell she was having problems with my story but her streamlined imagination was incapable of providing her with any acceptable alternative. Realising my hurried departure would only add to her suspicions, I paused at the door, forced myself to be calm and said, 'I'm really sorry I have to rush like this, Miss Courson, perhaps we'll get the pleasure of working together on a project at some later date?'

A strange light entered her eyes when I said that and she replied, 'I do hope so,' followed a moment later by, 'Hey, wait!' I froze, fearing that she had found a gap in my cover story. She dispelled my fears by saying, 'Look, I hate to ask, but if you're impressed by any of my programming, I don't suppose you could see your way to recommending me to your Project Manager?' I relaxed. Her interest was nothing more sinister than an ambitious underling trying to get another step up the corporate ladder. She continued, 'It's just that I'd really like to get a chance at working on some of the cybernetic implants. That's the real pioneering stuff.'

I noticed that her two colleagues were beginning to take an interest in our discussion and knew that I had to bring it to a rapid close. The other woman became downright hostile. She sneered, 'Put him down, Jade. You don't know where he's been. Honestly, I don't know. Are you really that desperate to work in the Nightmare House that you've got to throw yourself at every half decent looking exec that comes in here?'

Jade's eyes narrowed. 'Pay Dana no attention, Mr Leith. She's just trying to make waves because she got refused a transfer herself.'

'Right,' I said, pushing against the door in a desperate attempt to get out of the room. The last thing I wanted was to get involved in a petty squabble with one of her co-workers. 'Look, I can't make any promises, and I really must go now, but rest assured that someone will examine your work very closely.' With that promise, I hurriedly slipped out of the door before she could say anything else.

As I walked down the corridor I congratulated myself for handling the situation rather smoothly. I'd even told her the truth in a round about manner. I had every intention of showing those combat scenarios to some experts, just not the ones she expected.

That evening I called the old contact number I had for Georgio to see if I could get in touch with Vaughan. Childish as it might be, I felt like gloating. The fractal screen appeared almost immediately, followed by the gruff American voice. 'Yeah, what d'you want, buddy?' it asked before its owner recognised me. There was a sharp intake of breath punctuated by, 'Shit!'

I leaned back for a moment, silent, as I pictured a black evening dress clinging to a firm, feminine figure - the reality behind that electronically disguised voice. Then I said, 'Hello, Georgio. Would you be so kind as to tell Colonel Vaughan that John Dumas wishes to speak with him? I think you'll find that he's most anxious to have a word with me.'

I heard a snort of derision from the other end of the line. 'That's rich,' she said in the silky tone of her own voice. 'Don't you mean Kurt Brecht,

Europa City Vice, would like a word?'

'So my secret is out, is it? No matter. Just ask if he'll speak to me.'

'That won't be necessary, son,' Vaughan's voice cut in, 'I've been here all along. What do you want?'

I smiled, knowing he could see me even though I couldn't see him. 'How's business at Chromium Oxide? I heard there was a nasty virus going round.'

The fractals faded abruptly, replaced by Vaughan's snarling visage. 'That was you? You fucking little prick! You're a fucking dead man!' He paused to wipe a long stream of saliva from his chin. 'Damn Weill and his empty promises. You were supposed to be on a mortuary slab days ago.'

I smiled again. 'That wouldn't be Captain Weill of Internal Affairs, would it? Thanks for the tip off, Vaughan. It's always good to know who your enemies are.' I watched with pleasure as his face turned almost purple with rage with the realisation that I'd goaded him into giving away one of his contacts in the Department. The muscles in his jaw bunched as he struggled to remain silent, vetting his thoughts before speaking. I warned him before he had another chance to threaten me, 'This is just the beginning, Vaughan. I'm going to pull Tessler apart piece by piece while you watch. Then I'm going to come for you.'

'Don't threaten me you...'

I cut him off and sat there grinning.

Weill scowled angrily at the image of the assassin. He had just been on the receiving end of a highly abusive call from Vaughan and had decided to return the favour. 'I don't give a shit what sort of fucking problems you're encountering, my friend. I've just had my employer on the line tearing me a fresh arsehole because Brecht's still alive. If that wasn't enough, the bastard has only gone and broke into the headquarters of one of his companies and wiped out the network with a virus.' Weill pointed an accusatory finger at him. 'You're supposed to be the best, so why the fuck haven't you killed him yet?'

The assassin remained silent as Weill stared at the impassive features that he had come to loath and despise. The long jet-black and heavily oiled hair, the strangely ageless face with its unblemished skin stretched tight over the sculpted jaw and cheekbones, and the thin, bloodless lips that were permanently set in a disdainful sneer.

Finally, when he sensed Weill could bear the silence no longer, Sword spoke. 'I have already explained to you that he has protection. One of the Families has given him shelter and even I cannot take on what amounts to a small army. But don't concern yourself, he'll surface sooner or later and when he does I'll be waiting for him.'

'Like you were today?' Weill accused.

'No, not like today. That was unfortunate. I expected him to go after Vaughan directly. But the situation has its compensations. I now have sufficient information to pursue him.'

'Really?' Weill felt a fresh spark of optimism. Perhaps things were not as bad as he had feared. 'How so?'

'It's quite simple when you look at it objectively. Brecht could not have entered that building without some very specialist equipment to bypass the security systems. There are only two, possibly three people in this city capable of supplying that aid to him. All of who will be most willing to talk to me, I can assure you of that.' His lips twisted in their familiar mocking sneer and his normally dead eyes glittered, causing cold fingers of dread to walk up and down Weill's spine. 'And Weill?' he whispered.

'Yes?' Weill said, putting steel in his voice to counter his fear.

'I won't forget this conversation.'

The fat man heaved himself up on to his knees before promptly collapsing in a paroxysm of coughing. His leather clad tormentor stood to one side, flexing the fingers of his right hand while affectionately stroking the stainless steel knuckle-duster with his left. His victim had meanwhile recovered enough to make it back on to his knees. He rummaged in his mouth with a grimy forefinger and then spat out a couple of shards of tooth enamel mixed with blood and phlegm. 'How did you get in here?' he wheezed.

The assassin sighed and drew back his leg to deliver the toe of his steel shod boot against the fat man's ribs. The blow connected with a meaty thud, sending its recipient rolling over on to his back. 'You know this is in danger of becoming a catch phrase but I'll say it one more time. I'm the one asking the questions, understood?' The Quartermaster nodded and spat out a fresh mouthful of blood. His attacker nodded back. 'Good. I know you're the one who sold Brecht his new identity so don't even attempt to deny it. Tell me the name of that identity and I'll be on my way leaving you with nothing worse than a set of sore ribs and a hefty dentist's bill. 'Otherwise,' he punched the wall just above the Quartermaster's head sending a hail of plaster dust up into the air. 'I think I've made myself sufficiently clear.'

The Quartermaster cried out, 'Gunnar Leith!' in an attempt to forestall any further violence. 'But I don't think it'll do you any good, my dear boy. No, I shouldn't think so at all. He's already made use of it to infect the network at Chromium Oxide. It would be most imprudent for him to use it again, sir. Most imprudent.'

The assassin's lips twitched into a reasonable facsimile of a smile. 'My principal was far from pleased about that little incident.'

The Quartermaster pressed his corpulent bulk back against the wall with his hands held protectively in front of his face. 'I'm very sorry about that, my good fellow, but you must understand it was merely business. One doesn't ask questions when one sells the merchandise. Very bad form, don't you know.'

'Don't worry yourself about it, fat man. It's a matter of complete indifference to me whether or not my employer is happy. In fact, I would go as far as to say that the jumped up shit had it coming to him. But enmities aside, I think you have something else to tell me, yes?'

'Now you mention it. There is a back up identity - James Douglas Morrison. It's not as well-tailored as the Leith identity, you understand, but then again it doesn't have to be. It's sufficient to allow him to move credit around and to pass ID checks. Not the pinnacle of my art, of course, but good, solid craftsmanship nonetheless.'

'Excellent. I don't think it will be too difficult to trace Mr Morrison. What else did you sell Brecht?'

The Quartermaster sighed. He had violated his ethics this far and there was now no turning back. 'FD20 flechette auto. Hi-ex, fragmentation and nerve gas micro-grenades and some milspec stimulants. Nothing unusual, sir, but all top of the range.'

'I see.' The assassin crouched down beside him. 'You've been most helpful and so I'm going to let you live,' he paused, 'on two conditions. One, that you contact me immediately should you hear from Brecht. Two, that you make it widely understood that Brecht is now a non-entity. He is not to be sold or offered any form of assistance. To do so is to invite death on you and your family.' He stood up. 'Spread the word.'

The Quartermaster's hands shook uncontrollably as he attempted to punch in the number on the handset. When he finally succeeded, he switched to voice only mode and said, 'Hello, is anyone there. I have a very important message for Emmanuel Prinzi.'

A dark shadow fell over the screen, which then exploded. Everything went dark as the Quartermaster fought to stay awake following the explosion. He peered through the clearing smoke, which coalesced into the shape of the assassin. 'Give them enough rope, eh fat man? Thanks for the information. That's just what I wanted to know.' The assassin squeezed the trigger and sent the Quartermaster away from the light forever.

CHAPTER 14

S ajer cursed under his breath as he read again the entry he had just finished in Brecht's journal. He felt numb, not with surprise or shock but with the anaesthetic of cold fury. From their earliest days at the Academy, back when they had been friends, he thought he discerned a certain weakness in Weill's character. Nothing concrete or tangible, more of an impression, as though he was trying too hard to be seen to do the right thing. Now the proof of those suspicions lay written before him. The revelation that Vaughan's had paid Weill to do his dirty work provided the final piece of the puzzle, a scrap of information that suddenly made many things clear to him. He knew now why Weill had pressed so hard to secure the arms contract for Tessler, and force him into a position where he would have no option but to sanction Brecht. Much to his chagrin, he realised that he had played right into Weill's hands, the one consolation being that Vaughan could no longer benefit from all of his manoeuvring. Weill, though, was another matter entirely. In the light of Brecht's behaviour during the final days of his rampage, his journal would be inadmissible as evidence. But somewhere, Sajer knew, Weill must have failed to cover his tracks and it was just a matter of time before he found that evidence. Soon the Internal Affairs officer would be brought to book for his crimes.

Putting that particular happy thought aside, Sajer made a start on the next entry. A sense of intuition told him that he would find the remaining puzzle pieces within these final files.

26/11/85: I'm sitting in Marian's apartment as I write these words. The circles that I run in are becoming tighter and tighter and I know the end can't be far off. Marian is sleeping right now and in a short while, when Lady Methedrine comes for me, I shall leave her. I've already endangered her too much by coming here but I had nowhere else to go. The Damocles Assassin has threatened her once and I'm sure he wouldn't hesitate to kill her. If he can kill such powerful figures as the Quartermaster and Emmanuel Prinzi, what is the life of a common whore to him? Less than nothing, I have no doubt.

I am fed, rested, and have treated my wounds. The only thing I lack is the time to carry out my war against Vaughan. It is now a race to the death between the Sword and me. The stakes being my life against Vaughan's. I think it likely that we'll both be dead before this night is out, but death doesn't frighten me. I'd gladly die a hundred times over in excruciating agony if that is what it takes to stop Vaughan.

While I await Lady Methedrine's pleasure, it occurs to me that I should record in detail the events of the previous evening to provide an accurate account of what actually transpired. Here, then, is a factual testimony of the Rome Fire and the death of the head of the Prinzi Family. The journalists and news networks are already spinning the myth, distorting reality for the lurid mind of the public. The people cry out for sensation and that is all they receive. The truth is drowned. The truth has insufficient profit margin for consumption by the masses. But the damned and the insane may speak the truth without censor. And here is that truth.

A couple of days after my sabotaging of the Chromium Oxide network Emmanuel Prinzi visited my safe house on the outskirts of Rome. He arrived in place of my regular deliveryman with a supply of food. In addition to the provisions, he brought news of a most disturbing variety. The Quartermaster was dead. Shot in his own home. Once, straight between the eyes, with a large calibre pistol. The police had originally ascribed the killing to a disturbed burglar but as nothing had actually been stolen they were now at a loss as to motive. On the surface, to those unaware of his activities, the Quartermaster was an old fashioned gentleman, a pillar of the local community.

Emmanuel sighed as he placed a basket containing fresh bread, fruit and cheeses on the kitchen table. 'A bad business this, Brecht,' he said to me. 'Poor Ricardo. He and I went to school together. Heh, we stole our first car at the age of twelve. Got three thousand a piece for it at a local chop shop. My father was furious. He said a top of the line model like that was worth at least fifteen thousand broken down into spares.' He stopped to dab a tear away from the corner of his eye with a red silk handkerchief. After folding it fastidiously, he replaced it in the top pocket of his suit. 'I don't really expect a man like you to understand. Those were simpler days, before the Flood and this accursed conglomerate of a city. The real Rome was a beautiful place - not like this reinforced concrete monstrosity. People had respect for one another back then.' He laughed. 'Ah, listen to me, an old man rambling on about the "good old days". The point I'm trying to make is that Ricardo and me had history together. It don't sit well with me when one of my friends gets whacked. It makes me look bad. People, they say, Emmanuel Prinzi is losing his grip - can't even protect his friends from some punk killer.' Angry now, his face florid and red, sweat beading on his brow. 'And you, my friend, I think, bring me this misfortune.'

'There's much truth in what you say,' I agreed with him, selecting my words with care. 'Vaughan is a powerful man to make an enemy of and he will not rest until I'm dead. I've insulted him directly and his pride will demand nothing less. Perhaps it would be better if I went elsewhere?'

I knew from his expression that I had said the wrong thing. He savagely tore a piece of bread from the loaf and took a bite. His face redder than ever, he spat angry words at me. 'The fuck you will! I offered you my protection and now you insult me by suggesting that I can't provide it against a nobody like Vaughan? That's not why I come here tonight. You think I'd come here to beg you to leave my protection? You know me better than that, Kurt. I come to remind you that your enemy is my enemy. An' to offer you any help you need to bury this piece of dog shit. He needs to learn that he can't fuck with me. Nobody kills one of my friends and gets away with it. Not even his Holiness the Pope,' he crossed himself automatically, 'would dare to insult me so.' His speech finished, he sat glaring at me.

I reached out and gave his shoulder a friendly squeeze. 'I'm sorry if I've given offence. My words were ill considered and ill chosen. Rest assured, I will be happy to kill Vaughan for you. I'll make sure everyone knows they can't fuck with the Prinzi Family. The Quartermaster - Ricardo,' I corrected myself, 'will rest easy knowing I've killed Vaughan like the dog he is.'

Emmanuel nodded his approval. 'I must apologise also. I should have known I could rely on you. You understand the vendetta so well I often wonder if you have some Italian blood in you.'

'Perhaps I do. My mother never did say who my father was.'

Emmanuel laughed and slapped me on the back. 'A bastard and proud of it, eh?'

'Aware of it, anyway.'

At about the same time as Emmanuel and I were doing our male bonding buddy-buddy thing I guess Sword must have been occupied cutting up one of the regular deliverymen. At least, having later learned about the discovery of his skinned and castrated corpse, I assume that's how he obtained the location of my safe house. He had doubtless trailed me to Rome after worming my James Morrison identity out of the Quartermaster, allowing him to monitor my financial transactions.

Two hours later, Sword entered the conversation as we sat playing poker. I put down a thousand and told Emmanuel I would see him. He turned over three Queens and a pair of nines, beating my three Jacks. Cleaned out. Again!

'Want to borrow some more money?' he asked.

'No, no, I'm good.' I told him. 'I'm going to have to mortgage the houses of my descendants to the third generation as it is to pay back what I owe you.'

'I'll tell you what,' he mumbled round a cigar, 'kill Vaughan and we're quits. That way your great grandchildren won't have to pay me rent.'

Joke or not, the comment introduced a more serious note into the proceedings. I took a large swallow of wine and said, 'This isn't just about Vaughan you know. He may be pulling the strings but I've got an altogether different candidate marked down as Ricardo's killer.' I could tell the comment had piqued his interest and so I continued. 'The Police Department has put out a contract on me. They use an assassin code-named Sword who works for what is known as the Damocles Project. He quietly disposes of rogue officers and political undesirables with the minimum of fuss and embarrassment to the Department.'

Emmanuel put down the deck of cards, his expression grim. 'An' you think this "Sword" killed Ricardo?'

I picked up my wine glass. 'Yeah. He's already shot my ex and killed her new boyfriend by mistake. There's a good chance that he traced the equipment I bought back to Ricardo and held a little Q and A session with him. All of which means...'

I stopped as I caught a red glow reflecting off the side of my glass from out of the corner of my eye. Recognising the targeting dot of a laser sight, I screamed at Emmanuel to hit the deck and dived for cover. We were halfway to the floor when the window shattered inwards, littering the floor with shards of razor sharp glass. The back of the chair I'd been sitting in exploded into molten fragments of plastic an instant later. Something began taking large bites out of the floor beside me. I tried to yell at Emmanuel over the din. 'He's using explosive rounds - we're going to get cut to ribbons if we stick around much longer. Is there another way out?'

He shouted something I couldn't hear but his nod was affirmative and he started to crawl across the floor on his hands and knees. I gritted my teeth and followed him, ignoring the pain as fragments of glass sliced into my hands.

Emmanuel reached the spot of floor under the window and began tugging at a section of carpeting. He pulled it back to reveal a recessed manhole cover with a handle at either side. We grabbed the handles and struggled, due to the poor leverage of our crouched position, to pull it up. It came free at precisely the same moment that the firing stopped. I estimated that we had a couple of seconds while he changed clips and re-sighted. I looked down the hole and then at Emmanuel who indicated I should go first. Having no better option, I slipped into the dark.

A series of metal rungs fixed to the side of the duct provided access to the subterranean service ways below. The pitch black darkness and greasy rungs forced me to move cautiously and I'd only descended a few feet when I heard Sword call out, 'Aren't thermal imagers a wonderful thing?' I heard a shot and Emmanuel's cry of pain and immediately started back up the ladder only for him to wave me on.

A violent judder travelled from my ankles to my knees as I reached the ground unexpectedly. I felt my way cautiously forward and found myself in a narrow tunnel that I estimated by touch to be just over a metre wide and two metres high. The walls felt smooth, cold and damp, the floor even underfoot. Moving forward, I had to incline my head slightly to prevent my hair from brushing against the ceiling. Emmanuel dropped to the ground behind me with a heavy thud. In between panting gasps, he called out, 'Dragonfly,' and a series of lamps fluoresced to life in their overhead niches. Their dim, flickering light illuminated the tunnel with an ethereal glow.

Now that I had light, I could see that the service duct continued straight ahead for twenty metres before angling sharply to the left. A low moan caused me to turn round in time to witness Emmanuel collapsing. He left a long crimson stain behind him as he slid down the wall. Crouched beside him, I noticed the front of his shirt was soaked blood from a wound high on the left side of his chest. More blood pooled beneath him from the ragged exit wound in his back, making it obvious that he was not long for this life. His face deathly pale and his eyes fixed and glazed, he gasped out his words between ragged breaths. 'Sonofabitch shot straight through the wall. Caught me as I was entering the duct.' His voice trailed off in a ragged fit of coughing and thin streams of blood started to trickle from his nostrils. Another one bubbled from his mouth and flowed down his chin to blend invisibly with that which already stained his shirt. He clutched painfully at my forearms with the unnatural strength of a dying man.

'Must've punctured the lung. Guess I'm pretty well fucked, eh?'

'I guess you are.'

He fell silent and I thought he was about to pass away but then he uttered a final burst of advice. 'We're in the maintenance tunnels for the building's generator and recycling plant. You should be able to find an exit back on to the street at the rear of the building. Now,' another fit of coughing, a fresh fountain of blood from between his lips, a final low whisper, 'get the fuck out of...'

That was how Emmanuel Prinzi, Godfather of the Prinzi Family, died. Unmourned by his family in a service duct beneath a low rent apartment block. No impressive marble angels, no long funeral cortège, no mourning, weeping women dressed in black. Just a cold concrete tomb, followed later by an impromptu cremation.

I knelt beside his body lost in reverie. Being my friend appeared to have become a terminal condition. Then a voice from above shouted, 'Fire in the hole, motherfucker!'

I heard something metallic bounce off wall of the access shaft and started to run. A couple of seconds later a scorching hot fist slammed into my back and threw me to the ground. A wave of superheated air and smoke roared over my head, followed closely by a sheet of flame. I pulled my trench coat over my head and pressed myself as close to the damp floor as possible and started to pray. There was no air to breathe, sweat erupted from my pores, and I could feel my clothing starting to smoulder. My skin blistered in the heat of the explosion driven flames as I held my breath for fear of scorching my lungs. I held on for what seemed like hours but in reality was probably closer to twenty seconds. Then it was over and I became aware of the soft crackle-hiss of my burning clothes. A bout of frantic rolling extinguished the flames and I started to crawl, desperate to put as much distance as possible between the assassin and myself. I risked a quick glance over my shoulder as I regained my feet and caught sight of Emmanuel's black, withered corpse before turning the corner and heading into hazards unknown.

The corner turned into another corridor at the end of which stood a dull metal door. It may or may not have been locked, but I wasn't about to waste time trying it. I drew my gun and fired a couple of rounds through the lock plate. As I slipped round its edge a bullet tore a chunk out of the frame where my head had been a second earlier.

I'd entered the plant room for the building's water and recycling centre. A series of colour-coded pipes flowed from and returned to the boilers, filters and containment tanks, mounted on which were various digital temperature and pressure meters. Other instruments monitored acid and alkali levels and the percentages of chemical mixes. The overall impression was of a twenty-first century alchemist's crucible.

Another shot tore through the door and I realised I had done enough sightseeing. I also realised that the bastard was playing with me. The rules of game were simple – for me to run or hide until he caught and killed me. I didn't intend to make it easy for him.

Grabbing an overhanging red pipe, I swung myself into the shadows beneath it, burning the flesh of my already lacerated hand on its scorching surface. I let go with a scream and retreated further into the shadows. There I located the bubblepack of frenzy, pressed out an ampoule and crushed it against my palm so that it seeped directly into my bloodstream. An air-needle would have been better but sometimes you got to work with what you've got. I only hoped it would be enough to counteract the pain already creeping through my body now that my initial adrenaline rush had faded.

The assassin entered the room. I heard him call out softly as he stalked between the pipes. 'You can hide but you can't run, Brecht. Make this easy for both of us and come out. I'll make it quick for you. One between the eyes, you won't feel a thing.'

I said nothing, knowing he was trying to provoke a response in order to pinpoint my location from the sound of my voice. An old trick that I'd used myself on occasion. The use of such tactics finally gave me an insight into the psyche of my opponent. Under different circumstances I probably would have liked the guy. But not in the here and now. This, I reminded myself, was the man who had shot Hannah and killed the Quartermaster and Emmanuel. Remembering the blackened, strangely curled figure of his corpse, I summoned up my hatred. The killing rage that in conjunction with the drugs would give me the necessary edge. This man was my enemy and I had to destroy him.

I began threading my way through the network of pipes. Manoeuvring myself towards the exit by silently ducking below or stepping over the pipes as their relative heights required. All the while holding my gun at the ready in the hope that the assassin would cross my sights.

My fleet-footed stalking was perhaps a little unnecessary, the continuous rumble of the machinery sufficient to mask out all but the loudest sounds of movement. A double edged blade that cut both ways for hunter and hunted alike. The heat from that same machinery was the one other equalising factor that I had going for me. The random emissions swamped my heat signature on Sword's thermal imager. In this room my senses were almost equal to that of the assassin. Two cripples fighting it out. In such a situation the deciding factor became a question of who was hungriest for the kill. Capital gain verses revenge.

I began working my way round in a clockwise direction towards the rear exit. Where Sword was at this point was anyone's guess, but if he were even half the pro I thought he was, he would be sure to keep a line of sight on the exit at all times.

That knowledge kept me standing pressed against the wall some ten feet from the door as I weighed up the odds of being able to make it from the room without Sword killing me. A shot rang out, taking the decision out of my hands.

'Rule Seven - never stand still for too long.'

Sound advice but I didn't get much of a chance to consider it as the bullet shattered a pipe beside my head releasing a jet of pressurised steam. It fountained geyser-like from the hole, scalding the side of my face. Half blinded, my right eye already swelling shut, I staggered towards the exit firing randomly. My shots ricocheted from the pipes and tanks, occasionally rupturing one and releasing spills of human effluent or boiling chemical soup. These unidentified compounds hissed and spat as they ate their way into the concrete floor, sending up clouds of noxious vapour that mingled with the scalding steam jets to form a deadly mist. I held the back of my hand across my mouth and nose to protect me from the fumes and made my way to the door under the cover of the rapidly swelling chemical smog.

The assassin stepped from the hazy miasma as I reached the door. Raising his pistol, he said, 'Bang, bang. You're dead.'

I stood there frozen by the moment, unwilling to accept this was how it was going to end. My subjective perspective of time stretched out the tension filled second it took him to squeeze the trigger. Then all the fires of hell engulfed us.

Damaged by my random shots, one of the main sewerage recycling tanks exploded, showering the room with burning shit. Standing in the doorway, I was able to dive out of the way, unlike the assassin who caught most of the blast in the back. In spite of this, he still managed to fire a quick shot and I felt a burning sensation as the bullet grazed a couple of ribs. I rolled back on to my feet in time to see him come staggering after me, smoke rising from his smouldering leathers. He raised his pistol for a final shot. Having abandoned my gun I flexed my wrist and fired the snake-killer blade into his thigh. The corresponding fountain of blood suggested that I'd hit an artery.

Sword made no sound. He dropped his gun and clutched his leg to stem the flow of blood. I watched in horrified fascination as he widened the wound until he could force his thumb and forefinger inside and pinch the artery closed. The spray of blood immediately reduced to a trickle and he finally looked up at me. I met his gaze for a second and then broke eye contact, unable to endure the expression of pure hatred on his face, a face that showed not a trace of pain.

I retrieved my gun, took aim and fired. Instead of the expected deafening repercussion, I heard the dull click of the firing pin coming down on an empty chamber. I thrust the Walther back in its holster and started to run as a fresh explosion rocked the corridor.

The corridor turned to the left after a few metres and continued straight for maybe another twenty. Various doors led off on either side but remembering Emmanuel's dying words I continued straight ahead in the hope of finding another duct at the end that led back to street level. The frenzy started to kick in and I found myself sprinting along the corridor. My breathing came slow and easy and my head felt crystal clear. As I slid a little distance apart from reality I found myself convinced that even God couldn't feel better than I did right now.

A shot rang out and another bullet grazed me, this time burning across my right arm. Looking back, I saw the assassin hobbling after me, the fingers of his right hand still buried inside his thigh. Fate (or perhaps Lady

Methedrine) once again intervened to save me in the form of an exploding waste pipe that ruptured through the wall in a cloud of fire and flying concrete fragments. The explosion (possibly caused by a chain reaction of the flames from the sewerage plant igniting pockets of built up methane gas) sent Sword and myself diving for cover. I regained my feet first, the assassin hampered by only having one usable leg and arm. I had reached the end of the corridor by this time and could see another set of rungs leading up to the street. I grabbed hold of a rung at eye level and began to climb upwards, spurred on by the fact that I had to reach the upper level before Sword caught me cold in the duct. Halfway up a shaft of sodium light lanced down as someone lifted away the manhole cover. Having no other choice, I continued to climb, not knowing if friend or foe waited for me at the end of my ascent. There was the ominous rumble of an explosion below and the whole duct shook. Thrown off balance, the side of my head slammed against the wall. Cold, sticky fluid ran down my face as the steam blistered flesh burst and a wave of nausea gripped me. At the same time my foot slipped on a greasy rung and I felt myself falling, but only for a moment. Pale fingers latched about my wrist like iron bands and Lady Methedrine, demonstrating a somewhat unexpected strength of limb, hauled me clear.

I lay luxuriating in the sensation of the cool tarmac against my back, only vaguely aware of the nearby fires that raged through the apartment block I had been hiding in. A sharp toed boot kicked me in the ribs and Lady Methedrine, somewhat unkindly I thought given my condition, said, 'Get the fuck up. I didn't save your worthless hide just so you could lie around and die. This entire street is about to go up and I can hear your persistent friend climbing the ladder.'

'What?' I struggled into a sitting position only to be knocked over by the shockwave of an explosion from inside the adjacent building. Flying shards of glass littered the street and although several hit me not one of them touched Lady Methedrine.

She grabbed my wrist again, hauled me to my feet, and propelled me along the road. 'You must have hit your head harder than I thought. Come on, move it!' she hissed at me.

I followed her at a fast paced limp, glancing back now and then to see if the assassin had gained the street or if he had, as I hoped, fallen prey to the growing chain of explosions that continued to rock the street. 'It's a pity you didn't think to bring some transport with you.'

Lady Methedrine gave me a strange look and nodded thoughtfully. 'Good idea. Hold on a minute.'

To my amazement, she kicked off her boots and unzipped her catsuit. She shrugged out of the shoulders, reached above her head, and I witnessed the most bizarre transformation take place. Her features elongated, the nose and jaw extending as her eyes swivelled round to the side of her head. Her hair and skin faded to pale white. Her body contorted at the same time, expanding, the shoulder and hip joints changing formation. She kicked free of the catsuit and dropped to all fours as her hands and feet curled up and transformed into silver shod hoofs. Her arms lengthened and her body continued to expand, putting on muscle over a moving, re-configuring skeleton. A long flowing tail appeared, completing the transformation. A white mare stood before me, its sapphire blue eyes the only indication that it had once been Lady Methedrine. I picked up the catsuit and stared in wonderment from one to the other. Sheer disbelief had robbed me of the power of speech.

Her familiar sardonic and husky voice sounded directly in my mind, 'Look, we don't have time for you to hang about sniffing the crotch of my clothes or whatever else you had in mind. Your friendly cybernetic assassin just gained ground zero and I get the impression that he's severely pissed off with you. So I suggest you mount me - not from the rear I might add - and then we can get out of here.'

'Do you want this?' I asked, lamely holding out the catsuit.

'No. I can create another at will. Now, will you please fucking move it!' she snapped, her telepathic voice laden with urgency.

I leapt on her back and grabbed a handful of mane. With a spirited whinny, the Mare Methedrine reared and plunged before galloping off down the street. Clutching at her mane and gripping with my knees, I held on for the fastest ride of my life. Strange how natural it felt to be riding bareback, especially when one considered that I'd never seen a horse outside of photographs and films. Then again, this being no ordinary mount, it maybe wasn't so unnatural for me to demonstrate such horsemanship, Lady Methedrine herself being responsible for my sudden affinity and skill at riding. Certainly no stranger than many of the events I witnessed that night.

Another explosion sounded behind us and I felt a blast of warm air pass over me as we galloped into the night. Behind me, the fires rampaged unchecked through the outskirts of Rome colouring the sky crimson. The dramatic light show punctuated every so often by the rolling thunder of still more explosions. Rome was burning and this time there would be no mad Emperor to play a soft lament for her dying, only the discordant wail of sirens as the emergency services arrived too late. Their blue and amber lights provided a winking contrast to the ruddy tinted flames. No longer able to watch the chaos and destruction I'd indirectly wrought; I turned my head and rode on through strangely empty streets.

After some miles the Mare Methedrine addressed me, 'Are we merely running from something, Kurt, or are we running to somewhere?'

'I don't know,' I replied truthfully. 'Perhaps we should stop and consider our options? I reckon we've put enough distance between ourselves and the assassin - if he's still alive - to be safe.'

The Mare whinnied in a close approximation of horsey laughter, 'Oh no, Kurt. You can't stop now, once you get on the horse you're along for the whole ride.'

She increased the pace of her gallop, forcing me to cling tighter than ever, my head lowered against the wind. I noticed then that my mount had become piebald. Large patches of her mane, neck and flanks stained a rusty shade of red by my blood. And yet, though I bled freely from several wounds, I felt no pain. I felt closer to pure physical exhilaration. Free from immediate danger, that familiar sense of clarity gripped my mind and the Godhead came upon me again bringing with it inspiration. I told the Mare Methedrine to, 'Head for Amsterdam where my paramour awaits.'

The Mare Methedrine had me dismount a discrete distance from Marian's apartment block. She then transformed back into her usual feminine form complete with leather catsuit. A thought that had been bothering me earlier returned. 'If you could do that with your clothes why did you bother undressing earlier?'

She shrugged. 'Dramatic license.'

I shook my head, a major mistake that set off a series of pyrotechnics inside my skull and caused my knees to buckle.

Lady Methedrine caught me by the arm. 'Come on, you look fit to drop. We'd better get you wherever you're going.'

I might have questioned this latest sudden shift of attitude but I felt far too shitty to bother about her change from dominatrix to matron. My earlier euphoria had vanished within moments of dismounting the horse and now all of my injuries were crying out for attention, the pain further aggravated by an ache in my bones that seemed determined to prove the theory that the individual parts were greater than the sum of the whole.

We crossed the road and I used my electronic skeleton key to bypass the building's security door. By the time we crossed the foyer to the lifts, Lady Methedrine wasn't so much supporting as carrying me. I had gone from steadying myself by holding her arm to having my arm wrapped about her shoulders. The lift arrived and Lady Methedrine bundled me inside with the promise that she would be in touch. The door shut, separating us, and I punched the button for the ninth floor and prayed for the ground to stop spinning.

The door opened and I almost fell into the corridor. A little stumbling later, I arrived outside 909 and pressed the intercom. Marian's face appeared in luminous green on the tiny screen beside the keypad. Her voice sounded harsh and tinny through the speaker. 'Who the fuck's there?

Don't you know what time it is?'

'It's me, Garth, and no, I don't know what time it is. All I know is that I'm in trouble so please open the door.'

I heard the rattle of chains as Marian drew back the bolts and a man's voice asked, 'Wassa matter. What's happening? We're on an hourly rate here, babe.'

The door swung open as Marian replied, 'So I'll give you a discount. Now get out of my way. I owe this arsehole some serious grief.' As I staggered inside Marian launched into a full-on verbal assault. 'This had better be good because I had a long chat with your friends down at the Halls of Justice the other night and they had some interesting things to say about you – Kurt Brecht. I can't believe I've been fucking a Vice cop without some form of kickback!'

Her client, a paunchy middle-aged man dressed only in a pair of crotchless black leather knickers, leapt back as though he'd been burned. 'Christ! You've just let a Vice pig in? If I get busted I'll be fucked. My wife - my business associates - God only knows what they'll think.'

Marian ignored his bleating and grabbed me by the lapels, 'Well?' she hissed.

It was the last straw for my abused body. I said, 'It's a long story,' and then the legs went from under me. Marian's face swam in and out of focus as I collapsed to the ground, taking her along for the ride. She pushed me off and I found myself lying at the feet of her now silent client. I looked up and managed to comment, 'Nice scrotum ring,' before passing out.

CHAPTER 15

Weill switched off the TV set and pounded the top of the breakfast bar. 'I don't fucking believe it!' The "it" referring to the morning news broadcast of the previous evening's carnage in the Rome district. The newscaster had informed the world in a cheerful tone that casualties numbered two hundred fatalities and three hundred injured, twenty-percent of which were critical.

Weill sat and raged against the injustice of it all. Five hundred casualties and Kurt Brecht did not have the common decency to be one of the fallen. An entire street raised by fire and explosion and the bastard remained at large. Any minute now, he could expect a call from an irate Vaughan demanding to know what had gone wrong this time. He thumped the bar again and wondered how to explain his way out of it. He could imagine the conversation already. Vaughan shouting at him, 'Don't bother telling me Sword has never failed to complete a sanction, I'm not interested in your underlings. You, Weill, are his controller, and as such that makes you directly responsible. If the assassin cannot fulfil the contract then it's up to you to find one who can. End of story. No ifs, buts or other limp-prick excuses.'

Weill shuddered and pushed his bowl of muesli away. He had suddenly lost his appetite. Too early in the morning to deal with this kind of shit. He walked over to the socket for the vidphone extension and wound the cable about his hand a couple of times. He paused to look heavenwards and then yanked the lead from the wall. Weill had a sudden intuition that Vaughan would find him a very difficult man to contact this morning. In the interim, he was going to find Sword and ram a rocket up his arse over the Rome fiasco.

26/11/85 (cont.): I awoke some time later to find myself lying in Marian's bed. She had cleaned and dressed my burns and the bullet grazes on my arm and ribs. The smell of frying bacon wafted from the kitchen and my stomach growled in hunger suggesting I'd been asleep for many hours, probably under sedation. Marian certainly had enough pharmaceuticals stashed around her place to do the job.

I sat up, felt the room turn through a hundred and eighty degrees, and decided to lie back down. In this instance I reckoned caution to be the better part of valour and made no further attempt to move until Marian came through carrying a tray loaded with assorted breakfast items. Strange, I thought, that dressed casually in jeans and a baggy T-shirt, stripped of her usual heavy make-up, she looked far more attractive than usual. The sort of natural beauty all women radiate just from being happy and at ease with themselves. I took it as a good indication that she wasn't planning to start the day by bawling me out, that, or finding me relatively helpless, she had decided that she could afford to start nice before building up to the yelled accusations. The problem being that I probably deserved every ounce of scorn that she had in store for me.

Marian sat down beside me on the bed and treated me to a smile that looked as phoney as a twenty-seven euro-dollar note. 'Somebody gave you a pretty good working over, Garth. I wonder who?' she said, spreading a piece of toast with marmalade and handing it to me. I took a bite more to avoid eye contact with her than for any other reason. 'You don't have any suggestions, Garth?' I didn't like the way she kept stressing the pronunciation of my pseudonym but I let her continue speaking. She clearly had some theory that she wanted to put to me, or maybe she just wanted to put it to me in general. 'It wouldn't have been a certain leather-clad killer whom the police suspect of starting the fire in Rome last night?' Her voice had taken on the slow and deliberate patterns of an adult telling a child a bedtime story. 'A man last seen fleeing the scene in a hijacked ambulance.' She finished on an up tone, indicating she expected some sort of reply at this point. When I remained silent, she handed me a glass of orange juice and indicated that I should drink. She began forcibly cutting up my bacon and eggs. Marian paused in the middle of her task and said, 'Funny thing is, a man matching that description visited me some days ago. By visited I mean that he broke into my apartment and threatened me with a knife while asking where he could find Kurt Brecht.' She cut savagely through a fried egg at this point, the blade of the knife making a metallic scraping noise against the plate that set my teeth on edge.

'Ah. I'm sorry about that,' I started to apologise.

'Hush.' She held a finger to my lips to silence me. 'I'm the one doing the talking. As I was saying, he asked where Kurt Brecht was and of course I couldn't tell him. Could I? I didn't know a Kurt Brecht, or so I thought.

So he gave me a description, can you guess whose?'

'Mine.'

'That's right - yours.' She paused a moment to regain her composure before continuing her simpleton's narration. 'Of course once I knew Garth and Kurt were one and the same I found it a little easier to help my inquisitive caller. So I told him all I knew. Not much, just where you hang, that kind of shit. For one awful moment I didn't think that was going to satisfy him, but then he upped and left.'

I decide this would be a tactful time to try to show a little empathy and concern. 'Did you call the police?'

'Oh right on,' she sneered. 'Of course I didn't. What was I supposed to say? Can you imagine the conversation?

'Excuse me, officer. A knife-wielding maniac has just threatened me in my bed.

'Then we'd chat a little while he took my details before finally asking what my profession was.

'So I say, actually, I'm a whore.

'So he replies, I guess you should watch those S & M games. Some people let them get out of hand.

'Get real, Kurt. I kept quiet. What else was I supposed to do? But speaking of the police, they hauled me in a few days afterwards and started asking if I'd seen the elusive Kurt Brecht, Detective Sergeant of ECPD Vice. I hadn't, and they didn't have anything else on me, so they let me go.'

I looked at Marian. Not much else I could add to what she already knew. I certainly had no magic words that would suddenly make everything okay between us. Our acquaintance had always been one of convenience, a relationship founded on casual sex. Two people who mutually needed a body to be with. In fact, with no more than a slight twist of logic, it would be true to say that sleeping with each other was simply a job for both of us, she a whore and me a Vice cop. Before, she had always imagined that she was the one in charge and now she had to deal with the fact that on some occasions I'd simply slept with her hoping to gain a lead on a case I was working. Although that wasn't strictly true either. Like I said before, sleeping with her was never a chore. In fact I often had better sex with her than I did with Hannah. Perhaps because there was no peripheral stuff. It simply fitted into a physical framework. I imagine that's what gave her such a headfuck. I don't know - I'm not a psychologist.

Oh for fuck's sake! It's two in the morning and I'm sitting here theorising about male/female relationships while I wait for a visit from a woman who claims to be the anthropomorphic personification of the city's pain. Am I losing it big time or what? I'm supposed to be writing up the details of what happened after I made it back to Marian's apartment.

We sat there in silence for a while. Too long a silence I suppose.

Finally, she speared a piece of egg and bacon on my fork and said, 'Your breakfast's getting cold. Eat.'

I dutifully took the mouthful from the fork and chewed it slowly. Swallowing, I said, 'So why am I here eating breakfast when you could have just thrown me in the gutter the other evening? You don't owe me any favours and knowing me has already put your life in danger.'

'To be honest, I don't know. Maybe I just wanted to hear the truth from your own lips, and I guess I wanted some explanations. When somebody threatens my life I like to know the why of it. Besides,' she smiled, 'you're a great fuck.'

I laughed. 'Pour me some coffee and I'll tell you. At least as much as I know myself.'

Marian poured the coffee and I recounted everything I knew about the Damocles Assassin, Vaughan and Tessler. I'd long since grown tired of repeating the story but she proved an attentive listener and I figured I owed her the truth if nothing else.

After I had told her everything she simply nodded and sat in silent vigil at the end of my bed. A series of shifting expressions passed over her features, each one graver than the last, as she sat locked in some internal debate. Knowing better than to interrupt, I relaxed back into the pillows and studied her.

The curtains were slightly open at the top, allowing a ray of early morning sunshine to highlight her blonde hair with streaks of gold. I stared at her clothing, fascinated, seeing a microcosm in every crease and wrinkle, a world of light and shadow. All the little details that are so easy to take for granted when you believe you have your whole life ahead of you were suddenly precious to me. Was this some fearful premonition that my end must be near, or was my sense of doom merely the product of my usual morbid introspection? Hannah always used to say that my problem was that I thought too much. Perhaps she was right.

'Ground Control to Kurt, Garth, or whatever your name is,' Marian said, startling me from my brooding. 'That's better. I appear to have your attention now. Look, we're both adults, so I reckon we should just make a fresh start. I'm willing to chalk the past up to experience and let it rest at that. But,' I knew there had to be a but, 'by your own admission you're not a healthy guy to be around at the moment so…'

'So you're throwing me out,' I finished her part for her.

'Yes.' She chewed her bottom lip nervously. 'Well, no. Not immediately at least. You're injured. I couldn't throw you out when you're unwell. So, you know, take a couple of days. Get your shit together and stuff. Then go. Don't come back any time soon either.'

'I see. That's very decent of you, all things considered.' I took her hand in mine and she started to pull away before thinking better of it. Instead, she placed her other hand on top of mine.

She smiled and said in an attempt at her usual bluster, 'An' I just know you'll find some way to pay me back.'

I suddenly found another part of my body had gone stiff, although this time it wasn't due to bruising or over exerted muscles.

Brecht closed his com-unit and slipped it into his pocket. Gone half two and still no sign of Lady Methedrine. He began fidgeting with his pencil, turning it over the back of his fingers and then drumming it against the tabletop. He grew bored after five minutes and decided to go and make himself some coffee instead.

The design of the kitchenette was common to most of the city's apartments. Small and compact, with a series of built-in units constructed from cream coloured extruded plastics that concealed the refrigerator and cooking facilities. Brecht crossed to the sink, selected a relatively clean mug from the pile of unwashed dishes and switched the kettle on. Now he needed some coffee. He opened the overhead cupboard above the sink unit and found among the assorted condiments four plastic containers marked, coffee, tea, sugar and candy. He picked up the one marked coffee and pulled off the airtight lid to reveal a mound of dark brown chips from which rose the heavy aroma of freeze-dried coffee. He measured out a heaped teaspoon into his mug, thought better of it, added another and resealed the container. As he replaced it in the cupboard he spotted the candy container again and opened it. A wide smile spread across his face as he pulled out a pair of neatly folded wraps. Just the kind of candy one would expect to find in Marian's cupboard.

Brecht unfolded one of the simple pieces of origami, licked his fingertip and dabbed up some of the white powder. The familiar bitter taste confirmed the powder as some form of amphetamine. Just what the Doctor had ordered - an early morning eye opener. Good boys, he reminded himself, should always take their medicine. The only question being how best to administer the medicinal compound. He thought about snorting a few lines but decided it was too much effort. Instead, he dabbed up the remaining powder with a wet forefinger. After licking the paper clean, he crumpled it up and threw it in the sink. Breakfast, lunch and probably dinner having been served, he decided to wash it down with a cup of coffee.

Brecht carried the coffee back to the living room and sat down at the desk he had been sketching at. He held the mug in both hands feeling its heat against his palms as he watched curls of steam drift up from the surface of the black liquid. Occasionally he would take a sip and run his tongue across the front of his teeth. They already had that familiar furry feeling that seemed to emanate from inside the enamel. He heard a grinding noise and realised it was his own teeth making it. With a grunt, he stood up and began to pace. On his fifth traversing of the room he stopped to examine his watch. Three-forty and still no word from Lady Methedrine.

The vidphone receive light blinked red in the darkness and Brecht crossed to its console in record time, hurdling both the coffee table and sofa, he slammed his palm against the receive button. Lady Methedrine's head and shoulders flashed up on the screen, her eyes dreamy, her lips set in a pout.

'You been missing me my tired hero? Or has little Marian been seeing to your needs?'

'Let's just say I've been getting by and leave it at that shall we? More to the point, where the fuck have you been? Last time you called you said you'd be over between one and two this morning to collect me.'

Lady Methedrine stretched her neck and ran the fingertips of her right hand across her throat, down between her breasts and off screen to a place Brecht tried hard not to think about. A shudder ran through her upper torso and she told him in a distracted voice, 'Things came up - business. I'm afraid we're going to have to cancel our little date.'

'Fine,' Brecht snapped.

'Don't be cross.' Lady Methedrine giggled. 'I've got good news for you.'

'What? You're multi-orgasmic?'

'If you like. One of the main advantages of being me is that I can be anything it occurs to me to be. But that wasn't what I called to tell you. Isaac Vaughan's time is over. I have the address of where he's staying tonight. It should be a simple matter for you to kill him.'

'What am I, your pet mechanic?' Brecht growled, fronting big time. He was desperate to get Vaughan but did not think it wise to appear too eager for the kill. No point affording her any more leverage than she already had. 'I'll take Vaughan when I want, not before.'

Lady Methedrine sniffed. 'I don't think so. In case you've forgotten, I own you. That was a term of our bargain. Besides, you know I know you really want him dead. Quick, before he, Weill or Weill's pet assassin hurts anyone else you love. Marian was lucky, this time. Do you think the Sword will be feeling so generous the next time he has a little chat with her? It's simple, really. You take out Vaughan, which stops Weill, which in turn stops the assassin.' She glared at him. 'Well, what's it to be?'

'Fuck it. I hate it when you're right. Okay, what's the address?'

'Graceful as ever in defeat,' Lady Methedrine said, sticking out her tongue. 'He's staying in the penthouse suite of the Sartre Towers building in Paris. I understand you had an interesting experience in its basement not so long ago.'

'Not as interesting as Marcus Conroy. The poor fuck really got his mind expanded.'

'Well you ought to know, being the one who aerated his skull for him.'

'Don't remind me.' Brecht frowned. 'How the fuck did you find out about that anyway?'

Lady Methedrine smiled mysteriously. 'I know everything about you. Your mind's an open book to me. Not a very well written one, I might add. It sure isn't about to win any literary awards - definitely a pulp fiction.' She blew him a kiss. 'I gotta go now. You know the address; do the deed. Then we'll all be happy.'

'Except for the dead, crippled and maimed,' Brecht added darkly.

Lady Methedrine's voice carried over the static buzz of the disconnected line, 'But they're always unhappy, Kurt.'

Sajer sat brooding in his office after his off the record chat with the Commissioner. A knock sounded on the door and he shouted, 'Enter!'

The door opened cautiously and a moon-faced clerk whom Sajer vaguely recognised stepped forward. The man fidgeted nervously as he handed over a small parcel. His voice broke as he said, 'Internal mail, sir. Sergeant Brecht's sort code.'

'Hoom,' Sajer cleared his throat. 'I see. Was there anything else?'

'N… No, sir,' stammered the clerk.

Sajer raised an eyebrow. 'Then why are you still here?'

'Sorry, sir. Just going, sir.' The young man did a nervous about face and bumped into a chair. His arms windmilled frantically as he sought to maintain his balance before successfully recovering his equilibrium. Not attempting to recover his dignity, he hurried towards the door in what was to all intents and purposes a sprint. Sajer looked up and smiled as he heard the door close. Comforting to know that he could at least terrify the junior office staff.

His smile swiftly faded as he recalled the package from Brecht. He found it hard to imagine Brecht sending him anything other than a letter bomb after their last meeting. A theory he could discount because security swept all packages for explosives and similar life threatening devices or contaminants.

He picked up a brass letter opener, slit open the package and shook the contents out into the palm of his hand. A datakey wrapped in a sheet of paper with the printed legend "PLAY ME" spilled out. Sajer scratched his head and mumbled, 'Curiouser and curiouser.' He inserted the datakey into his terminal and downloaded the contents. Perplexed, he clicked on the first file and settled back in his chair.

Half an hour later he sat drumming his fingers on the desktop, his features set in a pensive frown. Like Brecht, he had interpreted the simulations as being paramilitary warfare tactics - hardly standard training for an urban police force. Not unless one was planning to place a city under Martial Law.

Sajer pondered how best to use the information. The Commissioner had already made his feelings about Sajer's lack of support for the arms contract painfully clear. Haynes would view any attempt by Sajer to discredit Vaughan and Tessler at this stage as sour grapes. He had no choice except to sit on the information until a window of opportunity arose allowing it to be used to its full destructive potential. Sajer hoped it would both be soon and not a case of "I told you so."

He wondered where Brecht was at the present time. Had the Damocles Assassin already slain him, leaving behind another John Doe in the morgue? Or was he still at large, awaiting his chance to strike at Vaughan?

Brecht waited cautiously at the junction that connected with the street containing his old apartment. He looked left and right, scanning the street for watchers, the night-time street dark and devoid of all visible life. He shifted his gaze upwards, eyes skimming across the sporadic dispersal of lights that shone from the various apartment buildings. If there was a surveillance team, belonging to either the Department or Vaughan, that was where they would be, ensconced behind one of those panes of glass.

Long minutes passed with no indication as to whether or not his apartment was being watched. Deciding he could afford to delay no longer, Brecht entered the street. Keeping to the dark shadows between the street lights, he progressed silently forward. Stopping a hundred or so metres down the street, he took a set of bearings from a fire hydrant and knelt down. Crouched in the darkness, he slipped his fingers through the gratings of a manhole cover. It required only gentle pressure to slide it back on well-oiled bearings, revealing a small keypad set into a stainless steel plate. Brecht typed in the six digit code and the plate slid back with a sharp hiss of as the hermetic seals broke. Stored inside the vault were the weapons he'd purchased from the Quartermaster, the Heckler & Koch FD20, spare magazines, micro-grenades and the nerve gas antidote.

Brecht examined his watch before opening the phial and swallowing its contents. He carelessly tossed the empty phial into the vault before closing it. Taking rather more care, he stored the weapons in his pockets before standing up.

He walked away at a brisk, purposeful pace, radiating a sense of calm that he hoped would dispel suspicion in the mind of the casual observer. Confidence was the key in performing such a procedure. Those that stare or hesitate always attract attention by the unease of their body language, emitting signals than even an untrained observer could detect on a subconscious level. Brecht's training prevented him from succumbing to such obvious traits of behaviour. His life undercover depended on his ability to bluff and adopt masks.

Pausing only to loosen the Walther in its holster, he hastened towards one of the district's main thoroughfares.

Brecht cut on to the road from a side street and raised his hand to hail one of the many taxis that plied their trade on the four-lane highway that fed into the district's notorious Reeperbahn.

The taxi drivers who served this area of sleazy vice were renowned for their discretion. Their dealings with the rich and influential had long since taught them the wisdom of silence. Within these cabs the laws and mores of society faded away.

Brecht boarded a white Mercedes and instructed the driver to take him to Sartre Towers. He relaxed into the leather upholstery as the engine, an old-fashioned combustion affair, revved up to full power.

Death was coming for Isaac Vaughan riding in a pale taxi.

30/11/85: It's finally over. Vaughan is dead and my race is nearly run. Tessler may well continue without him at its head but in the final analysis that no longer seems important. Lady Methedrine and Sword, however, are.

How did Vaughan die? As much as it pains me to admit it, he died well. Though I should have known that a man of his calibre would not go gently into that forever night. What follows is an account of our final conflict.

I paid off my taxi a couple of streets from Vaughan's penthouse to give me operating room and inventoried my equipment. FD20 fully loaded with three spare magazines. Walther PP10 fully loaded with one spare magazine. One fragmentation grenade, three hallucinogenic nerve gas grenades and two high explosive grenades; enough to stage a small massacre. But would it be sufficient to take out Vaughan's security?

Last time he had only his Arab assistant and his strange mismatched pair of minders. But I'd been a guest on that occasion. That and the fact that I'd since liquidated the three stooges led me to suppose that he might since have reviewed his security measures. I guessed he would also be keeping in mind the fact that I'd walked into the headquarters building of Chromium Oxide and totally fucked over its network. I was, in short, not his favourite person.

I paused in the entrance on the opposite side of the building to avoid observation and scanned the surroundings for opposition. One obvious candidate, a heavyset man in a loose fitting suit that suggested he was concealing some form of weaponry beneath it, most probably a flechette-auto similar to my own. He paced back and forth across the entrance to the underground car park that Vaughan had taken me to on my first visit. I surmised that his partner would be positioned in the recess of the car park itself. A few minutes later my suspicions were confirmed when another large man in a baggy suit stalked across the entrance and gave the first man the thumbs up sign. Ex-military types working the buddy-buddy system, covering each other's backs.

The first man took out a com-unit and uttered indistinguishable words into it. Some form of check-in procedure. To gain access to the building undetected I had to find a silent means of disposing of the two men. A nerve gas grenade was perfect for the job.

I timed the interval between each check-in. I had five and a half minutes to dispose of the two guards and reach Vaughan's suite before someone raised the alarm. Insufficient time for the lift to ascend the hundred stories to the penthouse. That left me exposed to the possibility that they might cut the power to the lifts as a precaution. I'd be trapped like a rat in a cage if they did. An unpleasant possibility but a risk I had to take.

I primed the micro-grenade and waited for the guard to make his check in before tossing it into the entranceway.

Borman heard the tinny clatter of something metallic landing close by and instinctively glanced down. There was a flash of bright light as the grenade's small magnesium flare exploded, temporarily blinding him. When the after images cleared from his eyes he found himself enveloped in a thick cloud of mustard coloured gas. His partner, seeing the flare, ran back to investigate, crying out, 'Rickard, what is it?' He stopped, frozen to the spot as the gas took effect, causing his muscles to lock. Then they came for him.

Huge, many-eyed tentacled beings, creatures that hid on the edge of human perception, occupying the spaces between molecules since time immemorial. They had waited aeons to gain ingress to the world of men. They were the Old Gods, those who wait. Madness and terror trailed in their wake.

He tried to scream but no sound came out, just a crash of purple light. Slimy tentacles wrapped themselves about him and squeezed. He felt his ribs crack. The pressure paralysed his heart and lungs.

Rickard Borman had always been terrified of spiders. His father, who had emigrated back from South America to the continent of his great grandfather's birth, had often regaled him with tales of huge, furry, poisonous tarantulas. The young Rickard had subsequently lain awake at night imagining them creeping through the dark, crawling up over his bedclothes and across his body. Spinning silken ropes to trap and smother him as they paralysed him with their venomous bites.

Now all his boyhood nightmares were coming true. The tarmac erupted and a host of giant spiders, half a metre across from leg tip to leg tip, crawled from the steaming crater. Fear rooted Borman to the spot and the creeping arachnids soon overpowered him. Mandibles clacked as the spiders spun a cocoon of silvery webs around his body. His panicked gasps drew its sticky threads into his nose and mouth until he could breathe no longer. For his terrified mind, trapped within an immobilised body, death by suffocation came as a blessing.

I commenced my assault the moment the grenade detonated. Rushing past the two paralysed guards, I headed towards the lifts, locating them in the darkened gloom by memory alone.

I readied myself for battle as the lift began its journey upwards. Taping the flechette magazines together in pairs to facilitate a swift change, I pulled back the slide and thumbed off the safety.

Time check; three minutes forty-two seconds. Lift carriage position fifty-third floor.

I primed another nerve gas grenade together with my final high explosive one.

Four minutes seventeen seconds - sixty-first floor.

I checked the Walther was loose in its holster and began to psyche myself up, picturing Vaughan's face, then his corpse, myself standing over it with a smoking gun in my hand. A cliché, but an effective one for all that.

Five minutes and thirty seconds - time's up on the eighty-ninth floor.

The moment of truth, would the lift continue or stop? Ninety, ninety-one, the lights continued marking off the floors on the control panel.

So they were going to let the lamb come to the slaughterhouse. Vaughan's goons were no doubt organising a welcoming committee for me on the hundredth floor. Well they were welcome to try. I was more than ready for them.

Bracing my legs against the sides of the carriage, I climbed up and released the emergency escape hatch. I had just scrambled out when the carriage stopped, rode on its shocks, and finally settled down. The doors slid apart and round after round poured into the small aluminium room. The bullets punched through the walls, shattering the recessed lights and destroying the controls. The damaged equipment fizzed and popped with the sound of electrical shorts.

Halfway through the barrage I threw the nerve gas grenade into the corridor and waited. Thirty seconds later the firing stopped and silence fell as a drifting cloud of gas wafted back into the carriage to mingle with the black smoke of the shorted wiring. Not trusting the damaged carriage to bear my weight, I swung myself forward into the corridor.

A strange composite of smells reached my nostrils. Ozone from the fire mixed with the spicy cinnamon and cloves odour of the gas. I checked the corridor for signs of life and discovered none. My only company that of three corpses. Big men in loose suits like the pair guarding the basement. Their faces set in disturbing grimaces of sheer terror, limbs unnaturally twisted. I'm no stranger to death but a gassed man is never a pretty sight. Realising that I was wasting precious time and giving Vaughan's forces a chance to regroup, I pressed on towards the door of his suite. Ten feet from the door, I primed the hi-ex grenade, threw it and pressed myself back against the wall. The roar in the close confines of the corridor was deafening.

I looked through the rapidly clearing smoke and saw that the explosion had completely destroyed the door and taken out a portion of the surrounding wall. Judging from the lumps of raw meat mingled with the scattered concrete and wood debris, it had also caught several men waiting behind the door. Was anyone left alive? Only one way to find out. I readied my gun and leapt through the shattered doorway. My first mistake during my assault on the building and, as is so often the case in these situations, almost my last.

I dived into the room, rolled to the left and came up on my knees in time to catch a bullet in the right shoulder. The impact spun me around and sent me crashing to the ground. I landed heavily on my back and watched helplessly as the flechette-auto skidded out of my reach across the floor. No pain. That would come later when the shock and the nerve-blockers in the frenzy wore off.

Vaughan stepped into view on the other side of the room; a smoking automatic gripped in his right hand. Georgio stood behind him, dressed once more in a sheer, black evening dress, pensive, drawing heavily on a cigarette. She gave me a lazy wink as I struggled to my knees. At the same moment Vaughan raised his automatic, his voice a laconic drawl as he said, 'You're shit out of luck, Brecht.' Then he pulled the trigger.

CHAPTER 16

Vaughan's smile of triumph turned into an expression of surprise, followed swiftly by anger, as the firing pin came down on an empty chamber. 'What the fuck's going on?' he snarled.

Georgio stepped forward, a strange juxtaposition of feminine grace and beauty against the carnage of the room, her smile now one of infinite cruelty. She raised her clenched fist and opened it to let a dozen bullets cascade to the floor. They bounced off the quarry-stone tiles with a metallic ping. 'The answer, Isaac dear, is simple. I emptied the clip, leaving only a chambered round.'

'Why?' Vaughan whirled round to face her, his face etched with lines of confusion and rage.

'Because,' she replied, and let her mask fall away to reveal her true self.

I could only shake my head in wonderment as her hair lengthened, her skin paled and her dress shifted from black to white. Georgio vanished in the space of a few heartbeats leaving Lady Methedrine in her place. Her transformation cleared up several similarities between herself and Georgio that had been troubling me - mannerisms and modes of behaviour, her willingness to betray Vaughan when they had clearly been intimate with one another. And yet Vaughan must have known her for years for him to place so much trust in her? While I had first met Lady Methedrine only a few weeks previously.

Vaughan's reaction proved far more prosaic than my own. 'Neat trick. How's it done, with holograms?'

Lady Methedrine subjected him to the sneer that I had come to love and hate. 'Poor little Vaughan, unable to accept the evidence of your own eyes. Georgio died two months ago. Since then,' her eyes flashed crimson, 'I've been masquerading in her place.'

Vaughan shook his head disparagingly. 'You've turned into a total fruitcake, Georgio. You know that?' He looked at the useless gun in his hand, then at Lady Methedrine, then back at the gun. 'Women,' he shrugged, 'can't trust the bitches.' Without warning, he lashed out with the gun and struck Lady Methedrine in the face. The foresight tore a long gash in her cheek and the impact sent her rocking back on her heels. Her head slammed against the wall and she slid unconscious to the floor.

I used the distraction to regain my feet and stagger over to one of the couches in the centre of the room. Vaughan turned away from the limp figure at his feet. He spoke without looking at me, almost as if to himself. 'This is what comes of relaxing my cardinal rule. I deserved this. Women make men weak and foolish, yet they are our inferiors - the slave sex. I let down my guard and I got my just reward. Perhaps I'll bury her with thirty pieces of silver. Kind of a shame 'cause I did like that dress.' He focussed on me once more. 'But what am I to do with you, my friend? You've caused me a great deal of trouble, you know that?'

'No shit,' I said.

'No shit indeed, Sergeant Brecht. Between having to reinstall the network at Chromium Oxide and hiring new staff every time you kill someone, you've managed to piss me off more than a little. And now, as a final insult, you've wrecked my home and destroyed several priceless art treasures.' He pointed to a broken sheet of glass with a torn print behind it. 'That used to be Melancholia, a fifteenth century print from the original engraving, one of Dürer's meisterwerks. It's irreplaceable!'

The idea that I might have driven the testosterone fuelled bastard over the edge crossed my mind at this point and I tried to look contrite about desecrating his gallery. Feeling helpful, I suggested, 'Hey, why don't you just let me go and take it out of my salary for the next thirty years?'

Vaughan loomed over me. 'Don't try and be cute, Brecht. It doesn't become you.'

'I guess,' I hastily agreed, stalling for time. Like most megalomaniacs, Vaughan was extremely fond of the sound of his own voice. The longer I kept him talking the longer I'd live. So I let him drone on while surreptitiously testing the extent of my injuries. Initial bodily responses confirmed that the situation was not good. My right arm was dead; the bullet had dislocated the shoulder and sheared away a good portion of the posterior deltoid muscle, making the snake-killer blade useless to me. It also made it very difficult for me to draw the Walther from under my left armpit. Any scrabbling motions made by my left hand would telegraph my intentions to Vaughan immediately, and he was far too big a bastard to risk getting to grips with hand to hand in my present condition.

Short of immediate ideas, I tuned back into his monologue in time to hear him say, 'I owe Hassan that at the very least. So you see, Brecht, or may I call you Kurt? It's just that I feel we're old friends now, after stalking one another for the past month. Anyway, as I was saying, I'm going to have to kill you, and honour demands that I do it slowly, piece by piece.'

He closed on me where I lay half sitting, half-slumped on the couch. I tried to avoid him but he proved surprisingly fast for a man of his bulk. His arm snapped back as he pistol-whipped me and there was a splintering sound as the butt connected with my left cheek. Unable to ride the blow, I tumbled across the arm of the couch on to the floor. Vaughan threw the pistol aside and leapt on me. Grabbing my lapels, he picked me up as if I weighed no more than a child and threw me across the room. I landed heavily, crashing through a glass topped display cabinet. I rolled over, aware of several fragments of glass that had impaled my back and chest. Still no pain, although I knew that wouldn't last. Vaughan grabbed me again, lifted me from the wreckage and pinned me against the wall. He was breathing hard, his nostrils flared, his lips flecked with bloody spittle. 'Are we hurting yet?' he snarled at me.

'I don't know. Are we?' I struck at him, slashing out at his throat with a long sliver of glass I'd retrieved from the floor. A thin trickle of blood appeared, the blow too weak to cause any serious damage.

Vaughan swatted the glass from my hand and laughed. 'Is that the best you can do, little man? This won't take long at all. How that fool of an assassin failed to kill you I'll never know.'

My whole body jarred repeatedly as he smashed me against the wall. Vestigial messages of pain began to reach my brain from the nerve endings in my ruptured shoulder, multiplying slowly like the cracks in the plaster each time my body hit the wall. On the verge of losing consciousness, I made a feeble attempt to draw the Walther. Vaughan, observing my actions, stopped pounding me against the wall and reached inside my coat. 'Well what have we got here?' he said, drawing the gun. He held it in front of my face as he flicked off the safety. 'Executed with your own gun, suitably ironic, don't you think?'

I would have died then and there if Lady Methedrine hadn't intervened. In my increasing haze of delirium I heard her call out, taunting him. 'Freud was right; the gun is a symbol of phallic power. You better get a bigger one, Vaughan, if you're hoping to make up for your deficiencies between the sheets. Needle-dick.'

Vaughan released his grip on me. 'Should have stayed down when you had the chance, bitch,' he said and fired.

The bullets struck her in the left breast, punching straight through her body to exit in a spray of visceral gore. The force of the impact threw her into the corner where she collapsed like a rag doll. Her blood formed Rorschach patterns on the walls - butterflies and skulls. The blood seemed to captivate Vaughan, who stood and stared at it, mesmerised.

Crawling on my hands and knees, I felt the familiar shape of a metal disc beneath my fingers, a micro-grenade - metallic purple - nerve gas. Vaughan turned as I activated it, the magnesium flare blinding me as he raised the gun. Then the darkness swallowed me.

Vaughan was lost in the desert at night. Tired, thirsty, hungry and cold as he staggered to the summit of yet another of the innumerable dunes. Overhead the stars were clear and bright, displaying the majesty of Heaven's vault. Ahead of him, the desert sands stretched limitless to the horizon - endless - barren. Disheartened, he fell to his knees and wept. Then the sibilant voice began its litany.

'Why did you kill me? I trusted you. We were like brothers.'

Accusation after accusation whispered by a dead man, one who Vaughan had personally dispatched to hell. He pounded the sand and screamed, 'No! No! No! It wasn't like that.'

Fingers erupted through the surface of the sands and Vaughan, terrified, scrambled down the side of the dune. A head, shoulders and torso followed until Major Wilson P. Brodie stood before him. His left eye and the rear quarter of his skull were missing, blasted away by a bullet to expose the pulpy remains of his brain. Two ragged holes, scorched around the edges and surrounded by the maroon of dried blood, punctured the chest of his combat fatigues.

The corpse grinned. 'Wasn't it, Isaac? You wanted my position, hungered for its power, and when I was injured you didn't hesitate to administer a mercy shot.'

'No! You're twisting it all. You were as good as dead anyway. You of all people should know that it's standard operating procedure when behind enemy lines. I had to do it. There wasn't any other choice.'

Brodie lunged forward, 'Liar!' he spat as his fingers locked around Vaughan's throat.

Vaughan started awake in bed. Unable to move, paralysed. Panic threatened to overwhelm him until he realised he had been bound hand and foot to the metal frame of the bed. Above him, the steel blades of the ceiling fan rotated lazily, chopping the heat of the arid desert air. He sighed. Only a nightmare.

The lithe figure of the Arabian prostitute moved rhythmically as she sat astride him. Vaughan closed his eyes and relaxed. He must have briefly drifted off to sleep as he had no recollection of the girl moving and yet he could now feel her tongue teasing at the head of his penis. He felt her teeth scrape gently against its base and then they clamped down just hard enough to break the skin.

His eyes snapped open and to his horror he realised it was not Scheherazade above him, but a white woman with pale skin and long black hair. Though he felt certain that he'd never met her, there was something strangely familiar about the woman. Something was also subtly wrong. It dawned on him slowly - how could his penis be gripped between this woman's teeth when she was sitting astride him?

The woman smiled and pain lanced through him as her bizarre nether-teeth bit deeper and she began to grind her hips. He tried to cry out and discovered that he had no voice. The woman bent closer to him and their eyes met. His were wide with fear; hers blazed with a cold, intractable fury.

Her mouth set in a cruel line, she whispered in his ear, 'Like many men you mistake violence for skill. Here is a taste of true sexual rage. I am vengeance. Part of me is part of every woman and child that you ever abused, tortured and hurt. This pain is theirs - feel it!'

Vaughan's voice returned to him in time to vent an agonised scream as the nether-teeth bit home, meeting together.

The woman slid from the bed and expelled his severed organ. She laid it beside him and calmly licked the mixture of blood and semen from her fingers. Then she walked away, leaving Vaughan to bleed to death.

There's not much else left to tell. I regained consciousness to find Lady Methedrine standing over me, her features as flawless and immobile as those of a marble sculpture. The gash on her cheek and the bullet wound in her breast had vanished. The only indication of their existence the now incongruous bloodstains that marred the front of her dress.

Vaughan's contorted corpse lay behind her. His face set in a similar rictus of terror as that of the guards I'd killed in the basement. I fervently hoped that whatever purgatory the gas had sent him to had made him suffer. Then I found myself capable of thinking little else as an entire host of aches and pains assailed me.

With Lady Methedrine's assistance, I managed to stagger my semi-delirious way from the wrecked penthouse to my new hideout in Berlin. An old Vice squad safe house that I'd managed to retain access to, dangerous in the long term but fine for the short term. Lady Methedrine remained silent throughout the journey, stoically refusing to answer my questions. She dumped me unceremoniously outside of the house and left without as much as a goodbye. A fact that chilled me for some unknown reason. I felt it boded ill for my coming confrontation with the Sword of Damocles.

CHAPTER 17

B recht felt weary. Gripped by a fatigue beyond all endurance. His bones ached to the marrow and the throbbing pain in his shoulder had risen in intensity to the point of being unbearable. His fingers scrabbled across the table as he reached for the bubblepack. Even this slight movement made him nauseous and his vision dimmed as unconsciousness threatened to steal over him. He knew he must be close to death (the crinkle of fingers on plastic) but that no longer mattered. He had killed Vaughan and that single act of vengeance was worth sacrificing his life ten times over. A fresh wave of light-headedness rolled over him (a click, the accompanying hiss) and he relaxed into it. Suddenly the pain did not seem quite so intense, while the effort of living seemed such a struggle. Death was no longer a great mystery, only part of the great cycle of life. It being as natural to die as to be born. And had he not finished his work?

Cool lips pressed against the blistered flesh of his own and he felt a surge of vigour pulse through his being. A soft voice told him, 'Not yet, my love. There is still work to be done. The Sword of Damocles is out there, in the night, and he will always hang over you unless you kill him. Remember Hannah - use your hatred to make you strong. This man will hurt and kill those you love unless he's stopped.'

'But I'm tired and weak and I can't fight any more,' Brecht whispered back.

A weight settled upon his lap, bringing with it a confusion of sensation, soft flesh against his thighs, the scent of cherry blossom and the tickle of long strands of hair brushing against his cheek. He opened his eyes and stared into the limitless blue orbs of Lady Methedrine's. Her lips brushed his again and soft hands caressed his back. Resting her head against his chest she said, 'No, you are strong. Now is not the time for you to die, because I do not will it. Your destiny awaits you on the night-dark streets.

167

Remember our agreement; it is I, and I alone, who shall decide when your life is over. Do you dare refuse to serve me?'

'You know I'd never do that.' Brecht felt his strength return with his reply. He had been on the shores of death but now he was returning to the living world, called back by a heady mixture of duty, lust and revenge.

The weight vanished from his lap and he sat up abruptly, causing something to fall to the ground. It landed with a dull, thudding sound. Reaching down, he picked up the hypodermic gun and placed it on the table beside the empty bubblepack. He felt clear and refreshed. All thought of rest vanished as he psyched himself up to hunt the Damocles Assassin. Only when he had taken care of that small problem would he be content to relax. Maybe - he had a dark suspicion that he would know no peace until he found a way to free himself from his servitude to Lady Methedrine. First the bastard and then the bitch, he promised himself, thumping the table for emphasis.

Accessing his com-unit, Brecht typed in the date, 21/12/85, and stopped. The words refused to come. He stared off into space as he tried to make some coherent order out of the mess of his thoughts and emotions, that he might translate them into words, but his muse had deserted him.

An indeterminate period of time passed as he sat, staring into nothing. The vidphone screen flickered to life, further scattering his already disordered thoughts. A nasal voice whined, 'Hey, Kurt baby, how are you doing?' A pause, 'Hmm, not good. Looking a little pale and drawn there. Not getting enough beauty sleep, Kurt. Shame on you.'

'Cut the shit, Slinky, I'm not in the mood for it,' Brecht snarled. The informer's rat-like features twitched in a sulky pout and Brecht, looking properly at him, thought he appeared mangier than usual. Drawing on the last reserve of his patience he said, 'Not looking so hot yourself, Slinky. So what do I owe the honour of this call to?'

'Oh, you'll like this one. It'll really get your rocks off,' Slinky enthused. 'Word is you're looking for a certain leather-clad psychopath. Fact is I know where to find him. Does that groove your truffles, man?'

Brecht sat upright. 'Oh yeah, I'm grooved. But I don't recall putting the word out or giving anyone this number. So you'd better do some fast talking before I have some of my friends pay you a visit.'

'Didn't think you had any friends left, not this side of the veil anyway. But hey, don't freak on me. Your kinky sick little fox called and gave me the news. Miss Ice Queen herself.'

'Lady Methedrine?'

'Whatever. The fucked up chick with the big hair and the white leather gear. Said this dude was out to off you and that you, naturally, wanted to get him first. I put the word out and got me a result. So if you want him?'

he left the question hanging.

'Course I'm interested. Where is he?' Brecht stopped as a sudden thought hit him. 'Wait a minute. You know my status with the Department - I can't pay you for this. What's going down here?'

Slinky looked decidedly uncomfortable and it took him several seconds to reply. 'No sweat. The lady paid for this one, since you're out of the loop as far as the ECPD is concerned.'

Brecht didn't like the pause. Perhaps he was just being paranoid, the explanation sounded plausible enough. He decided to accept it at face value. 'I'm certainly that. So come on, what are you waiting for? Give.'

'No way,' Slinky shook his head, 'not over the vid. I don't care if you think it's clean. I ain't risking it. Some of us aren't walking round with an expiry date stamped on our foreheads. We'll have to meet and discuss this, somewhere private.'

'For fuck's sake, where?' Brecht shouted, finally losing all patience.

'The alley, just off the Tiergrasse in Amsterdam. You know where I mean?'

'Yeah.'

'Good. Meet me there in half an hour.'

Brecht killed the connection. He glanced at his watch, reached for his com-unit and hastily typed a few lines. Checking the action of his gun, he holstered it before pulling on his trench coat, a procedure complicated by his wounded shoulder. Eventually, he had his clothing arranged to his satisfaction and made for the door. He stopped, walked back to the table, picked up the com-unit and slipped it into his pocket. After glancing round the room in some kind of bizarre ritual of self-assurance, he headed back to the front door.

Brecht paid off the taxi driver with a generous tip and stepped from the cab on to the cold concrete slabs of the Tiergrasse. Turning up his collar, he watched the lights of the taxi disappear into the steady flow of traffic and shivered. The cool night air froze the fever-sweat on his brow and made his clothing feel damp and clammy. He gathered himself and started to walk down the Tiergrasse, his gait little more than a shambling lurch. People hastened to move out of the path of this unwashed, bloodstained figure, fearful of having any contact with a member of that underclass of society composed of junkies, alcoholics and other degenerate homeless persons. Their disgust cut through the haze of Brecht's disorientation and he attempted to smile at a young couple, to explain he was one of them, but the muscles in his face appeared to have atrophied, rendering his smile as the rictus grin of a death's head. The man steered his girlfriend to one side and held out a warning hand.

'We don't want no trouble. Just keep away from us. Okay?'

Brecht stared at them, puzzled by their hostile reaction, and then stumbled on. A black space between two buildings registered in his memory as the entrance to the alleyway. Somewhere in his back-brain, a voice screamed a warning at him, telling him that something was very wrong. But it could not cut through the numbing mix of neuro-suppressants and physical stimulants that flowed through his body, a chemical cocktail that left him feeling as though he were somehow at ninety degrees to reality. In spite of this, some intimation of danger or age-old instinct proved great enough to make him draw his gun as he walked into the engulfing darkness of the alley.

Brecht's feet slipped against discarded bags of refuse and other less pleasant products of human waste as he made his way between the narrow walls. He called out softly into the darkness but received no reply and soon found himself facing a dead end. A footfall sounded behind him and he spun round to face an unseen terror. A hand clenched about his upper arm, sharp nails dug into his flesh, sending a tide of fear through his body. Lady Methedrine whispered, 'Now is the moment of truth, Kurt. Is your love for me strong enough for you to take him, or will you let me down at the last? A weak man is no use to me. I need a warrior who can fight. Think you've still got what it takes or are you like all the rest?' Her laughter still ringing in his ears, Brecht reached for his com-unit.

Sword watched Brecht with a growing sense of disappointment. He'd hoped Brecht would prove a worthy adversary but instead found him batting at the air and gibbering in terror as he confronted his death. A terrible anticlimax to have spared his life during their last encounter only to find the final battle so devoid of honour and glory. Had this shambling wreck really killed Isaac Vaughan? He had expected Brecht to provide better sport, but the drugs had finally got to him.

He raised his gun as Brecht stepped towards him, shouting gibberish; 'You won't get away with it. I've written everything down. They'll hunt you down for what you've done to me.'

Sword shook his head and fired, the silenced pistol barely making a sound. Brecht jerked and shuddered as the bullets ripped through his stomach, an expression of disbelief frozen on his face. His hyped up nervous system kept him standing for a second and then his legs slipped out from under him and he folded to the ground.

Sword crouched down. 'Last time I promised to make it quick, but since then you've put me to a considerable amount of trouble. Gut shot. Not a pleasant way to go. Enjoy.'

Something warm, wet and sticky adhered to Duvall's face. It clogged his eyes and dripped down the front of his shirt. At the same time as he registered his blindness, his mind informed him that he had heard the shot and since bullets travelled faster than sound he must still be alive. He scrubbed his face with his fingers and cleared the pulpy mess of tissue from his eyes to reveal a scene of bloody carnage.

Weill's headless corpse lay twitching on the floor in front of the desk, surrounded by an expanding pool of blood. Tearing his eyes from the decapitated body, he looked up to see a tall, shadowy figure standing in the doorway, observing Weill's death throes. The figure stepped forward giving Duvall his first clear sight of the assassin; a tall man with long black hair dressed in motorcycle leathers. His ageless face set in a habitual sneer. Fixing his dead eyes on Duvall he said, 'It would appear the captain is no longer in favour with his superiors.' He spat on the corpse before calmly walking away.

Duvall looked down at the mess of blood and brain tissue dripping from his fingers and started to vomit.

Half an hour later, Duvall found himself in a private interview room with Guyon Sajer. Still gripped by the shock of Weill's execution, he stared off into the middle-distance. Occasionally he would run fingers through hair still damp from frantic ablutions. He had been sitting like that when two officers from internal security had rushed into the room. Neither guard could account for anyone entering or leaving the building, or as having been in the immediate vicinity. The assassin, it would appear, had simply vanished.

Sajer handed Duvall a steaming mug of coffee and said, 'I suppose you would like an explanation, yes?' His voice soft and paternal, he tried to coax a response from the traumatised officer.

Duvall wrapped his fingers about the mug and looked up, wild-eyed. His expression made him seem very young, like a child punished by his parents for a transgression he could not understand. 'What kind of man calmly walks into the headquarters of the Police Department and murders one of its officers? How could he do that? Weill might have been a shit, so crooked he could fuck himself without bending over, but he deserved better than a summary execution. The evidence is all in the computer records for anyone to see. He used the Damocles Project, whatever the fuck that is, to have Paul Costello assassinated, just because he was making political waves he didn't care for.' His monologue complete, he looked at Sajer in askance.

'You have answered your own questions,' Sajer informed him. He wavered for a moment, uncertain how much of the truth he should reveal. Then, deciding Duvall deserved the whole story, he continued, 'The man who executed Weill - if man is still the correct term for what he has become - is known as Sword. He is the Damocles Project. A Departmental paid assassin who takes care of embarrassing problems for us. It's bad for both morale and our public image if we have to put one of our officers on trial. This way we transform our disgrace into a martyr, who remains another unsolved homicide.'

Duvall looked at him with a mixture of revulsion and shock. 'Guess your assassin botched the job with Brecht. I did wonder why the Department wasn't pursuing his case with any enthusiasm. Now I know.' He shook his head in disbelief and then sat upright as a new and unwelcome suspicion occurred to him. 'You knew Weill was dirty, didn't you? You're still running Damocles, even after you discovered he'd been used to murder innocents.'

'He's a tool, nothing more. He received his orders and carried them out. He had no means of knowing that Weill was using him for his own ends. Yes, I knew Weill was corrupt, just as the entire Arms Contract Committee knew Vaughan was dirty. Brecht implicated Weill as being involved with Vaughan in his journal but there was no way I could use that evidence. I had no proof until I ran my own trawl through financial records and discovered Weill's little peccadilloes. Then he became another embarrassing problem for Sword to take care of. That's how we do things in the real world. Barbarous as it appears, we need such systems to control the racial tensions of a mixed community of forty million souls. People whose ancestors spent the first half of the last century invading each other and bombing their cities back into the Stone Age. We like to pretend that we're all Europeans now - one language and one state, but in the final analysis that state is made up of Germans, French, British, Italians, Spanish and so on. They in turn are Protestant, Catholic, Muslim, Jewish, Wiccan or Atheist, which makes it easy to blame someone else when there are no jobs or food shortages. That's the real reason we have rioting on the streets every night, not because our force is inefficient, undermanned and antiquated.'

'So that's it, everything neat and tidy? I bet you'll even turn up at Weill's funeral wearing a suitably grievous expression.'

'Yes, Weill will be afforded a police funeral. White gloves, full honour guard, another brave officer killed in the line of duty. I sign one piece of paper and an embarrassment becomes a martyr. Bad publicity transformed into good. That's how it works. I don't blame you for feeling cynical or cheated. There's no honour in how we uphold the law, just necessity. You are either going to come to terms with that or quit.'

'I can't do that. It's my life. It's the only thing I've ever wanted to do. But we're supposed to protect and serve the people, not be their keepers.'

'If you ask me,' Sajer said, 'you've already made your decision. But take a couple of days leave and think it over, then let me know how you feel. If it makes things any easier, this was a result for the good guys.'

'How do you work that out? Brecht is brain dead and his killer is probably getting ready to take care of the ECPD's latest embarrassment. That kind of suggests to me that there aren't any good guys.'

'Simply not true. The fact that you care puts you on the side of the angels. As for victories won, Brecht achieved much through his sacrifice. Unintentionally, perhaps, but nonetheless valid. Tessler Corporation is bound by contract to supply arms to this Department for the next five years - with or without Isaac Vaughan at the helm. Now that Brecht has removed him we can assume control of Tessler, shut down their illegal operations and concentrate on their legitimate research.'

Duvall stood up. 'And the world keeps turning? Well, I'll let you know my decision shortly.' He paused. 'Can I say something off the record?'

'As you wish.'

'I want you to know that I think this whole business sucks. I'm not so naïve that I believe in black and white absolutes, but you've taken the grey areas to the extreme. Perhaps there's no better way but if there is one I'll find it.'

'One man can make a difference, eh? Keep on believing that, Duvall, and who knows what you might achieve.'

EPILOGUE: POINTS OF INTERSECTION

The Heidelman Psychiatric Foundation: 18 January 2086, 10:19

The receptionist glanced up from her desk as she heard the sound of high heels clicking against the floor of the corridor. Their rhythmic, staccato beat heralded the approach of two women. The receptionist swivelled about in her chair and regarded the pair with a scrutiny that went beyond politeness.

The first was a middle-aged black woman of average height, dressed in a well-tailored suit that showed her figure to be trim despite her years. The other, a white woman, about half a head shorter than her companion. Little more than a girl, in her teens, with a shock of red curls spilling down to her shoulders, dressed casually in tight fitting denims and a cropped T-shirt that revealed her pierced navel and brightly tattooed arms. A pair of ridges beneath the close fitting cotton stretched across her breasts suggested her nipples were also pierced. The phrase "Little tart" passed through the mind of the receptionist as she examined the girl, along with other less socially acceptable ones. She sat up a fraction more primly as the black woman approached her desk. Putting on her best PR voice, and nearly going cross-eyed with the effort of metaphorically looking down her nose, she asked, 'How may I help you, Ms?'

'Doctor. Doctor Claudia Rae. I've an appointment with Doctor Wilsdorf. I'm here to finalise the adoption of the Buscato children,' Claudia explained, her tone intimating that she could adopt just as many airs and graces as this upstart of a secretary.

The receptionist, whose name badge identified her as Veronica, did some hasty mental back-pedalling as she re-evaluated the two women. Her expression neutral as she enquired, 'And the young lady?' barely hesitating on the last word.

'Miss Anastasia Bousfield, my ward. We're both expected.' Claudia said, putting a little more iron into her voice as she added the last statement.

'Of course you are,' Veronica replied, attempting a cheerful smile that turned instead into a sickly grimace. Hitting the switch of the intercom system, she held a quick, murmured conversation before returning her attention to Claudia. 'Doctor Wilsdorf will be happy to see you both. His office is through the swing-doors, first on the right.'

Claudia thanked her brusquely before marching smartly in the direction of the swing doors. Anastasia lingered long enough to put on her most saccharin smile as she told the receptionist, 'Don't worry, I had a bath before I came out.' Leaving the woman open mouthed, she hurried after Claudia.

The Reeperbahn: 18 January 2086, 10:19

Slinky tossed the credit card up in the air and watched as it spun end over end. It flashed silver and gold along its parabola until it reached the apex of its ascent and surrendered once more to gravity. He looked away as it fell; he had never liked the "must come down" part.

Ten thousand; a lot of junk, a lot of forgetfulness, but no forgiveness. Ten thousand - that was how much his friend's life was worth. His father had been right when he called him a plague rat. He brought death and suffering to all those that he touched. His acquaintance always appeared beneficial in the beginning but eventually it proved fatal. Born in death, he thrived on death. It never had been and never would be any different, but with a family like his you couldn't expect anything less.

He wondered why his betrayal of Brecht bothered him so much. Kurt was hardly the first friend he'd ripped off or let down. Was it because Kurt had seen something of worth in him? Some spark of humanity that Slinky had long since forgotten, or at least thought that he had.

He looked at the card on the ground. Not too late to get back in the game. He could still walk away, try to put the past behind him, or he could stick a spike into his vein. As be bent down to retrieve the card he sang softly to himself, 'Because it makes me feel like a man when I...'

Halls of Justice: 18 January 2086, 10:19

Duvall paused outside the door and read the freshly inscribed gold on its glass, "Commissioner's Office". He knocked once, firm and loud, and a stentorian voice called out, 'Enter.'

Guyon Sajer was sat at his desk examining a framed photograph when Duvall entered his office. He put the photo aside as the young man came smartly to attention in front of his desk and clicked his heels and saluted.

'You may stand at ease,' Sajer assured him. 'I gather you wish to speak with me?'

Duvall clasped his hands behind his back and spread his legs. 'Yes, sir. I submitted a formal request for transfer back to the SPF. I was wondering if you had reached a decision, sir.'

'Ah, yes,' the newly appointed commissioner called up a file on his workstation. Concentrating on the screen, he said, 'A bad business that with Captain Weill and Sergeant Brecht and the Damocles Project; one that I think would be best forgotten by all parties concerned.' He subjected Duvall to a questioning look.

'Yes, sir,' Duvall hastened to agree with him. Ignoring one of Sajer's unofficial commands had resulted in his original transfer to Records.

'Good. I see you're learning at last, Duvall. One has discovered that several weeks of performing dull, repetitive tasks can focus even the most obtuse of minds. You've obviously given up your foolish notion of quitting the force.' Sajer typed a few lines on his keyboard and then looked up again. 'Officer Duvall,' the young man snapped back to attention, 'I am pleased to inform you that your request for transfer to the SPF has been granted, effective immediately. You may resume street patrol from zero hundred hours on Monday.' He stretched out his right arm and Duvall shook the proffered hand. 'Good luck, son.'

'Thank you, sir,' Duvall responded, struggling to contain his smile. As he turned to leave he caught sight of the photograph again. It showed a young woman with blonde hair. Feeling he should make some polite conversation before leaving he asked, 'Your daughter, sir?'

The question had an immediate effect on Sajer. His shoulders sagged as if under an invisible weight and his voice grew weary, 'No, that's Sara Brecht. She was Kurt's mother - a most remarkable woman.'

Saint Jude's Infirmary: 18 January 2086, 10:19

Doctor Nystrom's neck gave an audible crack as she stretched. A nine hour surgery followed by rounds had taken its toll. Ten, possibly fifteen minutes more, and she would call it a day. Go home, open a bottle of wine and relax in a hot bath. Her breath escaped in a plaintiff sigh as her com-unit trilled out its summons: Emergency. Ward 9. Room 101. Her brow furrowed and then she made the connection – Kurt Brecht. Fatigue fell away as she sprinted along the corridor in the direction of the lifts.

A nurse stood frozen in front of the EEG monitor, the waves of which were going off the scale. Nystrom recognised the cycles as theta waves, a dream state.

'How long has he been like this?'

'Only a couple of minutes. I called you as soon as I noticed the change.

Is he waking up?'

Nystrom extracted a pen torch from her coat and pulled back Brecht's left eyelid. The pupil dilated in reaction to the light. She repeated the procedure with his other eye and then stepped back to examine the EEG. The frequency of the brainwaves started to increase.

Brecht raised his hand against the stinging powder that blew off the white dunes. It clogged his nose and mouth, making it difficult to breath. He squinted through his fingers at the towers and minaret's of a distant castle. A mirage or a safe heaven amidst the desert wastes? He walked on, body angled against the wind. The castle drew near, coalesced from shadow into glittering ice. He pushed open the intricately sculpted gates and entered a long crystalline corridor. As he walked along its length the walls reflected back a series of distorted images. The mirrors revealed a thousand separate futures each the result of a different choice in life. Architect, doctor, husband, father, the fractal patterns of lives that might have been. Brecht shrugged the images aside, his purity of vision strong enough to justify any sacrifice.

The corridor ended abruptly and he found himself in a sparkling throne room. Lady Methedrine sat sideways on the throne, her legs draped across one of the armrests. Her eyes narrowed with displeasure.

'You failed me, Kurt. After all I've done for you. I gave you the power of a god but you were too weak to use it. Shot down by some geriatric assassin. Such a disappointment.'

'I'm sorry.'

'Sorry is no use and neither are you.'

'Wait! Give me another chance and I'll prove myself. I won't fail you again.'

Lady Methedrine stepped down from the throne and descended the steps of the dais. She cupped Brecht's chin between her thumb and forefinger and raised his head. He met the blue of her eyes with a frightened glance.

'Are you so certain you want to do this again? Maybe you ought to quit while you're ahead.'

'Give me another chance. Please.'

Doctor Nystrom flinched as Brecht's hand locked about her wrist, the grip impossibly firm for muscles atrophied by disuse. She prised the fingers apart and stepped away from the bed. On the periphery of her vision the EEG readout displayed beta waves. Brecht opened his eyes.

AFTERWORD

The genesis of "White Vampyre" has been a long and protracted affair. It started life in 1993 as a short story (also included as part of this edition) inspired by a poem written by a close friend and by September 1995 had grown into a fully fledged novel, having collided with one of my rejected proposals for the series of "Judge Dredd" novels then being published by *Virgin Books*.

After a number of unsuccessful attempts at finding a publisher, I concentrated on my career as an electrical engineer and consequently the novel did not become publicly available until 2003, produced as a Print On Demand paperback by *Booklocker.com* in the United States. Needless to say, it underwent extensive revision in the interim.

The end product was difficult to find and expensive to buy, as a result of which I withdrew the book in 2005 in order to revise the text and find a publisher capable of marketing and distributing it to its full potential. I intended to use a new publishing venture titled *Writers of Worlds* to fulfil that role, but the company unfortunately failed to get off the ground. I would be remiss, however, if I did not thank Oliver Low, Elizabeth Waddington and Sarah Jennings for their editorial input into that unpublished edition, most of the amendments of which I have carried forward. I owe a debt to Oliver in particular for inspiring me to produce a further novels set within Europa City.

Following the above failure to launch, the book lay in a state of woeful neglect for a number of years. A condition that might have proved terminal if not for the growth in social networking sites and the eReader revolution started by devices such as the Kindle. The book was accordingly published by Kindle Direct Publishing in December 2011. I am now pleased to offer it once more in print format via Amazon's print on demand service.

Leon Steelgrave

September 2020

THE WHITE VAMPIRE

urt felt the familiar rush of energy as it rose from the pit of his
stomach and triggered a jackhammer pulse inside his skull. An
increase in the backbeat of the music assailed his ears
simultaneously, but all of these sensations paled when he looked across the
dancefloor and caught site of the White Vampire. Lady Methedrine sat
alone at one of the club's small tables. Her dark hair hung like rags about
her shoulders, contrasting sharply with the white of her ballgown. Their
eyes locked and her lips curved in a sensuous smile, the sight of which
invoked a wealth of memory and sensation. Of all the loves of his life she
was without doubt the most demanding. Lady Methedrine granted all of his
desires, but always at great cost. Yet her favours were an expense that he
bore willingly in spite of knowing where their affair must inevitably lead.

The White Vampire moved across the dancefloor with an inhuman
elegance and grace. Kurt, responding to her summons, downed his cognac
before following in her wake: entering an arena of the young and
disaffected, the fringe members of society who had come here to lose
themselves in the beat. People like him, seeking to free themselves from
the mundane restrictions of city life. As he joined with them in their
symbolic rituals the heady brew of flashing lights, pounding rhythms and
cloying odour of dry ice enmeshed his senses. Time became meaningless as
he indulged himself in a cathartic release of energy, only emerging from his
trance when the DJ selected a song that jarred with his mood.

Sucking air into his lungs, Kurt sought to locate his lover on the
dancefloor. When this proved fruitless, he redirected his energy to scour
the remainder of the club. A short while later his suspicions were
confirmed; the White Vampire had eluded him once more. He would have
to seek out and pay the Man if he wished to continue their subtle game of
cat and mouse.

The Man liked to believe he was the Lady's master but in reality, like everyone else who dealt with the Vampire, he was subservient to her needs. Lady Methedrine wore a hundred different forms and employed a thousand courtiers to spread her word. She offered succour to the hopeless while infecting them with her disease. Her aim was to enslave an army bound to her by an insatiable hunger that only she could feed.

Kurt had sworn to overthrow her, electing by way of reasoning to fight the Lady on her own terms, choosing to deliberately infect himself with her disease and thereby better comprehend what it meant to be in her thrall. He had known success at first, gaining an insight into her nature that he might never have otherwise realised. But circumstance proved cruel and he found himself sharing the fate of her other slaves before he could use his newly acquired wisdom. The once bold idealist, like so many before him, had become a puppet vassal of the Vampire.

These memories twisted through the confused landscape of his mind as he located The Man and paid him for the key that would unlock the barriers that stood in the way of his pursuit of the Lady. Familiar sensations of doubt and trepidation filled him before taking the key. Once having left, the White Vampire would not return that same evening. He would need to seek her elsewhere for his search to be successful.

Outside a thick fog had rolled in from the sea to shroud the night time streets in mystery. It was reminiscent of the club's dry ice and Kurt found it strangely comforting. Up ahead he could see the diffuse glow of a multitude of lights, which seemed to beckon. Could this be a sign from the Vampire? He would trace their source and find out.

The lights led to the city's street of delight, which cajoled him with promises of indulging in all pleasures of the flesh. But their entreaties were as dust compared to the favours of his mistress and could not sway him. Steeled by his craving, he ran the gauntlet of the Reeperbahn, shunning its hedonistic delights to emerge untouched on the other side, where he beheld the Lady Methedrine. The Vampire's ice-cold smile spoke silently of Nirvana.

Kurt licked suddenly dry lips, 'You've led me quite a chase, but I've cornered you at last. Foolish to meet with me alone, for you must know that I intend to put an end to your vile reign.'

The Vampire's laughter was sweet and melodious, yet somehow it managed to remain without a shred of warmth. She spoke in tones rich with mockery. 'My dear Herr Brecht, you are such a postulating fop. I do believe you've quite missed your vocation in life. Surely anyone possessed of such a fine sense of melodrama as you should be upon the stage.' She flung her arms wide. 'Ah, but I forget, the whole World is but a stage.'

'Can't you do any better than to mock me? I expected more from you.'

'Herr Brecht, or should I call you Kurt, for we have been so very intimate, have we not? But your choice of appellation matters not. As for your question, search your heart. Can you honestly say, after putting yourself in my power, that you deserve anything better than mockery? Of course not. Like all my servants, you gave into some innate weakness or craving. The fault is quite your own.'

Kurt felt his resolve weaken and said in desperation, 'Liar! Deceiver! You're a cancer eating at the heart of society. All you exist for is to take. I know your guises. I know your methods. I can break free of your web. The circle will be broken!'

The Vampire shook her head sorrowfully. 'Such self-deception. I pity you. You didn't find me this evening, I found you. Once again you've accepted my gift and now you must pay the price.'

Kurt stood still as Lady Methedrine advanced and enfolded him in her bittersweet embrace. She had raised him up on high and now the time had come to cast him down again as she leeched back every ounce of power she had given him. But her hunger was great and the return of her favours alone never enough. She must continue to feed until she had drawn the power from the very wellspring of his being. Tomorrow his enervated body would seek her favours anew, receiving the brief illusion of power before the Vampire forced him to return it with still more of his essential being.

Kurt knew all this but remained powerless to prevent it. He heard the grinding gears of the wheel of fate as it slowly turned its circle. Shudders wracked his body as he surrendered to the Vampire's embrace.

She stepped away from him, shimmering as she dissipated back into her own world. He would surely remain enthralled until the end of his days if he let the Vampire escape. But what if he took the final key, the secret one that would open the door to the realm of delirium? Might he not then confront the Vampire and put an end to his slavery? Further debate was useless; he would use the key and be damned.

The once comforting fog had now become a living entity, a snarling creature that threatened to engulf him. Its icy fingers clutched at his body, searching for some point of ingress. This beast was without doubt an agent of the Vampire, sent to prevent him from traversing the planes as he searched for her realm. She would not find him so easy to dissuade. It would take more than an incorporeal being to halt his quest. The road shivered beneath him, undulating like a giant snake. The White Vampire had sensed his challenge and sent more of her minions to stop him. The houses on either side reared up, corroborating his assumption. Their windows glared at him while the doors snapped open and shut like hungry mouths. Kurt tried to back away only to find himself pitched into one of the gaping maws as the road gave another reptilian shudder beneath him. A kaleidoscope of sounds and colours, a roller-coaster of sensation that became one with him as he fell towards the darkness, assaulted his senses.

Consciousness returned with an agonising slowness, bringing all of his senses with it; allowing him to see the empty sky above and feel the dry dust beneath his body. He clutched at the dust as he struggled to his knees, realising as he did so that a vast field of white powder surrounded him. This could only be the realm of the Vampire.

Despair washed over him as he surveyed the barren plane. Here there were no signs to point him in her direction. He might wander endlessly in this timeless place without ever finding his quarry. Yet the Lady must be omnipresent in her realm and already know of his arrival. The Vampire would surely find him if he waited, seeking payment for that which he had just borrowed.

Time passed. How much he could not say for there were no yardsticks by which to measure time or distance in the realm of the Vampire. He heard the drumming of hoof beats. The sound drew nearer until he could distinguish the shape of a white horse galloping towards him. The pale horse stopped, its hooves digging up flurries of dust. 'I am the white mare, Horse,' she said. 'You must ride me if you would confront the Lady Methedrine.'

Kurt stared at Horse in wonderment for several seconds before managing to ask, 'You know where the Lady Methedrine resides?'

Horse tossed her head, 'All aspects of the Lady know where her other forms may be found. Whether they are the Snow Queen or Mother Methadone the Surrogate. All are one. One is all. But come, you waste time, for a mortal may only exist in the realm of the Vampire for a short while before coming down.'

Kurt reached up and gripped her mane to assist him in mounting. Horse felt his weight settle on her back and said, 'Hold on tight, for the ride will be fast and dangerous.' The mare reared up on her hind legs before launching into a gallop.

The ride was everything she promised and Kurt revelled in a rush of pure adrenaline as they sped over the white field, oblivious to the cold winds that tore at his clothing or the faded images from his past that blurred around him. Then as suddenly as it had begun it was over, leaving behind the aching desire to ride Horse again. But she was already vanishing as he dismounted. Disappointed, he looked up and saw that she had brought him to the gates of a sparkling palace carved from ice. Its minarets and crenellated walls reminded him of a fairy tale castle.

He pushed aside the intricately sculpted gates and entered a long crystalline corridor. As he walked along its length the walls reflected back a series of distorted images of him, causing him to wonder if they were mere mirrors or a gallery depicting different aspects of his personality. A test to see if he was willing to confront the darker side of his psyche, that which most people prefer to ignore, choosing instead to maintain their delusions of inner purity. Such images held no terror for one who had long since acknowledged his spiritual sickness. Kurt faced each leering gargoyle with indifference or acceptance, depending on which emotion felt the most appropriate. Dispelling the images one after another until he found himself without warning in a glittering throne room.

At first glance he mistook the figure sitting on the throne for the White Vampire. Closer inspection revealed subtle differences. While the Lady's ballgown was of unadorned silk, this woman wore a dress brocaded with a myriad of sparkling jewels. And then there were the eyes. The Vampire's eyes were of a sapphire blue and twice as hard as that precious stone, while the throne's occupant had honey coloured eyes with a hypnotic quality that snared the heart. She spoke in a mellow and languorous voice. 'So, you have sought my company at last?'

'Forgive me, Madam. I know not who you are. Horse brought me here because I seek the White Vampire.'

'Foolish child. Have you not yet realised that it is your search for the Lady Methedrine that binds you to her in chains stronger than adamantine? If you would be free of her clutches, simply abandon your quest. Give yourself to me, Mistress of Illusion, and I will provide succour from the Vampire's wiles.'

Kurt tried to consider her words but the hypnotic tones of her voice caressed him like a lover until coherent thought became all but impossible. Her honeyed tones reverberated inside his skull, gradually gaining in volume with each echo as they rose to a melodious crescendo. This was the secret of the Mistress's magic, the manner in which she transformed her words from sound into glorious visions.

Kurt stood agape as bizarre reflections of reality manifested themselves from the writhing air. He felt as if some long forgotten door in his mind had opened allowing him to perceive the world with greater clarity. Motes of dust floating in the rarefied atmosphere formed miniature solar systems with microscopic moons orbiting tiny planets that in turn revolved around their model sun. Cracks in the walls and ceiling expanded to become the contours of long lost continents that would only be defined when Kurt had walked upon them.

A voice reached him from far away, 'See what I offer? Won't you join me for forever and a day?' entreated the Mistress. This final enticement proved her undoing for it broke the spell she had woven around him.

'I'm sorry Mistress, but I must decline your offer.' Kurt enunciated each word slowly and with great care as he struggled for control. 'My business is with the White Vampire and with the Vampire alone. Now, at the risk of appearing rude, I am told that my time here is limited. If you would kindly point me on my way…'

The normally serene features of the Mistress clouded at his announcement and then her usual calm returned with a heady sigh. 'So be it.' She pointed to a door partially concealed by her throne. 'Yonder is the Vampire's boudoir. Your lover awaits you, sir.'

Kurt gave her a stiff bow from the waist before hurrying inside the boudoir. He beheld the Lady as she reclined on a four poster bed of bone and ivory. Its drapes were of gossamer thin lace and its sheets of the finest samite, overlaid with winter fox furs. She wore a simple nightdress cut to reveal the swell of her breasts. Her eyes were full with the promise of pleasure. Faced with her enticement, Kurt forgot his purpose and staggered towards her waiting arms.

The scene shifted and faded before he could reach her and he found himself lying on his back while fluorescent lights flashed overhead to the accompaniment of whispered voices. The squeak of rubber heels on linoleum and the clink of glass on steel. Voices urged him to stay with them but he could not resist the call of the Vampire. He found himself back in her embrace, his skin burning hot against her cool flesh as she urged him to greater efforts. The rhythmic thrusting of his loins matched the pounding inside his head as he reached the fiery approach of his climax. He screamed with the agony of his release as the Vampire sucked him dry. Draining every drop of his will and vitality, she rejoiced in her final triumph.

The harsh light and whispering voices returned. 'It's no use, he's going into arrest. Give him ten CC's of adrenaline - set for one-twenty - stand clear.' The meaningless phrases buzzed around his body like insects as Kurt slid towards a warm, comforting darkness. The dark beckoned him to surrender, offering a return to the primal womb. A jolt of pain tore through his body, threatening to drag him back from this sense of blessed relief. He fought against the pull, a salmon swimming upstream, driven by instinct. Another shock ripped through his body, its call less insistent as he continued his slide towards oblivion.

Kurt awoke to an impenetrable blackness. Without form or substance, he could only assume himself trapped in limbo, cast by death into a timeless void where he would at last know peace.

He had no sooner reached this conclusion than a familiar voice whispered, 'Thou shall have no refuge, not even in death.'

Kurt knew then that he was truly damned.

ABOUT THE AUTHOR

Leon Steelgrave is the author of the *Europa City* series – hardboiled science fiction that traces its genealogy back to the pulp stories of the 1930s. This dark and satirical world serves as a warning of the dangers of ecological disaster and totalitarian regimes.

Leon's early work includes articles and reviews for music fanzines *Take To The Sky* and *Glasperlenspiel*. But it was his attempt to secure a commission for writing one of a series of *Judge Dredd* novels published by Virgin Books that kickstarted his fiction writing career. Although ultimately unsuccessful, the editorial feedback was sufficiently positive and encouraging for him to complete his debut novel *White Vampyre*. He has published a further three books in the series and is currently working on the first of a new series set in the wider *Europa City* universe.

Leon is a member of the Alliance of Independent Authors and self-publishes his work through Ice Pick Books – fiction to make your ears burn!

Writing being a solitary profession, Leon loves to engage with his readers, so feel free to join his mailing list for releases, updates and exclusive material.

Printed in Great Britain
by Amazon

18903875R10119